I am not dedicating this book to anyone. This is my own work.

Disclaimer: This is a fictional book, and even though it may contain content distressing to the reader. It's fictional, and I take no responsibility for anyone's interpretation of the book.

This book in no way is an attempt to cause friction to any ethnic minorities, or any other minority groups. This book is not an attempt to be anti religious. This book in no way is a slur against any minority group. I thoroughly support them in their aspirations. This book might contain chapters that explore different cultures. I have tried to be inclusive to all cultures. I have in no way, intentionally or unintentionally tried to create confusion in the identity of any minorities. Any genders, or any differences. I am working hard to ensure my book remain in regards to the laws regarding. Residing with internation law, state law. The first amendment, and human rights laws.

Further disclaimer: This book in no way is trying to violate anyone.

This book, is about a detective, who is investigating crime. It follows through twists and turns.

Introduction,

A guy called Giles Hemingway is standing trial for murder of Louise Grey.

Chapter 1

I am down town in Detroit. My name is Lucas. I am investigating the murder of Louise Grey.
Miss Grey was murdered in cold blood whilst she was walking to a friends house. She was stabbed in the chest. I am a detective. I walk into the office.

2

Detective Bruce Davis. My associate. Is researching the information. I said to him, 'it was a stabbing, not a shooting, are you sure?' He said, 'yeah'. I said, 'I thought all of the stabbings happened in England?' He said, 'that's what I thought, and that is what didn't make sense from my point of view.'

I said, 'any other lacerations?' He said, 'no, none, just the initial wound. Fingerprints over the weapon. Bladed article in forensics. We have a male in custody called Giles Hemingway

I said, 'I'll walk over to the interview room, and speak to him.' Bruce said, 'by all means, I am coming with you.'

We walked down, and met him. Hemingway was cold as ice. Long hair, *hadn't seen a barber on over a year and a half*. Neither had he shaved for that time. He had acne all over his neck. He was a rough sleeper. Figured he got the bladed article from a theft.

The previous theft wasn't noted. He was sitting with. Lawyer. Maria Davidson. She was a black woman.

I slammed the paperwork down, which in 2020. When we talk about paperwork. Which we don't usually do that anymore. Yet, having said that. It still helped sometimes. I said, 'right, we are starting the interview.' I switch on the CD

3

recording device.

I said, 'Mr Hemingway, Louise was stabbed last night, in cold blood. One straight stab to the heart. She died almost instantly. She was 21. Time of death around 22:00pm.'

Mr Hemingway nodded. I said, 'please note this interview suite is also video recorded.' He nodded. I said, 'so we are trying to get to the bottom of what happened. Now is your chance to tell us your version of events.'

Hemingway opened his mouth, I felt sorry for him. Regardless of if he did do what he had allegedly done. I looked at him with empathy. He paused, grazed his neck and stuttered. He eventually spoke. He said, 'I was walking out through the town in Detroit. Begging for change. Hustling. Doing my own thing. Louise, was a local in the area. She walks up to me. She spits in my face. And calls me a 'dirty tramp.' I pushed her away. As I did this, she grabbed my knife from me, in an attempt to attack me. There was a struggle, and as an accident, I stabbed her, in the chest once. I admit the stabbing, but it was an accident sir.'

I coughed. I looked at Maria Davidson, and I could see an awkward look. This would seriously lesson the charges, and would go from first degree. Right down to

4

self defence. It's even unlikely a manslaughter charge would be applied. But possible. Or we may be looking at third degree murder.

I said, 'are you just saying this for a reduction in sentence. The best way for a reduction is to tell the truth.' He said, 'this is the truth.'

I said, 'so if there was a struggle. How come we noticed no bruises, no marks. No lacerations on your hands, or body. No bruises or lacerations on her body. The only mark on her body was the stab wound.'

He said, 'I don't know, it was cold, it was dark. Can you look more closely?' He pulled out his arm, and showed me a bruise.

I sighed and said, 'explain please.' He said, 'this is where she slapped me multiple times on the arm.'

I said, 'just suppose what you are saying is the truth, and all of this happened.' He said, 'is it the truth.' I nodded. I said, 'just explain one thing. Why did it get so heated? This young lady had just graduated from college. A smart girl. Wanted to be a doctor.'

Maria Davidson objected and said, 'listen, her occupation or desired occupation is not relevant to this case.' I said, 'maybe not, but I am just trying to get to the bottom of what has happened here. So she slapped you did she Giles?'

Giles nodded. I said sympathetically, 'why?' He said, 'there was an argument. She didn't like me begging for change. She said it was 'her estate'.' I sighed and said, 'which isn't true, I mean you resided there also. You were living on west 89 street. Past the boulevard. You quit your job as a postal worker, because of a redundancy. You were laid off, couldn't pay your rent, you slept in your car. For 4 months. You sold it for money, in which you solicited cocaine. From a local dealer, called Maxwell Clark. You were begging for change every night. Did you know Louise before this?'

Giles said, 'of course I did, she used to walk passed, every evening. It was her route.' I said, 'were you friends before, any history, anything happen?'

Giles said, 'yeah, we used to talk, she took pity on me for some time.' I said, 'yet that changed?' Giles said, 'well the older she got, and the more grades she was getting in school. There more arrogant she got. She used to hang around with Sophie Edwards. She was a high school drop out, and they used to score dope, weed, anything. It changed them.'

I said, 'in what way sir?' He said, 'it turned them into good people, and made them monsters. The laugher I heard. The cruel jokes they used to subject me to.'

I said, 'are you sure you didn't commit a revenge attack. Because of this alleged harassment?'

He shook his head and said, 'no, I didn't. I liked her.'

Everyone looked stressed, and I was in no rush to charge him. The DA had been generous and given us a couple of days at the very least. We were not that rushed. So I paused the CD recording. He looked emotional and went for a coffee with his lawyer. I regrouped with Bruce Davis. We spoke in the office. Got the elevator on the way.

I said, 'what do you think?' Bruce said, 'I think he's telling the truth, I have looked through Louise Grey's record. She had previous for harassing this guy. One count. She served 30 days in jail.' I said, 'what, really?' He nodded and said, 'she had previous?' I said, 'what is Giles Hemingway's previous?' He chortled and said, 'oh come on, you know how it is. Crack cocaine use, misdemeanours. Nothing that outrageous. Yet the harassment that he received. On the hands of Louise was a felony.'

I said, 'no shit.' He said, 'yes shit. Because it was aggravated. She pulled a knife on him, but the knife was dismissed due to lack of evidence.'

I said, 'not the same knife.' He said, 'no, a small pocket knife. The judge said there was lack of evidence she used this on him. Yet he claimed she did. She also admitted charges of battery, and assault. The felony was the criminal damage to the window behind him. The others were misdemeanours'

I said, 'it doesn't make sense, she was a good student, studying to become a doctor. College student. Applied to University. Took two gap years.'

Bruce Davis said. 'Cut it out. That means nothing. She led a double life.' He showed me photos of her, from the CCTV. At the day of the attack. Showing her taunting this homeless guy. One of the male friends was urinating on him.

I said, 'okay, I have seen enough. This is just going to mean we charge him with third degree murder.'

Bruce Davis said, 'the judge may dismiss it, and may file a manslaughter charge. He will do 4-10 years at the very most.'

I said. 'If we let him go, we are not helping him.'

Bruce said, 'the guy needs a barber, they have those in jail.'

I laughed and said, 'I kind of can see all of the positives in this now.'

Chapter 2

We restarted the interview. Giles Hemingway had calmed down. He was still looking upset. I said, 'so, we have heard more about this little escapade. Turns out, your story checks out. If we charge you, it will be on one count of third degree murder.'

He said, 'that still sucks, why not charge me with manslaughter.'

I looked at Bruce Davis and I said, 'because you still decided to use the knife. You could have pushed her away. You could have called us. From a payphone.' He said, 'I understand, hindsight is always 20/20.' I felt kind of stuck. Kind of helpless really. He looked like the kind of dude who would only respond when provoked. I felt angry at this female. Louise. Some kind of pretentious student. Who felt she could trample all over this guy.

I said to Giles Hemingway, 'look sir, with all due respect. If you do go to jail. You will get the help. That I think you need. Look at this as a blessing in disguise.'

He said, 'that girl hounded me.' I said, 'I know, and forensics have paged us. Your story checks out.'

Bruce scoffed and said, 'look. We charge

you. You go to court in a few days time. We sit in there with you.'

He said, 'will I get bail?' I said, 'no, unfortunately not because we need to get this sorted.'

Giles said, 'so you are remanding me.' I said, 'well, it's highly likely we will. It's more cost effective than those electronic tags. Besides. You could just cut it off.' Maria was angered and looked angry. She didn't say anything.

Bruce looked at me, and said, 'cut all of this bullshit, we are just talking.'

Giles Hemingway said, 'look, I understand. Is there anything else you want to discuss?' I said. 'Why her? Of all people. Why not just walk away. Do something, go to a different district. Call us.'

He said, 'I was getting no help in the community.' I said, 'no shit, but you could have tried to help yourself. Get another job. Do something with your life. Now you're looking at 10 years maximum here.'

Giles said, 'I understand, yet Louise was a nasty piece of work.'

I said. 'I know dude, but she doesn't look much better on an autopsy slab.'

Giles said. 'What do you mean?' I said, 'they are cutting open her chest. Looking at her body. Taking down DNA. Doing swabs.'

10

Giles said, 'I regret what I did.' I said. 'Right that's fine.' I cut the CD player. I said, 'right, everyone out. I need to go up to the office now.'

Everyone left. I was taking the stairs. I felt a bit dizzy. Needed some light exercise. Even though at the top. Kind of wish I had taken the lift. The detectives office, which I am working in. Is on the third floor.

Chapter 3

Booking this guy was difficult. Resources were stretched. He was anxious. The desk sergeant read him his rights. We took him to a remand block. Up on high passed the district.

That would have been in the end of seeing Mr Hemingway for a while. Yet, having said that. When the court date arose. I was due there. Sat on the third aisle. Staring at this guy. He was nervous. He was anxious. He looked like he hadn't had a good nights sleep in months. His lawyer, the same lady. Maria, was with him. The prosecutor. Was a man called John Smith. John was looking at the jury. He was also looking at some sobbing in the background, from the bereaved. Sounded like a fuckin' choir. You know.

Not that I blamed them. I just wanted

this circus to be done with.

The judge, Julia Cartwright. She was looking very stern. At this point in time. I was called to the witness stand.

John said, 'so what is your job?' I said, 'I am a detective in Detroit' He said, 'were you the arresting officer?' I said. 'No I was not.' He said, 'who was the arresting officer?' I said, 'Chuck Jenkins'

John said, 'was Chuck alone?' I said, 'no sir, Chuck was with Gary Jones. I said, 'who dialled the 911 call?'

I said, 'I believe it was a neighbour from above one of the buildings.'

He said, 'was the arresting officer conducting himself properly?' I said, 'we are a professional team sir. Minimal force was used.'

John said, 'what force was used?'

I said, 'they read the guy his rights. They said they were going to handcuff him. They asked him to put his hands behind his back. He was compliant. Handcuffed. He was then placed gently into the cop car. Chuck placed one hand on his head, for safety. The other hand was placed on his arm to guide him in the cop car. In the back.'

John said, 'was there any blood?' I said, 'sir, there was a lot of blood present at this was a fatal stabbing.'

John said, 'how many litres?' I said, 'it's

impossible to say, some spilled out onto the side walk. Louise bled to death. I would say an unprecedented amount.'

He said, 'thank you, no further questions.'

Next to interview me, was Maria Davidson. She said, 'Lucas Davis Jones. How long have you been a detective?' I said, 'thirty years'. She said, 'were you uniform before then?' I said, 'yes, for three years.' She said, 'you got promoted quickly then.'

I said, 'I was studying a masters during those times, and in criminology. I gained a masters degree in Criminology. I was highly respected and professional.'

She said, 'so you know what you are doing. You do things very thoroughly?' I said, 'of course.'

She said, 'tell me more about Louise Grey.'

I said, 'she seemed to lead a double life. A hard working girl during the day. Yet at night, she used to score illicit substances. Consequentially had history.'

Maria said, 'do you mean criminal history?' I said, 'yes I do mean that?'

Maria said, 'what criminal history did she have?' I said, 'criminal damage, assault, battery, and harassment. She spent 30 days in a county jail.'

Maria said, 'who was she convicted of

harassing?' I said, 'Giles Hemingway.'

She said, 'no further questions.' I stepped down from the stand as I could hear gasps. Julia Cartwright, the judge. Slamming the hammer. Ordering a recess. I got my coffee from a Cappuccino machine. I sit down. John Smith sits down next to me. Wanting a social.

He said, 'tough day?' I said, 'you could say that, yet I am coping.' He said, 'something doesn't add up.' I said, 'what do you mean?'

He said, 'in a murder trial, where the victim has previous, for attacking the alleged suspect.'

I said, 'it's an unusual case.' John Smith, was a slim man. 6 foot. Black hair. Combed back. Very intelligent looking. A kind of mysterious look about him.

I was the same, 6 foot, almost looking identical to him. I had light brown hair. I was 58. He was 49.

John said, 'we go back in there, and we sit down.' I said, 'watch the rest of this. This isn't a theatre show John.' John laughed as we stood up and said, 'the only reason I became a prosecutor, you know that reason?'

I said, 'because you can't afford theatre tickets?'

He said, 'no, because it's better than theatre tickets.' I said, 'interesting.' We

14

both walked in the court room. I whispered. 'Theatres better.'

Everyone assembled. You could hear the judge shout, 'all rise.'

Chapter 4

Now was the opportunity for more questions. Which was going to happen. Giles is looking tired. A neighbour who witnessed the dispute is called to the stand. Called Marie.

John said, 'Marie, what did you witness?' Marie said, 'a lot of blood.' John said, 'is that the first thing you saw?' Marie said, 'no it is not.' John said, 'so tell me what the first thing you saw is?' Marie said, 'I saw and *heard* an argument.' John said, 'elaborate please.'

Marie said, 'Giles Hemingway, of no fixed address. Was begging for change. Louise walked over, and spat in his face. Giles was angry. He pushed her back.'

John said, 'was Giles provoked?' Marie said, 'not really. I then witnessed Giles, brandish a 10 inch bladed article. Looked like a butchers knife. He dug it sharply into Sophie's chest. She fell to the floor, and blood trickled everywhere.'

John said, 'were you the neighbour who called 911?' Marie said, 'yes I was.' John said, 'do you think that Mr Hemingway, used excessive violence?' Marie said, 'without a shadow of a doubt.' John smiled and said, 'no further questions.'

Maria, Davidson, was interviewing Marie. Maria said, 'Marie, in all due respect, did you know Mr Hemingway?' Marie said, 'very well.' Maria said, 'what was your impression of him?' Marie said, 'he was a nice bloke. Misunderstood. He had a crack cocaine addiction but he never troubled me with it. He used to get harassed a lot, by the cops..' Before she had time to finish talking. John shouted. 'Objection, argumentative.'

Julia Cartwright, the judge said, 'Overruled' She said with an almost bewildered fashion. She said, 'I will let Maria proceed with caution, and I will let Marie proceed. Providing they get to the point.'

Maria said, 'Marie, I have a question for you. Do you think there is any chance, that Mr Hemingway, could have tried to use self defence?' Marie said, 'well it's possible yes.' Maria said, 'He was getting harassed by Louise?' Marie said, 'every day.' Maria smiled and said, 'no further questions.'

Everyone was looking tired. Another recess, and everyone walks out. I am feeling tired and frustrated, and walked over to John. I said, 'why did you try objecting?' I said in rhetoric. John said, 'oh come on, '*harassed by Police*'. That is one of the oldest defences in the book.' I said, 'it's still a defence.' John said, 'yeah I know, but it wasn't the case.' I said, 'how do you know that? The guy is homeless. We train our officers to the highest standard. Yet we have to be clear here. What Marie was saying was perfectly lawful. It was her opinion sir.'

John smiled and said. 'You really feel for Hemingway, don't you. You think he's a victim of circumstance. A victim in disguise of a suspect.' I said, 'not really, but we have a job to do. We have to do it properly. Don't go pulling any stunts like that again.' John looked angry and said, 'I am doing my job. I suggest you do the same.' I smiled, with anger, and he walked away to the coffee machine. Maria walked over and said, 'what was all that about?' Maria was a very beautiful black lady. Slim, a curvaceous figure. I said, 'just politics.' Maria said, 'well, this court room is turning into a circus.'

I said, 'things got heated. I wouldn't worry about it.' Maria said, 'we just have to be professional, yet there are some things we can't be sure of yet.' I said, 'like what?'

Maria said, 'like the fact that John just seems to be intervening all of the time.

17

You should see this guys history. High conviction rate. Higher than mine.' I smiled and said, 'he's out of his depth, I wouldn't worry.'

I walked towards the canteen. There was two, and away from John Smith, attorney at law. I got some fries, and a hand-burger, and sat down. This was my break, and I was enjoying it. Ketchup also.

Chapter 5

The courtroom was amazingly built. Even the actual court itself. It's almost like if God had landed there, and created it.

Detroit, was a busy city, and we sure worked hard. You looked over, and saw all of those cars driving passed. Most of the traffic was okay. You some times got the motor enthusiasts who liked revving the engines.

Traffic used to be my specialty when I was a beat cop. Not anymore. I am working as a detective. Yet, this whole case was one thing I was working on. I wanted the best for Giles Hemingway.

The only problem is, if he got outside. Part of society wouldn't feel the same level of sympathy for him; They would want him hung from the trees. Possibly

18

castrated also. There were people protesting outside the court.

I was the one who had to make the statement. Resources were stretched. There were some rebel protestors. Who were moved along by cops.

We had around thirty to forty police officers in uniform. Holding a line between the protestors and the court room. There was a blonde female cop pushing this angry man back. Assertively. She was not smiling, however, she had a glint in here eye. That she was able to cope.

My officers were coping well, but then all of my detectives showed up. James Hamlin, detective. Along with some other ones in the background.

James said, 'Lucas, I appreciate you are trying everything you can do to help. Yet please sort this circus out.' I nodded.

I shouted, 'right, I want to make a statement.' Everyone simmered down, and amongst the protesters were thirteen reporters. All from different news crews. CNN, Washington Post, New York Times, CBS News, and some others. Sky News were there also.

I said, 'My name is Lucas Davis.' I cleared my throat. My blonde hair swimming over my pale white freckly face. My latte in my hand shaking and dripping

19

over my wrists. My black tie, loosely trying to hold onto my white shirt. Coffee stained on my shirt, ever so slightly. Black polished shoes. Slim build. My notebook in my pocket, and my braces tightened. My wrist hurt, and I was feeling stressed. I was showing it but deep down, I didn't mind.

I continued, 'Giles Hemingway of no fixed address. Was arrested On Saturday the 2nd of May 2020. At around 22:00pm. He has allegedly caused serious and fatal injury to victim Lewis Grey. He has been charged with third degree murder.'

I can hear some gasps at this point, and the same protestor who was making a scene. The same one who was shoved back by the female blonde officer. Quite a handsomely large chap. Brown suit. Looked almost too sophisticated to be a protestor, and definitely wasn't part of the news crew. Looked like a loner who wanted to travel to express his opinions. He yelled, 'this is an injustice'. He is throwing his arms around almost like he is swatting flies.

The sun is shining heavily on him, and the news crew scoff at him. I carry on speaking.

I said, 'please questions and comments at the end. We are taking this matter extremely seriously. Unfortunately at this stage. As everyone knows, it's innocent until proven guilty. I can't discuss too much about this case. Because I couldn't do that.'

The male in question is deeply remorseful for what he has done.'

At this stage, a female protestor. Looked like she was a tad shy, and had blonde/gingery hair. Looked like a liberal lady. Around thirty five. She shouted, 'there is no justice in that.'

I coughed, I said, 'I appreciate tensions are high right now. Detroit Police are taking this very seriously.'

I had prepared a longer speech than this. Yet I had to let people vent. It was getting too much. The more I spoke. The more agitated and angry people got.

It was clear that Giles Hemingway, in the public's eye. Was the suspect. He clearly was in my eye also, albeit, it wasn't my training per se that caused me to pity him. It was my overriding knowledge of his history. Having known the man for years. He was not a shadow, like the press and public wanted to portray. 'As a shadow'. I mean, he was more than an outcast, or some 'deranged lunatic' the public wanted to display.

First to ask questions was CNN news. CNN news. Big man, looked very well built. He said assertively. As he cleared his coffee breath, stubble, his brown tie. Plaid shirt. Almost indistinguishable to the fact that it was grey and white. His shiny Rolex watch, that looked second hand.

He said, 'Lucas Davis Jones, you have made it clear this is an ongoing investigation. It has surpassed charges. How long is this court case going to last? And what do you think is going to happen?'

I said, 'at this stage, we are not sure how long the court proceedings are going to last. We expect that justice will be swift, and we will be able to cope with this. We will give another statement post possible sentencing'

The same reporter chimed in again. Looking very restless, and looked like he really need to drive the question home. He said, 'so you think he will be convicted?'

I said, 'he has plead guilty, and there is a lot of evidence that suggests he has caused a fatal stab wound to victim Louise Grey. However, there are mitigating circumstances.'

A woman in the background. Dark brown hair. Smartly dressed. Looked like she had decided to protest. Middle class. She said, 'oh excuses, excuses, what mitigating circumstances?' She said robustly.

I said, 'Louise Grey, in the public's eye. She was a lady who was a good student. Straight A, almost. Yet, she was harassing and taunting this man. She had previous for a felony charge. She lead a double life. I can't say any more than that.'

Fox News chimed in. A black lady, smartly dressed. She said, 'you can't say anymore than what you have said?'

I said, 'unfortunately not because this is an ongoing case. Please be assured when the jury reaches a decision. And if the judge issues a conviction. I will be able to be more clear in my speeches. Please be assured Detroit Police are working hard on this matter. No more questions.'

As soon as I said, 'no more questions.' The protestors were shoved away by Police. The compliant protestors were pushed into taxis. The non compliant protestors were shoved more aggressively. Yet, like always, there is always one person who over steps the mark.

Some kind of free lance journalist. Looking very upset, and is giving spiel of how he has children. He is disgraced. He is shoving Police. Almost nine of them. He has a handsome man, who looks angry. Dark jet black hair. Can't tell if dyed. Brown suit, and looks very angry. He pushes my police officers, and we push

23

him into a police car. The sirens and lights are on, as the cop car drives passed some anxious civilians. Just watching the protestors. Some recording, others not, just stuck in traffic.

James Hamlin said. 'Well handled, let's get back to work.' He said assertively.

Chapter 6,

Going back to the courtroom, after the onslaught of press and protestors; It was a bitter pill to swallow. I hear Julia Cartwright shouting, 'all rise'. There was some silence for a bit.

Next to the witness stand was Giles Hemingway himself. Blistery eyed. Hadn't had a nights sleep in over a week. Excluding the naps in the custody block and remand cell.

John started the questioning. He said, 'so Giles, how long have you been homeless?' Giles said, 'about a year now sir.'

John said, 'ever thought about getting some work?' Giles said, 'I did work as a postal worker. I was made redundant.'

John said, 'so you then decided to sleep on the streets.' Giles said, 'I had no choice.' I stood there shocked at no shouts of objections. I guess people were intrigued.

Giles said, 'look I know what I did was wrong.' John said, 'what exactly did you do that was wrong?' He said, 'I murdered that girl in cold blood.' John smiled and said, 'no more questions.'

Next up was Maria, she said, 'Giles, you have had a troubled life.' Giles said, 'of course.' Maria said, 'you and Louise Grey had history?' Giles said, 'of course. She befriended me, she was nice at first.'

Maria said, 'then what happened?' Giles said, 'she turned nasty. Got in with the wrong group of people. Had a felony charge, for assault, battery, and criminal damage. I was vulnerable, yet she was this 'dual personality'...'

John getting arrogant chimed in and said, 'objection, Julia is not here to defend these allegations.' Julia Cartwright said, 'sustained, please, have some respect for the deceased. Move on with your questioning Maria. You are overstepping the mark.'

Maria said, 'so Giles, was it your intention to kill Louise Grey?' Giles stammered, 'not at first. I was goaded into a reaction.'

Maria said, 'how did she goad you?'

Giles said, 'pulling my hair, the felony charges. She was a negative person. I didn't like her. The day of the alleged murder. She was hostile. Spat at me three times. Right in the face. Lit me on fire. That has been suppressed.'

Maria said, 'now you have to be very clear, were you provoked?'

Giles said, 'yes.' The court was in complete hysterics. Not laughter. The court was in uproar. The judge. Julia Cartwright, was slamming her hammer on the table. Shouting, 'order, order, please.'

John shouted, 'this is not fair.' Julia said, 'John settle down before I hold you in contempt of court.'

I chimed in and I said, 'look this is not fair.' The court was in recess. Everyone was angry, and I was not going anywhere near John.

I walked over to Maria, and I said, 'good questioning.' John walked over, a short, stubby little guy. He looked kind of angry. He said, 'you get what you want, don't you Maria?'

She gasped and she said, 'what exactly do you mean?' John said, 'oh come on, don't play me the hooker with the heart of gold. That guy is guilty as sin. Putting him out there, on the witness stand. Pertaining self defence. He could get let off completely. The judge could dismiss the whole thing.'

Maria said, 'I am just doing my job.'

Giles was being led out in hand cuffs, and ankle shackles to his cell. Julia, the

26

judge, ordered everyone, including me John and Maria; Into her chamber.

She reaches for some scotch. She said, 'look, this whole thing is getting out of hand. I want you all to calm down. Or I will fine you all with contempt of court.'

Everyone was quiet at this point. I chimed in and said. 'That is understandable. Yet John's attitude is completely unacceptable.'

Maria said, 'it's true'. John said. 'oh come on, now they are ganging up on me.'

Julia said. 'John, the amount of times you have objected, and objected, and objected.'

John said, 'it's my job.' Julia said, 'it's my courtroom.'

Everyone returned to the hallway. I sat down. Coffee in hand. Looking upset. John walked off and scoffed. Julia was with me, she said, 'behave yourself.' She sat down. I said, 'this is turning into a circus.' Julia said, 'I know, I know it is. Yet we have to do it. It has to be done.'

I said, 'so now what?' Julia said, 'a break.' We were given a two week break. Which doesn't sound like much, but the media kept calling me. All of the time.

Chapter 7

I lived in a luxury house, with my wife,

and kids. Children both grown up. Still saw them sometimes. My daughter, Isobel, 23, married with Jonathan.

My other daughter Sophie, married with a guy called Steven.

My son, Alex. Not married, 17 years old. Typical teenager.

Keeps on playing the Xbox, and I opened the door. I said, 'look mate, you are going to need some fresh air.' He said, 'I don't feel like it.'

I said, 'yet this whole routine we have here. It's not going to help. You dropped out of college, grew your hair. This isn't the son I wanted.'

At this stage, I wasn't going to lecture him. It wasn't the time. I gave him a $20 dollar note for a take out. He ordered pizza. I could hear the pizza man at the door. I grabbed a slice, and sat in front of the TV.

I had my notebook with me, and I was just trying to make sense of this. I had audited a copy of the sketch of Giles Hemingway. A scruffy looking man. It just didn't make sense. I had written notes that concluded of how I felt. 'This does not make sense. Mitigating circumstances.' Amongst other stuff.

My red carpet, and furniture around me. My beige sofa. I just felt trapped. Like my options were limited. I had to make sure I was being appropriate in the response of this case. I couldn't afford to get too wrapped up in it.

So I switched my radio on, and I could hear chatter similar to, 'drunk male outside the corner shop, has a weapon, armed.'

I grab my pistol, put it in my holster. My wife is spewing something about 'be careful', yet it's inaudible. I walk towards the brown door. I walk out, and I chase it. As it's next door, and I want some peace.

Male, mental health related. Distressed. He looks mentally ill, and I put a wire in my radio, with an ear piece to calm him down. I said, 'look sir, we can sort all of this out.'

He was black, and I had studied all of the equality and diversity training modules. My friends in The Police had done the same. He had an afro. He was skinny. Looked like he was using. I trained my staff to accept cultures. I fired anyone who showed prejudice. I had the ability to do that. We knew this guy well. His name was Floyd. Daniel Kyle. Looking over at me, looking tearful. He shouts, 'I can't cope with this anymore.'

I said, 'you can't cope with what sir?' He said, 'this demon inside me.' I said, 'it's not a real demon.'

He said, 'it feels like one.' His loaded

gun, is pointing up towards his neck. His pistol is real because I can tell by the make. He eyes up my pistol. Worried I might reach for it. At this moment in time, I said, 'sir, how about we have a chat on the pavement.' He said, 'you won't write me a citation for jaywalking?'

I said, 'no, it's my discretion.' He sat down next to me, and he said, 'look, this whole thing is messed up.' I called off additional units with my beeper. I stayed with him, and covered my pistol with my coat. To make him feel secure.

I was not alarmed at this point, yet I kept getting radio chatter. I turned my radio down a bit. I said, 'life's tough isn't it'. We could see the side walk, we could see the sun. We could see the clouds. Yet the loneliness etched on this man's face. He was only 30 years old. Into his rap music.' I said, 'I have known you for ages. You don't want to do this.'

He said, 'try me'. I knew that the longer I spent with this guy. The more anxious the control room was going to get. I had to take his gun off him and arrest him. I knew I did, but deep down. I couldn't. Not right now. Not with his hand close to the trigger. His hand was stammering.

Cuts and bruises on his hands, glass, broken glass. Bits of shrapnel from fist fights.

I said, 'let me guess, is it women trouble?' He said, 'how did you know?' I smiled and I said, 'it always is with us men. How about you give me the gun?' He handed the gun over.

I said, 'I am going to have to arrest you now.' He said, 'really?' I said, 'well, yeah but let's wait until uniform arrive.' They were taking ages. They were stuck in traffic.

I shredded the gun of it's bullets. Loaded magazine of 8. Not a barrel. It was a magazine. My pistol was a barrel but I was old fashioned. I said, 'seriously dude, you wasting your money buying these things.'

He eyed up my gun and said, 'what about yours?' I said, 'I joined The Police. I have a permit and we're authorised to use them. Hell it's just like a novelty to me really. Feels fun to hold it in my hand, but it's just like any antique.'

He said, 'so this whole boys in the hood, stuff. This is not how I should live?'

I smiled and said. 'Not really. But you learn. Look. I will put in a good word for you. You co-operated. You were good with me. You tried to run up this liquor store. You were suicidal. I'll cut you a deal.'

Daniel Kyle said, 'what kind of deal?' I said, 'just call my number.' I walked off as uniform arrived. He was cuffed and placed into a police car.

I walked away feeling good about the situation, yet I had more work to do. I return home, and I switch on the TV. Like I had just put another bit of money on the electric metre. Or I had just dialled up for a pizza. It was just how I did things. I didn't include emotion.

I watched the TV, whilst thoughts going around in my head. Sometimes it was easy to let all of the drama in your life consume you. Don't get me wrong, we used to get angry liberals attack us all of the time. Play mind games with us, and it carried on like that. I didn't mind them, but it got annoying. Then you got the far right nuts. Who used to go to rallies, and they were just as annoying in my opinion.

My TV. Switched on. Watching certain programmes. Commercials switched on of advertisements like Rogaine and Viagra. Vitacin, Vitamin supplements. Vacations. Long walks in the park, followed by medicine adverts.

The TV reverted back to this wild wild west movie. Where the cowboy was roaming through the dessert. Cool as a cucumber, finding his damsel in distress. Putting her on his horse, and riding off.

I kind of thought at this time that I was going to have to keep occupied. For some reason or other. It hadn't crossed my mind.

I crept into bed, and I could feel kind of disorientated. All of that thickness of skin you had as a cop, and all of the day to day things. We had. The adventures, and the talks. The long drives, and even the mental health visits. Entered our brains like knives, and came out like butterflies and moths. I slept like a tranquillised horse. I woke up, and I got some milk from the fridge. The real good stuff. I was just drinking that for ages.

I took some aspirin because I had some kind of headache. The wife was making scrambled eggs.

My wife was called Fiona. Fiona was 56. The curly strawberry blonde hair. The way she cooked those scrambled eggs on toast. I had my blue tooth set in my ear.

I was talking to my detective Sargent He was briefing me on an incident, which included someone shooting up a convenience store. Holding everyone hostage. I said, 'look, I will go and pay a visit.'

I grabbed my coat, with my bullet proof vest, and walked over to my car. I drove up next to lots of cars. Police cars.

Chapter 8

Police cars arriving at the scene. The convenience store was being robbed. Some man called James Clive. Had decided to rob this store. Take all of the money from the cash register. I was getting ready, and I had my other gun. My pistol, the antique looking one, in one holster. My other pistol. The proper one. For emergencies, in the other holster.

I also had my taser, my handcuffs, and I looked like uniform. With a blue jacket. Hiding behind my car, and other squad cars. A newbie cop called Owen Marks, said, 'look sir, what do we do now?' Asking for my command.

I grabbed the loudspeaker, and I said, 'this is the police. Please, come out with your hands on your head.'

James Clive wasn't co-operating. We had three hostages. A woman and two children. The convenience store owner had escaped with a bullet in the butt cheek. I was feeling kind of confused at this point.

I shouted again, 'James Clive, please come out.' We weren't firing at this point. SWAT came in, and sharp shooters. Flying above us. Helicopters. Everything. They took over, and they shot James Clive, dead within seconds. Through a window. We were under resourced, and it was for the victim's safety.

Another rookie cop, called Sarah, said, 'okay, good move.' She said sarcastically. I walked right up to her, and I said, 'what did you just say?'

She said, 'oh good move sir,' she backtracked a bit. I said, 'that man needed to be stopped. We don't have time to babysit him.' Fiona said, 'just like you babysitted Floyd' I said, 'that was different, he was compliant. This is a different scenario.'

Fiona walked away and I said, 'another word out of you and you are up for review.' She turned around and she said, 'you are not internal affairs. You can't do that.'

I said, 'try me. I have more power and influence than you think.'

Sargent James Watkins comes over. A detective, and looks at Fiona in disgrace and said, 'what on earth is going on?' He said with bitterness.

I said, 'Fiona is trying to put a spanner in the works. Trying to throw us all off balance.' James Watkins said, 'just leave it, okay.'

Fiona said, 'okay'. James Watkins said, 'what the hell was that about?' I said, 'no idea, she's well in over her head.' James said, 'well to be fair, you have been a good detective.' James was an amiable man. He was very well dressed.

I said, 'look sir, we come here time and time again. It's the same store. It's the same thing. We don't have time for all of these shootings.' James said, 'what's the alternative?' He said. I said, 'there is none, and I will continue to do my job sir.' He said under baited breath, 'if I see that rookie cop, again, she's going straight to my office.'

I said, 'I know, but you won't. I have so many cases right now.'

James said, 'you feeling stressed?' I said, 'not a chance.' He had his badge on his belt. I said, 'it's an adrenaline rush.' He said, 'yeah, we are all Adrenaline Junkies aren't we.' He said, 'something like that, deep down, behind those brown eyes of yours. I kind of have a yellow tint in mine.'

I said, 'gotta watch out sir, you might be a werewolf' He said, 'I doubt it, not with all of this going on. The only thing I have noticed about all of these crimes. All joking aside. Is that we have to get back to that cheese dick in custody. What's his name. Hemingway?'

I said. 'Yes'. He said, 'why all of the sympathy for him. I don't get it.'

I said, 'I don't know sir, I guess it's mitigating circumstances.' He said, 'maybe, but you do your job.' I said, 'alright, of course I do.' He had a blue jacket on. Slim build. I was looking kind of podgy. Yet he was the real deal.

I said, 'look sir, in all fairness. You look

around at the nights sky. The TV I have is still switched on. Life isn't fair sometimes boss.'

He said, 'sure it is, what have you got to grumble.' He touched me on the belly, and he said, 'you got a lot going on, but when you retire. You will get everything handed back to you.'

I said, 'and no early retirement for me, still working on things.'

He said, 'that's how you have to look at it. These bread and butter cases we have. Robberies, armed robberies, other things, hit and runs. Murders. The list goes on. Yet the bottom line is this. At least you are still good humoured.'

I said, 'I try to be sir, I try to do the right things. Yet it doesn't always work out. Not all of the time. Crime is rife in Detroit. This life we live, and it just feels strange you know. Like the easiest option is also the most painful.'

He said, 'what are you alluding to?' I said, 'I feel like I am fucking up a lot sir.'

He said, 'don't think like that, you are a great lead detective.'

I said, 'I know I am, but some things don't stack up. I say the wrong things. Get into trouble sometimes.'

He laughs and he said, 'we all do, I was up for review once.'

I said, 'with IA?' He said, 'yeah with IA.'

I said, 'what for?'

He said, 'I took a loaded gun, with me, during this hostage negotiation. Not this one. This was years ago. There was a man inside his house. Holding his wife hostage. The orders were not to shoot. I fired three times at him. One in the leg, one in the arm, one in the neck. He ended up in a coma for three days, and it was referred to the DA's office. I could have served jail.'

I said, 'did you serve jail?' I said, 'did you?' He said, 'no, the DA ruled self defence. Yet I was given misconduct charges. Suspended for 23 days. Almost like a fucking omen. Could have lost my wife, my house, and my kids. Could have had to travel to some shitty estate block and work security.'

I said, 'and someone bailed you out.' He said, 'his name was Johnson, he was a strange guy. He was a police informant. Didn't even want to give his first name. Think it was Craig Johnson. He was a good bloke. He called me late one day. I was watching TV, with my wife.

He said he had a word with the inspector. Said that his information would continue if I was on the force. We were paying this guy huge stacks of cash for information.'

I said, 'so a police informant saved your

skin.'

James Watkins said, 'yeah, and I am grateful, yet looking back. Looking at the police officer I am now. I changed. I am more sarcastic, not a bad thing, but more cautious.'

I said, 'sarcasm is not a bad thing sir.'

He said, 'sure it is, gets you into trouble, but it's how you cope. You have to look at people with disgrace. You have to assert what you believe is right. Yet deep down. It changed me. I became different inside. It wasn't a bad feeling also. It's almost like I learnt from the experience.'

We moved to the lake and were skimming rocks, and drinking beers.

I said, 'so you put a positive spin on it.' He said, 'not really, it was age more than anything else. Life experience. Feel that I can't go into a situation heavy handed.'

The sun started to set, a crimson glow almost shadowed the pond we were skimming rocks in. I said, 'look, in all fairness here. I am just as terrified as you are over this Giles Hemingway case.'

He said, 'fuck if I am terrified. It's a slam dunk, he'll do time.'

I said, 'self defence entered the court room, turns out he may even be out in two years. Then he has a different battle on the streets.'

James said, 'let's take one step at a time.

I don't want you messing this case up.'

I said, 'I won't, but what do you mean?'
He said, 'oh come on, you know. The way
you behave sometimes. It's almost like
you are almost too laid back for the job.'

I said, 'oh come on now. I thought that
was the way it was supposed to be?'

He said, 'not really. You have to use your
gut. You know. Go in there and assert
what you want to believe in.'

I said, 'it's hard work. It's tiring and I
can't see sense sometimes. Not all of the
time. I keep looking back, and I keep
thinking. My decisions have either been
boring or fucking wild. Nothing in the
middle, except for the anger I feel.'

He said, 'you don't have any mental
health issues do you?'

I said, 'none whatsoever, I would know if
I did. I am very good at thinking in grey
areas.'

He said, 'so what is the problem then?'

I said, 'just sometimes, this police work.
You look at the stars, you look at the glow
in the sky. Then you wander why people
argue in the first place. That people tense
up and you forget who your friends are.'

He said, 'it doesn't have to be that way.'

I said, 'oh come on, chasing after
butterflies like this with you. It doesn't
square with me. Life is strange, and I feel
like I am regressing.'

40

He said, 'you have to be a great leader and a male role model. To hell with the past.'

We clanked Heiniken beers. I said, 'listen sir, for all I know, when this case is over. Then we have to face the onslaught of the media.'

He said, 'they are a piece of cake, take it from me. Tell them what they want to hear.'

I laughed and I said, 'it doesn't always work like that. They are smart people.' He chortled and said, 'oh really, pencil dicks, standing around with a video camera. Recording and asking questions. I wouldn't classify that as super smart.'

I said, 'I don't know, you should see some of the hot blondes who do some of the reporting. Must have got into the job some how.'

He said, 'to be honest with you, there are good reporters out there. Yet the bad ones. The bad ones linger around, like, I don't know. We can't swat them.'

I looked distant. The whole case with Hemingway was stressing me out. Didn't want to show it. I could look over the twilight. The crimson glow on this golfing lake.

I could look at the birds in the distance just flying over my head.

I said, 'you know, the amount of

resources that are being placed into Hemingway is inordinate.'

James Watkins, still looking alert. Even though we had been off duty for almost an hour now. Coming up to an hour and a half.

James said, 'listen, we can talk all of the time about Hemingway. We have a god damn job to do. Yeah sure, this court case is a circus. Yet it will end, and when it does. There will be a press release.'

I said, 'yeah well the press will be able to understand all of this.'

James Watkins, his moustache, his wretched face. His lack of enthusiasm. He said, 'nature of the world. That is how it is. It's like Beauty and the Beast. Some kind of twisted tale. The news will be all over this.'

I said, 'I get what you mean, it's just weird is all. Nobody used to bother Hemingway. At least not until I knew him. He was a smart man. I remember his days as a postal worker. Never used to bother anyone. Now we look at what has happened now. Deep down. I kind of blame him a bit, but the guy's only human.'

James said, 'I know but he committed one of the cardinal sins known to man. This is not a walk in the park for him. Prison is going to take some adjustment.'

42

I said, 'I am not visiting him in prison. I have my work cut out.'

He said, 'come on man, think about this, you have the opportunity to turn someone's life around. You didn't even know Louise. She was a hypocrite.'

I said, 'if only we could bring felony charges on the dead, that is not going to happen.'

James said, 'so you are in agreement with me?'

I said, 'no I am not. I mean she was the victim in all of this. Besides, that felony charge, and the things we look at here.'

James said, 'are you a criminologist or a police officer?'

I said, 'right now, it's almost like I am both. That was the way it was supposed to be, right?' I said rhetorically.

I continued, 'the way I see things now have changed. We look at all of the sins mankind has done. We look at all of the wrongdoings, people have done. *Some things* don't chalk up.'

James said, 'well I guess we are going to have to do our damn jobs.'

It was unusual at this point. The sun was setting. I had never seen so much peace and calm. As the warm sun, was setting in a tranquil fashion. Glowing over the lake. I had seen so much positivity. I had seen so much hope. Yet deep down inside. I just wanted to feel normal again.

The summer's breeze was accommodating the sun. I looked over at the golf lake. The old mower just outside, that the gardner forgot to put away. The freshly cut grass, with the weed outside it. The muddy water of the lake, slowly churning away, from the light rain coming from the grey clouds.

We could see some thunder, and lightening, miles and miles away. Almost in a different state, as the sun was setting gently. Leaving the sky red. As the clouds dispersed I would sit there. In my grey suit. My ankle biters, just lingering above my hair ankles.

My polished black shoes. Which seemed to almost fit my grey suit. My black tie. My $100 dollar watch. The wife bought for me at a Christmas fayre one year.

My DKNY bag. My leather ruck sack. My golfing equipment in the back of my car. My Chevron, seemingly just sitting at home. Whilst my black BMW. Seemed to linger there. Parked next to James Watkin's antique car.

That was silvery grey, looked like if he had driven it anymore. It would all fell to pieces.

I looked at James, a surly faced man. Around 50 years old. Wretched look, and you could tell experience had shaped him in ways *I could never imagine.* I looked at the twilight. I knew, deep down, that the Hemingway case. Would be over soon.

James, in his whole attire. Black suit. Grey striped tie. The federal detective badge, on his belt. Overwhelming his black leather belt. You could see his years of experience glow in his face.

I said, 'James, it's been lovely to chat.' I patted him on the back.

He said, 'likewise.'

I said, 'just have to leave it there.'

He tapped me on the shoulder. He said, 'don't stay up too late.' He left in his silver Porsche, late 94 edition. Surprised the whole thing hadn't fallen to shreds, and at this point I left.

I drove my BMW home. My second car. Black BMW. My first car was a silver Chevron.

I returned to my wife, and had to watch more TV. I fell asleep in front of the TV. I woke up with breakfast. Nothing seemed to be phasing me. That was the life of a cop. If I am being honest. There was one pet hate, and I didn't like to tell people this. But I disliked the protestors. Because it's not crime, and it's not helping.

We have limited powers in Detroit. We have breach of the peace laws. Had some dudes a while back protesting over human rights.

45

Accompanied by other protestors, also claiming that we weren't helping.

I knew I had to get back to Hemingway. As the days passed by, I grew even more tolerant. Thick skinned and I made my return.

Chapter 9

When I say a return. I am in the court. Not the court room. We are outside. Just waiting. The judge is late. I have John breathing down my neck. The stocky, short man syndrome. The alpha induced hostility. He was a fiery one. I looked away from him and didn't want anything to do with him.

I thought back to the old days, when things used to make sense. Now it seemed everyone was either an abusive alcoholic, or on some kind of methamphetamine drugs. We nicked this guy the other day for being on polycotton. We nicked this guy the other week, for being on TCP. I had never seen someone so aggressive before.

I had seen dudes, so high, on skunk, they had passed out on fire hydrants. I had seen dudes so drunk, that they had fainted on the streets. I had seen domestic abuse victims battered and bloody. Victims of hate crimes, bloodied up, and abused. Graffiti, drugs, dog attacks. You name it.

The court has this vibe that we had a lot going on. In the most politest of respects. The suspect, in the name of Giles Hemingway, walks bregudgringly over in shackles. With Julia Cartwright. Almost like she is babysitting. We all return to court.

Now here comes the speech from Julia. Julia, said, 'look, I know this is hard for you to swallow, but we have to get on with proceedings.' Everyone was obedient and compliant. Deep down nobody wanted a contempt of court fine, or any unnecessary recesses.

Next up was some photos. John was standing over there outlining the injuries and the fatal stab wound to Louise Grey. Right in the chest. You could see her chest all bloodied, bruised, and broken. Her white bra, still remained intact, but was broken.

The attack wasn't sexually motivated. Hemingway wasn't the sort to attack children. He just lost it.

I looked at him in the box he was in. I looked at him in an almost curious way. Almost suspicious of his motives. I wandered if he was latching onto the 'mitigating' circumstances thing. Deep down when I saw the bruises. There must

47

have been more of a struggle. But it made me think he must have pinned her up against the wall.

We then, had to question him again. I chimed in, I was not questioning him. I said the following. 'Look, please let's just carry on with this.'

John said, 'she had bruises on her chest. There was a struggle.' Giles Hemingway said, 'no struggle sir.'

John said, 'so explain the bruises.' Giles said, 'she must have already had them.' John said, 'I have heard a witness statement, you pinned her up against the wall. Is that true?' He said, 'no sir, I would never do that.'

I said, 'oh come on, you hated her. You didn't like her. She made your life a misery. You had motive. You used that motive to use deadly force. You could have dealt with this in a different way.'

He then looks to the jury and he said the following, 'members of the jury. This is not an act of self defence. This is the act of a man who wanted to take revenge.'

Maria gasped and said, 'this is not the case.' She said assertively.

Giles said, 'okay, maybe there was a struggle.' John said, 'so your story keeps changing. So there was a struggle.' I said, 'oh come on.'

Maria said, 'objection, this is

entrapment, you have already questioned him.'

Julia said, 'no, carry on, overruled.' John said, 'so was there a struggle or not?'

Giles said, 'there may have been. I was high at the time. On some heavy cocaine. She wouldn't stop hitting me. I fell to the floor, I blanked out. I pinned her against the wall.'

John smiled and said, 'funnily enough cocaine addiction is not reasonable excuse.'

This comment was so outrageous. Julia said, 'right that's enough, another recess. This is absurd.' She slammed on the hammer.

I said to John, sarcastically. 'Nice work there John, nice questioning.' He said, 'well someone has to do it.'

I said. 'Look, the guy is troubled. I never even met Louise Grey. I saw her dead body on the autopsy slab. That was it.

I knew Giles for years. He was provoked. I don't care how pretty that lady was. She had a nasty temper.

John said, 'in all fairness, you know what the jury is going to decide?'

I said, 'what's that then John?'

He said, 'the jury is going to find him guilty.'

I said, 'then it's up to the judge to use discretion. The man's troubled. Homeless.

He's already shaking and on some kind of comedown. We can't feed him cocaine in prison. Don't rub salt in the wound.'

He said, 'I knew Louise Grey, for three years. She didn't have a violent bone in her body.'

I said, 'well that's your opinion, but you could be wrong.'

He said, 'fuck if I am wrong. There was nothing wrong with her.'

I said, 'what about the Felony charge. Was that a trumped up load of horse crap?'

He said, 'the female judge issued that to be smart. There was minimal damage. That whole thing was a circus.'

I said, 'just like this one. What's your point?'

He said, 'there is none, look, the jury is going to decide on the verdict soon.'

I said, 'bullshit, we are just getting started.'

Chapter 10

I entered the court room. More forensics reports. More questions, and many more things to say. At this point Giles Hemingway was breaking down. Just as Louise Grey's mother and family in the background were also.

It was an emotional time for everyone

involved. The court room, was almost delicately entwined Soft furnishings. Big oak settings. The judge, on this great big oak chair. As the jury all stood next to each other in this oak, shiny box. All on red leather seats. Upholstery. The seats I was sitting on were big leather seats.

It was far too sophisticated to be a court room, it was state of the art. With windows, opaque looking. With the sun light glimmering in. The only sense of freedom Hemingway had. As the opaque glass would shine the light.

The big atmosphere. The big court room. The high building with a big chandelier hanging over us. Two in fact. Big oak doors.

The hammer the judge had also. A big hammer, and lots of paperwork. The wig on the judge, and the wigs on the lawyers. All curly and white.

The artist, was drawing more pictures of Hemingway. Like we had enough of him already, he was also drawing lawyer John Smith. The jury also.

He sold the drawings onto the media for profit. A professional artist. He let me keep a piece.

I was next up to the witness stand, again. Talk about being thorough. John was first in line. He said, 'Lucas Jones, how many cases of alleged murders have you dealt with in your 32 years of detective history?'

I said, 'too many to count.'

John said, 'take a wild guess, are we talking a thousand, two thousand?'

I said, 'no, we're talking around, 10,000, at the very least. We do murder enquiries all of the time. Wouldn't be surprised if it was 30,000. In my line of work.'

John said, 'were you lead detective all of the time on these cases?' I said, 'no, I have been lead detective for the past 10 years.'

John said, 'so before that, were you still involved in murder investigations?'

I sighed and said, 'look, ever since I joined The Police. Even as uniform. I have and had been involved in murder investigations.'

John said, 'so is it fair to say you are highly experienced?' I said, 'yes, absolutely.'

John said, 'is there anything unusual that stands out from this case?'

I said, 'of course there is. Most murders are premeditated.'

There is a typographer typing all of this.

I continued, 'must murders are premeditated. Planned. Sure there have been some moments of passion, but they are few and far between. Usually get transferred to uniform if we are busy. Are detective department deal with a lot of

52

premeditated murders. This is one of the few murders, that I have been heavily involved in. That was no premeditated.'

John said, 'but when Hemingway, Giles, decided to strike. He struck with menace, did he not?'

I said, 'perhaps he did, but he was provoked. I also don't know why Louise Grey had a bruise on her chest. I am guessing she attacked him also.'

John said, 'so who is the victim, and who is the suspect here?'

I sighed and I said, 'in the Police, in my department. We don't think just in terms of those two narratives you have outlined. It's possible for someone to be a victim and a suspect. It's possible for someone to be a suspect and a victim. It's also possible for someone to be framed. There are so many different variables here. We would call Giles Hemingway, a victim and a suspect. A victim of circumstance, yet a suspect of the alleged crime.'

John said, 'what would you call Louise Grey?' I said, 'well predominately she is the victim. Having said that, she had been the suspect of felony charges against Hemingway in question.

Battery and assault. This is a complex case.'

John said, 'so do you think Hemingway, Giles, decided, intentionally to kill Louise

Grey?'

I said, 'in my honest opinion. I think he blacked out. He panicked. She was harassing him, and he wanted to get away from the situation.'

John said, 'why didn't he just call 911, or just pushed her away.'

I said, 'because there was a struggle. No payphone near by. The guy doesn't/didn't have a mobile phone. Nor has he had one prior to this.'

John said, 'so you are on Hemingway's side?'

Maria shouted, 'objection your honour, argumentative and prejudicial.'

Julia Cartwright said, 'sustained. John Smith, please. Stick to your line of questioning. Don't be argumentative. Rephrase or carry on.'

John said, 'okay I will rephrase. Who, in your humble opinion is more guilty. Giles Hemingway or Louise Grey?'

I said, 'Giles Hemingway, because as you said. He should have used less aggressive force.'

John smiled, and he said, 'no further questions your honour.'

Maria frowned at me. Maria walked up, and said. 'Lucas, how long have you known Mr Hemingway?' I said, '11 years.' Maria said, 'that is a long time, what was your first interaction with him?'

I said, 'it was a DUI stop, the man was under influence of alcohol. In his own private vehicle. Way before his homelessness. We seized his car for no insurance also.'

Maria said, 'did he get the car back?'

I said, 'in the pounding lot the next day, he chalked up the cash, and renewed his insurance contract.'

Maria said, 'so how many interactions have you had with him in 11 years?'

I said, 'countless, maybe, 50, 100, even 500. The man was, troubled. We were always going out to speak to him. He had a cocaine addiction. Misdemeanours, and he had been the victim of multiple attacks. We had to take statements from him. Sometimes he had to sober up in the cells overnight to do so.'

Maria said, 'who attacked him?'

I said, 'everyone, kids, neighbours, anyone and everyone. Especially during his homelessness.'

Maria said, 'so you gained a rapport with him?'

I said. 'I did indeed.'

She said, 'what have you learnt about him over the years.'

I said, 'that he's a nice person. He struggles with impulse control. He regrets the homelessness situation. We tried getting him housed but it fell through at the last minute.'

Maria said, 'do you think he intended to kill Louise Grey?'

I said, 'yes, but he was provoked?'

Maria said, 'how much so?'

I said, 'we have CCTV footage, of Louise Grey headbutting him and spiriting at him.'

The whole court went into uproar again. John shouted, 'oh it's funny you should mention that now. This footage was never subponead'

Julia Cartwright slammed the hammer on the desk. She said, 'I am ordering a subpoena for that footage. It will be in court next.'

Maria said, 'no further questions your honour.'

Julia continued and said, 'okay, we are going to take a couple of days break now. I await to see that footage.'

We all walked out. John is snarling at me. I drive away in my BMW. I don't have time for this. I go back home, and I switch on the TV. As a tear runs down my cheek, as I hide it with the evening news. The smell of the coffee, the smell of the freshly printed paper. I was human.

The smell of orange juice, but the smell of the courtroom air, and dust. Stuck up my lungs, like a bad smell I couldn't get rid off. I fell asleep in front of the TV. Very hostile and angry with myself. I felt like I was letting the court down. I woke up to more scrambled eggs on toast. This time with some jello, and some little peanuts.

Mind you, it was more like poached eggs this time, as I switched my radio on. Burglary in progress. I wasn't taking it.

Chapter 11

I had a few days left until the court case was going to be reopened. I had the press knocking on my door. Every hour of every day.

I am not responding to the burglary. Not right now. I needed to regroup. Do something. A knock on the door and James Watkins was there.

He said, 'tough break'. I said, 'tell me about it'. He said, 'when is that court case going to end?'

I said, 'soon, perhaps.'

James said, 'well I hope so, because it really is annoying me.'

I said, 'I saw you sit in. The last session.' He brings a plate of Doritos and said, 'look, it's tough, but it's life.'

I said, 'so going back to trial, then having to wait until the Jury decides. That could take hours.'

James said, 'trust me, you are not alone on this. Some things just take time.'

The sun was shining in our eyes. I kind of felt a bit resentful. The court case should have been a slam dunk, but it was being dragged through the mud.

James said, 'look, I'll be there in the courtroom, when the case begins.'

Alex my son, walks down the stairs. Looks like he has been up all night playing Xbox. He said, 'dad can I have money for a pizza. I am starving.' It was a Friday night.' James laughed and said, 'pizzas are in the fridge.' Alex said, 'take out is much better.' James said, 'it's cold take out, probably just as good.'

Alex pointed at James and said, 'were you on TV last week?' James said, 'for a bit. We are working with the FBI right now on tax fraud. It's not much stuff, because it's Detroit. But we try to assist them when we can. Seems like the media loves us.' Alex said, 'no way.'

I said, 'Alex just grab the pizza, and go upstairs, we have business to take care of.'

His hair was long and blonde. Dragging over his eyes. He refused to go to a hairdresser. In his mind, he thought they were all out to get him or something. Wanted to stay in his room, and play stupid video games.

I said to James, 'kids, right?' As Alex scrambled upstairs. James said, 'my daughter is just the same, wants candy,

58

crisps, anything. Then she's upstairs having sleepovers. It's cringeworthy because I want the house to myself to watch baseball.'

I said, 'no shit, you know what's going to happen don't you?' James said, 'no but I feel like you are going to tell me.' I said, 'the red socks are going to beat New Jersey.' James said, 'I don't care about that. I just can't seem to switch off from this Hemingway case. It was like Fiona the other day.'

I said, 'what the rookie cop who wouldn't take no for an answer. We don't want IA breathing down our necks.' He said, 'she is exactly the person who is going to attract IA. Her attitude was off the wall.'

I said, 'she was angry that we took SWAT in, and we took action. She should have been a babysitter. Not a cop.'

James said, 'is that so, so we are not babysitters?'

I said, 'no we're not. We have a job to do. I don't mind doing welfare checks, but I refuse to hold people's hands.'

James said, 'which is more reason why once the Hemingway case is done and dusted. You move on. The last thing I want is for you to do more than the job requires of you.'

I said, 'which means, waiting on the

judge, and jury. It's almost over. Like I want to visit that shmuck in prison. Even though I might have to.'

James, sporting this black tie, and grey kind of shirt. Black shoes. Looking more and more confident for some reason.

I said, 'go red socks right?' James said, 'it doesn't add up.'
I said, 'it's baseball. Why does it not?' James said, 'no the case, itself. Louise Grey. Have they buried her yet?' I said, 'fuck if I know.' James said, 'she has any friends we can question?'

I said, 'don't think so, might be a few. You mean that old college, right down near the lake. Kind of made me think like going down a trip down memory lane.'

James said, 'she was a pretentious college student. Not calling all college students pretentious. Yet she lead a double life. What if she's the suspect.'

I said, 'we have been through this already. We can't bring the dead back to life and hold them on trial. Besides, what did she do, stab herself?'

James said, 'it's possible.' I laughed and said, 'it's possible? Not really. Besides. We have fingerprints nailing Hemingway to the weapon.'

James said, 'it's just eary is all, it doesn't make sense. Unless she staged it, or something happened. Or it was a set up and they tried to pin it on Hemingway.'

I said, 'Friday night conspiracy theories, featuring yours truly. James Watkins.' He laughed and he said, 'well maybe I am wrong.'

I said, 'Hemingway produced the fatal stab wound. Wait.'

James said, 'what?' His cornflower tie hanging over his grey shirt. I paused and he nudged me and said, 'what?'

I said, 'I just forgot. The court wants the CCTV.' James said, 'okay, so let's go up tomorrow, and get it.'

I said, 'obviously we will watch it first. Because I personally only sent it through.'

James said, 'why didn't you process this when you had the time. Not four weeks after.'

I said, 'I didn't think we needed it. It's just the judge kicking her heels. Trying to make something out of nothing.'

James said, 'well it's important.' He grabbed his suede coat. Dangled some keys, and said, 'we are going now.'

I said sarcastically, 'who's going to babysit Alex?' James said, 'come on, let's go.'

James had another car, and for reasons I had noticed. It was nothing like a Chevron. Looked like an old Jaguar car. We drove to the detective office.

I grabbed the tape out of the cabinet. A

DVD type tape-CD.

I pressed pay.

Chapter 12

The tape was showing Louise Grey spitting and shoving Giles Hemingway; She was with 3 other women. All college friends. I didn't recognise them.

Then we look at Hemingway, he pulls out the knife. As we expected. There is a struggle. He shoves the blade in her chest. The other girls look scared and run off.

James said, 'well this confirms everything. I thought she was alone.'

I said, 'me too, but chasing down those other ladies isn't going to pay credence.'

James said, 'what is the college?' I said, 'Oaksville, by the lake. Some posh college. They work hard but that group. I pointed to the CCTV paused. That group take drugs quite readily.'

James said, 'they might have more information.' I said, 'no we have everything we need. This is just the judge trying to stamp her feet.' James said, 'do you have names and addresses?' I said, 'sure I do. Sophie Brightman. Angelina Hoffman. Sarah Dickinson. All straight A students. The same people who have done these drugs. The same people on the CCTV.'

James said, 'leading double lives.' I said, 'sounds like it.' James grabbed the DVD. We both ran down to his car. We drove to Sophie Brightman's house. Some blonde female. 21. We flashed our badges. The father. A grey, husky, and dark shadow of a guy, and the mother in her 50's. Some small, woman.

I said, 'Sophie, we can we speak to you please?' She said, 'sure.'

I said, 'Sophie, we have seen you on CCTV the night of Louise Grey's murder. It shows you with a group of other girls. Taunting Giles Hemingway. What can you tell us about this?'

Sophie said, 'well, we were walking home, and Giles became aggressive.' I said, 'let me stop you there. That wasn't all that happened. Were you provoking him?' She said, 'no.' I said, 'oh come on, you expect us to believe this was a misunderstanding.' The mother was looking over quite fiercely James said assertively. 'Look, the court case resumes on Monday. Is there anything you want to tell us.'

Sophie said, 'that I lost a best friend.' I said, 'oh cut it out.' She said, 'excuse me?'

I said, 'this is a circus.' James chimed in and said, 'I think what my colleague is saying is we have information. Giles was provoked.'

Sophie said, 'well that's what he is saying, but he always liked to play victim.'

I said, 'so take us back to your relationship with him. What did he try doing? I have known this guy for 11 years. He's not the person you are trying to make out.'

Sophie said, 'on the night of this attack. He was drunk, agitated. He was angry. He wanted cocaine. We didn't have any on us.' I said, 'continue, please.' Sophie said, 'he became violent, he was blaming us for everything. Thought it was our job to go to the bakery, and get him something. He wanted us to babysit him. When we ignored him and walked away. He turned hostile.'

I said, 'the CCTV shows Louise Grey spitting at him.' Sophie said, 'yeah okay. Louise wasn't all that nice. We just put up with her.' I said, 'but you still did drugs with her?' Sophie was silent. I said. 'Oh come on Sophie. We know your history. Class A possession, we know you did Cocaine. It's pointless lying to us. We won't arrest you for personal use. We just want to know what is going on here.'

Sophie said. 'Okay there was cocaine involved. Yet that wasn't what the argument was about.'

I said, 'oh come on, your story keeps changing. I want to know facts. Was

Hemingway provoked or not?'

Sophie said, 'yes, by Louise Grey, but I tried pulling her away.' I said the CCTV camera doesn't show you doing that. Just shows you laughing.'

Sophie said, 'well out of nervousness Does the CCTV have audio?'

I said, 'no, it doesn't, but I can lip read. You called him a cunt.'

Sophie said, 'tensions were high.' I said, 'well, so what? Tensions are high, but this implicates you slightly. I am going to recommend you are charged with harassment'

Sophie started crying and said, 'oh what? Really?' I said, 'yes, really, because you didn't help this situation. This murder charge, and then we talk in circles here. You think this is an easy job for me?'

Sophie said, 'well what can I do?'

I said, 'give us intelligence, and we'll turn a blind eye to the harassment charge.'

Sophie said, 'what if I don't have any intelligence.' I said. 'Look, let's talk practicalities here. Something is going on. I want to know what.'

Sophie said, 'okay, that knife. That Hemingway had. Two weeks ago. Louise Grey bought it for him. Said he would keep him safe. She tried setting him up.'

I said, 'but he was the one that stabbed

her?'

Sophie said, 'well of course, but I don't think she was expecting that to happen. She just wanted him out of the way. Jailed. Maybe for a few years. She was sick of him.'

I smiled and said, 'thank you, that goes a long way.'

Me and James walk towards the door. The gruesome mother still howling at us.

Sophie said, 'wait.' I said, 'what is it?' Sophie said, 'do you want me to testify in court.'

I said, 'no, don't worry about it. We have all the evidence we need now.'

James whispers in my ear and said, 'might not be a bad idea.' I sighed, the mother growling at us, had left. I looked at Sophie. I said, 'Zip code, 3030, Detroit Court. Down town state. Estate Lane. 10am. I'll let the judge know you are arriving.'

Sophie said, 'okay.' She smiled, and we left.

In the black Jaguar. Back to my house with James. With the DVD, a cooberating witness. More snacks. James said, 'the way you handled that situation was great.'

I said, 'this whole thing will get sorted.'

James said, 'I hope so.'

Chapter 13

66

Back in court, it wasn't what it seemed. The evidence was emerging. I played the DVD on a TV screen. With build it DVD player. Everyone watched with horror as they saw what had happened.

Sophie, was sitting there. She was called up to the witness stand. John said, 'so Sophie, how long did you know Louise Grey?' Sophie said, '8 years, all the way through secondary school, and college.' John said, 'did you get on well?' Sophie said, 'sure.' John said, 'describe the night of the attack.'

Sophie said, 'Giles was angry. He was very upset. There was an altercation between him and Louise. A scuffle ensued. And he stabbed her. Fatally.'

John said, 'describe the stabbing?' Sophie said, 'it was fatal, aggressive. He didn't do it to wound. He did it to kill. She was lying on the floor bleeding for ages.'

John said, 'was it you who phoned 911?' Sophie said, 'I phoned 911.' John said, 'when did The Police arrive?' Sophie said, 'it seemed like 10 minutes, but it was probably only 4.'

John said, 'what did Giles do after using that knife?' Sophie said, 'he kept repeating, sorry, sorry, sorry. He kept stammering over and over the same apology. He seemed shocked, and he

67

stood back.'

John said whilst pointing at a picture of the wound. 'Did Giles intend to kill Louise?' Sophie said, 'without a shadow of a doubt.'

Maria was next to question Sophie. Maria said, 'Sophie, you knew Giles for how long?' Sophie said, 'a few years.' Maria said, 'what was your impression of him?' Sophie said, 'he was a loner, he used to score drugs, and alcohol. He was a nice guy, but he had an angry side to him.'

Maria said, 'tell me about that murder weapon. Is it true that Louise Grey, bought this weapon for Giles. Two weeks prior, to try and set him up. To frame him?' Sophie said, 'that is correct.' You could hear gasps.

Sophie said, 'she tried setting him up for possession of the blade. She didn't want him around any longer.'

Maria said, 'why's that?'

Sophie said, 'Giles was seen as a threat.'

Maria said, 'oh come on, a homeless guy is now 'a threat', what kind of cannabis had you been smoking the night of this attack?'

John piped in and said, 'objection, argumentative.' Julia Cartwright said, 'sustained, please. Maria. Rephrase the question.'

Maria rephrased. She said, 'okay, so I

68

will reword. Were you intoxicated the night of the attack?'

Sophie looked at me, all glimour in her eyes. A look of guilt resonated on her face. Her blonde hair, her blue eyes. Her childish mannerisms. There is no way this girl was brought up in a loving household. The way she was acting.

Sophie said, 'we were all high on skunk. Me and all of the girls.'

Maria said, 'sorry, my knowledge of strains of cannabis, is not very good. Being a non smoker. Describe 'skunk' to me?'

Sophie said, 'it's a very harsh strain of cannabis.'

I interjected, and said, 'right this is enough. We are not getting anywhere with these questions.'

Julia slammed her hammer down on the board. She said, 'look, please, let the questioning finish.'

I said, 'this is bullshit, and you know it. There is no way they were sober on the night of attack. Not them, nor Giles Hemingway.'

Julia glared at me, and she said, 'right that's it, my office now.'

I was escorted by security to Julia's office. She was sat in her chair. Brown, leather. She said, 'so what exactly are you doing? Making my court room out to be

69

some kind of joke?'

I said, 'this type of questioning is getting old. Those girls antagonised Giles. I call bullshit on the whole thing.'

Julia said, 'isn't that up to the Jury and me to decide. You're a detective. One hell of a good one, but you have to let everyone do their jobs here. She was your witness. You called her in.'

I said, 'yeah but I didn't realise she was going to spin a whole opera music on the whole thing. This thing went from crazy to god damn lunacy. Do you expect me to believe they were just high the night of that attack?'

Julia said, 'so what do you think happened?' I stammered and said, 'the whole thing stinks of a set up.'

Julia said, 'the CCTV, that does not lie?'

I said, 'I don't know, I didn't want to say this because I didn't want to interfere'

Julia said, 'you didn't want to say what sorry?'

I said, 'the CCTV looks like it's been tampered with.'

Julia laughed and chortled and said, 'oh ho ho, do you seriously expect me to believe a pair of naïve college students were able to pull a stunt like this?'

I said, 'maybe someone else was in on it?'

Julia said, 'like who?'

I said, 'when I spoke to the DA, they mentioned a tall guy, called Russel Blakely. Russel wasn't the usual type of guy. Very hidden. Didn't speak much. He was connected to those girls. Sophie's uncle. Ex marines. Very professional. A bit of a vigilante. Always tried giving us tip offs, that we used to laugh at in the office. The more I think about it. Russel Blakely. He must have put a video on the CCTV lens or something. I have been doing this job for years. I remember a voice mail. From him. Threatening me. Said that he didn't' want me to jeopardise the trial. Maria had the same message. We didn't want to mention it to you because we didn't want to distract you.'

Julia pressed some kind of buzzer on her phone, she said, 'bring Maria in please.' Maria walked in looking shocked. She said, 'what's going on?'

Julia said, 'please, take a seat.'

Julia said, 'is this true, Russel Blakely. Sophie's uncle. He has tampered with evidence?'

Maria said, 'I don't know, but I am sure you have heard of the voicemail.'

Julia said, 'right that's it. I am calling of the prelim. We suspend this trial until we find out how to reach this guy.'

I said, 'I am sorry, but this trial. Has been suspended, and cut, and stopped. So many times.'

Julia said, 'it's a murder trial, not a traffic violation hearing. We do things by the book. I want to know who this Richard Blakely guy is.'

I said under baited breath. 'Some type of asshole.' Julia said, 'I am sorry, do you have something you want to say?'

I said, 'no, I am okay, if it's okay with you I am going home.'

Maria said, 'well, I will come with you.'

It was me, Maria, James followed behind us. We also had this big muscular guy from the DA. Some lawyer called Mark Clinton Jones. We all arrived at this warehouse.

Things got heated, and these men, big men, arrived. With Richard Blakely following. All his comrades. 8 of them. Gangsters.

Richard Blakely was wearing all leather. Tooth pick in his mouth. He said assertively. 'You tried getting my niece involved in this trial?' He said arrogantly.

Another guy from the DA, Russel Travis Jones Clive, arrives. Massive guy. He said, 'look, let's take the heat out of this.'

Richard Blakely draws a pistol, and said, 'take the heat out of what gentleman?' We all draw our pistols. Russel Clive, draws his, and I am reaching in my holster for ages for mine.

I said, 'look, Richard, we have information you have tried jepordising this trial. The CCTV is bogus. You played something else. A previous clip. This whole thing stinks of a set up.'

Richard laughed and said, 'oh yeah, but it's going to take you ages to find out what I did.'

I said, 'I know what you did, you taped a previous incident. Recorded it, edited some bits, and used some prior footage. We know Hemingway punched Louise a few months before the attack. All you had to do was edit the footage. What software have you got? Good editing software. You don't fool me.'

He smiled. I said, 'plus the gun firing off. The CCTV is not audio. But there is no shrapnel. Nothing.'

Richard lights a cannabis joints and blows it in my face. I said, 'you are some dumb animal. I will tell you.'

James Watkins said, 'listen here, it's time you went into custody.'

Richard said, 'try and stop me.'

SWAT arrived. We had around 50 SWAT people. Take this guy down. Rubber bullet in the chest. The rest of the guys were dead. We brought him in for questioning.

Into the cell block. Straight out. Me and James not looking impressed. I said, 'listen, you are looking at 100 years in a state jail without parole.'

He said, 'so why the fuck should I start snitching now then? Not that you wanted anything to do with my tip offs.' Me and James laughed. I said, 'now we do, we will reduce your sentence. We may even let you go. But we need to know. What you did.'

Richard said, 'you will drop all charges.' I said. 'Yes sure.'

Richard said, 'The CCTV is a set up, and it wasn't Hemingway who killed Louise Grey. It was me.'

Me and James were pushing each other, trying to get near to this dude. I had reach first. I punched Richard in the face. I said, 'listen, this is what you have done?' Another punch to the face. More blood comes out as the guy has a sore lip.

James smiles and said, 'that is enough, put him back on his feet.'

We put him back. He scrambled and sat down.

I said, 'this changes everything now.'

Richard said, 'oh I wouldn't do that if I was you. I have a guy on the outside.'

He picks his skin and underneath his skin. Is some kind of remote control device. He said, 'the guy on the outside, you don't want to mess with.'

I said. 'You try messing up this case.'

74

James said, 'don't go near him.'

I said, 'what is that device.'

He said, 'it's contraband. It's a cell text message activator. I have pre set a text message for my man. Clyde Mark Parkinson. To kill, Sophie.'

I said, 'you don't get on with your neices or something?'

He said, 'it's a bargaining chip.'

I said, 'what do you want?'

He said, 'I want a million dollars in cash, and to be out of this office.'

I said, 'we can get that arranged. Just don't hurt anyone.' I called a hostage negotiator in called Frank Owen. Frank said, 'listen Richard. I know you are angry right now.'

Richard said, 'angry or greedy?'

Chapter 14

Frank said, 'okay, so we can sort this situation out.' Richard said, 'have to make it quick.' I said, 'look Richard, this is getting stupid now.'

Frank Owen said, 'what do we have to do to make this work?' Richard said, 'I want a billion dollars in cash.' Frank said, 'we can get you that money.'

I took Frank outside. I said, 'look, this is getting ridiculous now. There is no way this is happening.'

Frank said, 'we can't take our chances. It's not a lie.' I said, 'maybe not, but this whole thing has gone stir crazy.'

Frank said, 'what is your idea then?'

I said, 'we call his bluff.' Frank said, 'bullshit, if Sophie is in danger. We need to tell her.' Frank did a dialling gesture to a female detective called Paula.

I said, 'we get him the cash, and then what? We let him walk.'

Frank said, 'well do you see any other alternatives?'

Frank walks in the interview room, and said, 'right, we will get you the cash.'

Richard said, 'I want it in 50's.' I said, 'fine, no problem, now please give me that device, and call it off.' He handed over this microscopic telephone. Almost like an auto text generator. It was so weird. He must have dug it underneath his skin.

This guy was ex marines but this was crazy. I said, 'we'll get you a doctor to sew up your arm. Despite the fact you tried pulling this stunt.'

A female doctor came in and gave him stitches. I said, 'this is absolutely crazy the way you have orchestrated this.'

Richard said, 'oh well.'

I am feeling kind of confused, as we deliver him his money. I am feeling disorientated. Once the money is delivered. That is not the end of it. He also

76

has some words he wants to say to us.

He gives us this spiel about self preservation as he walks out of the door. I am literally tongue tied, and I don't have time for this.

Frank said, 'I can't cope with this much longer.'

I said, 'neither can I. This whole case is ruined.' James said, 'maybe.'

An impromptu stop to Mcdonalds. I couldn't shake the feeling in my head. Neither could James. Fries and handburgers. The fries were nice and salty. I had ketchup, kind of felt like comfort food.

Deep down, with my strawberry milkshake, and my sense of optimism slowly fading away. I was left confused. We had no case. Richard Blakely was away. We had absolutely nothing.

James said, 'still worrying over that shmuck Blakely. What an arrogant son of a bitch.' I said, 'he sure did play us, but we will catch him.'

James said, 'look our detective unit, has been cut, resources are sparse. It wasn't how it used to be. It's just me and you on this right now.'

Ironically as he said this, a detective behind us. Chief Detective Ryan Coleman. He shouted, 'boys.'

We stopped. He was around my age.

Maybe a year older. At best. Though wouldn't stretch it that far.

He got out of his Rolls Royce. Big chap. Bigger than me, and I was just carrying an extra stone. He must have been packing an extra 7 stone. At best, maybe even 9. Yet his charisma, made up for it. Bushy tailed. Bright eyed. Friendly.

He said, 'they've assigned me to this case.' He said with his assertive look. His grey coat.

He said, 'we are trying to find Blakely. Yet we won't be able to exonerate Giles without getting Blakely into custody. The trial has been suspended until further notice.'

I said, 'do you know where Blakely has gone?' Ryan Coleman said, 'sure I do, he's still in Detroit.'

I said, 'no shit, really?'

Ryan said, 'call in a helicopter.'

A helicopter was flying above our heads. We were looking all over for this guy. We find him in a parking lot. Underneath some boxes. Sweating, nervous, and high. It was just him alone. We cuff him, and we take him into custody. I am getting really tired and I say the following.

'Look, you son of a bitch, what exactly is *going on here?*"' I asked.

He said, 'shit got out of hand.' I said, 'it's time to bring you towards the DA. I have had enough of you.'

DA officer Justin Kyle, gripped this guy, and bundled him into the cell. It took convincing but we were able to exonerate Giles Hemingway. I was taking that guy to a barber shop. For my own sanity. I drove him there, and he got his beard done. His hair done. He was looking a million dollars. Ironically we lost that.

I said, 'you are a changed man. Turned out the asshole who killed Louise is in custody now. Do you know anything about this.' He shook his head.

I drove him down to an apartment on west thirty eight street. I was able to pay for him to stay there for a year. Whilst he was able to get his postal work job back.

I climbed into my Mercedes and I drove back to the DA's office. I said, 'Blakely, you son of a bitch.'

He was due in court. He was found guilty, of perverting the course of justice. He was then found guilty of murder also. He was serving 100 years in a state prison. With chance of parole in half of that time. Yet he kept yapping. That's all he did, and all I could ever remember him doing.

I said to James, 'this is getting unreal.' James said, 'it's how it is. Just how it is.' I said, 'time to meet Giles Hemingway.'

We pulled up to meet Giles, and he was getting on okay. He had a postal work job.

He was successful. He a car. Well I bought him an old Porsche Out of my own money. I said, 'lucky those girls can't bother you again. Shame about Louise.' He said, 'shame I was set up also.'

I said, 'I got you out of it.' He said, 'of course you did, you are on excellent detective.' I said, 'yet that is all I am to you. An 'amazing detective'. Not your friend. I said in a jokey way.' He said, 'of course your my friend.' I said, 'look, for all I know, everything we have ever discussed. We won't know the full facts here. But that lunatic Richard Blakely, was able to doctor that CCTV footage. He was able to do it in a way which could try to fool the jury. It was him who stabbed Louise.'

Giles said, 'I know all of this.' He said in a tired kind of way. I said, 'do you know how difficult it is being a detective?' Giles said, 'no.' I said, 'running around all day, having people lie to us at every opportunity. When I worked in uniform. All I got is lies, lies, and lies. It was part of the job. And I accepted this. You know, and as the years went on, I decided to never believe anything anyone ever said. Always look into things. At first I was going stir crazy. I couldn't get it out of my head. It wouldn't make sense, and I sure as hell couldn't shake it. I used to have

80

some sleepless night also. Just as long as you are safe.'

Giles said, 'yeah of course I am safe. That dude Richard Blakely is in maximum security pennsylvania.pennsylvania Jail.'

I said, 'I know, and he's probably wound up someone's bitch.'

Giles said, 'that's it? No remorse on his part.'

I said, 'probably not, no. People like that can't change over night. If ever.'

Giles Hemingway laughed. He said, 'it's pretty crazy stuff isn't it. Go and visit him in jail.'

I said, 'I am not visiting that shmuck in jail.'

Giles said, 'why not?'

I said, 'because I don't feel like it. I don't want to know anything about this dude. Nothing whatsoever. That is how it's going to stay. Until we get things sorted out. At least.'

Giles said, 'he's got you running around worried.' I said, 'no he hasn't. I really am not that concerned about him.'

I said, 'so hows the postal work going? You with fedex?' Giles nodded and said, 'yes I am, and it's great. I am meeting so many cool people. I go the extra mile to make my customers happy.'

I said, 'that's good, yet this whole ordeal has been a lot for you to take in.'

81

He said, 'yeah but I am over it. It's not a problem.'

I sat down next to him, and I said the following. 'Look sir, time and time again. Everytime something happens. Every time the radio is on. Every time I run out of gas. Every time I have to make a phone call. It's always the same. Back to work. Yet it's not like that anymore. I feel like I have made a friend.'

Giles said, 'yeah you have said that twice now, but you forget everything else in-between'

I said, 'like what? I am not going to grab those drawings of you, and make you out to be some celebrity or something.'

Giles said, 'it just pays credence to the fact that you are going to have to meet people like me. Time and time again.'

I nodded and left the building. I walked out, and down the stairs.

Chapter 15

I was at home now. Just eating peanuts, watching TV. Another western, and man if those things got boring. Some armed robbery just comes live on the radio. 'Shots fired, all units.' I radioed in and said, 'not attending.'

Ryan Coleman shouted, 'come on, make it happen.' I said, 'can I finish my god damn peanuts first?'

Ryan said, 'of course. No rush, only safety to the public.' I sighed. Every Saturday night. That was how it was. I was settling down in my pyjamas, watching a movie. Then this bullshit happens.

I change into some suede trousers. I put on my DKNY shirt. My tie. I walk outside, and into my Chevron. It needed to see the inside of a car wash.

I drive to the shooting. Some dude is robbing a convenience store. Again. Time and time, I have to put up with this.

SWAT are on the way, and I am handed the megaphone. Ryan Coleman whispers, 'talk to him.'

It was some loner in his twenties. Kind of a loose canon. It had mental health written all over it.

I shouted, 'sir, come out, and put your hands on your head.'

He shouted audibly, 'go away right now.'

I rolled my eyes and I said, 'sir, please, come outside.'

No response, a shot fired through the window. Ryan said, 'he's a cheese dick, give me that megaphone.'

Ryan shouted, 'right, this is the Police. Come out with your hands behind your head.'

No response. He had held someone

hostage. I think it was the convenience store owner. An asian man.

SWAT arrived, I rolled my eyes and shouted to commander Lee Oniel. I said, 'take it from here boys.' Lee said, 'right okay.' SWAT launched a smoke flare. They ran in. Two rubber bullets were fired. One in the chest, one in the leg. He was arrested

Ryan said, 'nice work.' Lee took a different attitude. 'Everytime there is a shooting in this damn county, and damn, district and state. You ring us up. Next time, it's your mess to clean up.'

4 members of SWAT around him agreeing. A guy in the background also shouting, 'yeah that is what I am talking about. We are not your slaves.' Lee said, 'shut up.'

He looked towards me and he said, 'next time, deal with this yourself.' He handed me his bullet proof vest. He had taken off. I ran over, and threw it back at him, and I said. 'What's all this fuss about?'

Lee said, 'I am working double shifts. We have more pressing business.' I said, 'the guy was armed sir.'

Lee shouted, 'every god damn person in the USA is armed. You are not understanding my point.'

I said, 'I am understanding your point. You can't be bothered to take this call. We have professional men on this. Yet we are busy with other stuff. Take your ego out of this.'

Lee got right up in my face, and he said, 'you don't understand the week I have had. We are not robots.'

I said, 'I thoroughly understand the week you have had. Yet it's not that simple. You think us guys don't work hard? I am comforting eating with peanuts In my room, just eating fries. Watching shitty Western movies here. Whilst you are and you 'army' are acting like you are God's gift. Give me a break.'

Lee said, 'one call to Internal Affairs. One fucking call.' I said, 'IA won't do anything. Stop blaming all of this mess on us.'

Lee said, 'the fuck I am, we have a job to do.'

Ryan pushed his way in and said, 'look, everyone go your separate ways.'

Lee gave me a look of disgust and left. Ryan said to me and James. 'Look, just ignore them, throwing their weight around. We did the right thing by calling them.'

I said, 'did we? Did you hear what I was saying. I am comfort eating in my room. Eating peanuts. Just watching some Western movie. My radio goes. I attend the call. I make the appropriate referral.'

Ryan gets pissed off and said, 'I worked hard also the last few years. Let's all just regroup.' I said. 'I am going back home. I have a movie to finish.' I drove back in disgust. Pulled out of the parking lot, as you could see smoke everywhere.

James Watkins followed me and said, 'wait up, I left my car at the station. Can I have a ride back home?'

In the car he said, 'look, I know things got heated.' I said. 'I know they did, but that's the line of work we are in.'

Ryan said, 'everything seems like it's failing in our department. The last thing I want is IA poking their noses in.'

I said, 'that's not going to happen. Don't worry about it.'

I left, feeling upset. I drove home. Continued watching the Western movie. Fell asleep in my own clothes.

Chapter 16

Nothing made sense anymore. Nothing whatsoever. I was able to know what I thought about the world. I was able to take guesses. I was able to realise what was happening.

I couldn't really feel anything anymore. It's almost like the wind had swept away from my hair, and left me breathless. My whole life I tried to put on this front. That

I was some good person, when in actual fact. Part of me felt like I was turning too nice.

Taking pity on random people, and my life had no opportunity for growth. So I could just remember how life was. I remember a time when life was easier. Now with all of this going on. I had a lawful duty to visit Richard Blakely in prison.

I walk up to the grounds. Looks like a fortress. It's a big building and I look over at it in amazement. When I go inside, it's a different story all together.

Cell mates shouting at each other. A lot of hostility. Blakey's cell opens, and I speak to him. I said, 'you almost got away with that. Well you didn't succeed.'

Richard said, 'I tried,'

I said, 'the way I see it, everything now is in the past. Yet you won't see parole for ages. Then you have to convince them you have changed.'

Richard said. 'We go to the exercise yard. Every day, and I play basket ball. The people in here want me dead.' I said, 'I am not surprised.'

He said, 'you don't care do you?'

I said, 'I do, it's just you have been very annoying of late. I have been told I have a lawful duty to speak to you.

Every fortnight, I play golf, with James

Watkins. Nice bloke. Sometimes the chief detective Ryan Coleman joins us also.

I can swipe ages for the ball to go on the green. Sometimes it doesn't make it, yet I have the energy to at least try and make it.

We walk around with the golf clubs, and cart. The sun is shining, and it's a slice of freedom.

Yet I do this job, and it changes. It turns into something I haven't really experienced before.'

Richard said, 'you trying to say life is easy on the outside?'

I said, 'no, not really. I am just saying how my lifestyle is. Us cops, we socialise and we talk. Even outside of work. We talk about lots of things. Sometimes names get shared. Sometimes they don't. Yet the bottom line is we try our best to make ends meet. That green. It resembles something to me. Hope, dignity, and the ability to be able to get things done. We are not all negative in our presumption of this life. I guess I can be faithful I won't have to see life. As you did. Inside a cell. Correct me if I am wrong, but that's how you see it?'

He said, 'not really, it doesn't work that way with me. I find it difficult to keep a straight face with everyone kicking on off in here. That slice of freedom you talk about. Sure I will be damned if I ever see it again. Yet it's going to make me feel kind of worried, moving forward. Not everything is as you mention.'

I said, 'these conversations aside, the amount of tricks you tried to pull on us. Turns out exonerating Giles was a slice of pie. A piece of cake. What exactly did you think you could do? You do know the FBI and IA keep tabs on us. You think this was a walk in the park.'

He said, 'it wasn't supposed to.'

I said, 'so you figured you could just run in, tamper with evidence. Frame Hemingway. Get money, and just play the system like a fiddle. It doesn't work like that.'

I handed him a cheese sandwich. He ate it very quickly. As if it was the only decent amount of food he had had for a while. I handed him an apple. Some Lays crisps, and I stood right facing him. As the guard impatiently wanted me to hurry up.

I said, 'you did the crime, you do the time. Enjoy your lunch.' I left and walked out. The gates were buzzing, and I hope into my Mercedes. I drive off.

Chapter 17

Nothing could stop me thinking about the life I was leading. Being a detective and deep down. I was okay with that. Yet there were certain things I couldn't do.

89

There were certain things I couldn't say. I took a step back and looked at myself. I wandered what life had in stall for me.

I could see glimouring faces and good people, and deep down. I didn't know what to expect anymore. It's almost like life had taken a turn for the worst. I deeply wanted to become involved in more investigation work. Yet I disliked getting called to these robberies all of the time. It was uniform's job. Yet they were always so stretched.

I looked my drive. I looked at my silver Chevron. I looked at life, and I saw things in terms of what I wanted. I wanted a health retirement, and at times I am not sure if that was going to happen or not. With this case lingering over my head. Deep down, sometimes you just wanted the best for your victims/suspects. Yet I deeply wanted to know where life was going.

I walk back into my room, and I go to bed. The wife is still asleep. You know. I keep waking up to different breakfast meals. This time it was some kind of oatmeal or something. I wasn't used to it. Yet I still ate it. The wife said I had to monitor my cholesterol or something.

Life was different now. Yet I was willing to work with what I had. You could hear lots of things. The radio dispatch going. The long pauses in conversations. All of the commitment and effort, you had put into your work. Just to make sure it was paying off.

Things weren't squaring well with me, and I wasn't sure why. I looked around and appeared kind of distant. In a way. I kind of felt it. I had a lot of energy, even in my older years. Yet my mind was going ten to the dozen. Not all of the time, and some times you wouldn't know how I felt. Deep down I kind of resented how I was working. Working long shifts, just to do so much. Yet nothing was really making sense. I look at the world through a lens of what I have to do.

My Motorola radio. My sense of humour, and all of the people I had met. As I looked over the scaly front yard and the porch. Almost ghost figures seemed to walk passed, as I seemed even more concerned with the notion of the branches. Just hanging over the cars outside. As nature seemed to blossom around me, and my power of positive thinking. It was reaching an all time low. I couldn't help but look back in hindsight. I guess sometimes that didn't work well. At least not all of the time.

Yet in some results. I kind of wish life was working with me. Out of all of the decisions I had made. My body felt it was aching. I was giving up everything I had longed for. I had abused my body too much and fed it with random crap. I was a broken down vehicle. Even though it's pathetic to describe it like that.

All of my policing work, everything I had done was for good. Everything I was doing was to help people. I get no thanks, and no rewards whatsoever. None of the help I do is appreciated. I was never invited to the late night dinners when I was first in uniform. Sure it took me a while to build up people's trust. I can't describe to you what a period of depression feels like. Especially as a police officer. You have to see so many traumatic things. I was burning down inside. Once was an oiled machine, was a vacuous mess. I was abusing my body, drinking alcohol. The flash backs, the nightmares of the work I had done. The visions of all of the suspects I had apprehended Yet the doctor was okay with the notion. It wasn't serious. It would go away. It's in human nature.

You can shake all of those thoughts away, you can live your book by your own design. Throw the rule book away and do what you want to do. Because that is what you want to do. It wasn't about hard work anymore, even though that was a contributing factor. It was just about, the motion of moving forward. In a linear way.

Feeling kind of alien to the world and what the world expected of me. I didn't want to associate with pseudo intellectual liberals. I didn't want to associate with the dregs of society. Just following me around like I was god's gift. Yet this depression was effecting my own performance.

I see the police psychiatrist, and he issues me with this medicine. He tells me it's not anti depressants. I take it from him, and I open it up. It has to be some kind of joke. Because inside. I can see what it is. It's tablets. Take 1, one a day, for a week.

That was it. I open the door and I said, 'what is this, valium?' He said, 'no, lithium.' I said, 'are you out of your mind here?' He said, 'no.'

I said, 'this is going to knock me unconscious.' He said, 'that is the whole point. You have to get to sleep somehow. All of this dozing off. Taking calls to robberies. How can you respond to a robbery if you are already half asleep? They wouldn't take you on board, besides, you'd probably think it was a lucid dream or something.'

I said, 'you're very smart.' So there it was, for one solid week. With the DA's

93

approval, and all of the other top sharks above my head. I was able to take these tablets, and fall asleep. Like someone had knocked two bells out of me. The first night I took it. I could hear a robbery in the background. I could hear them calling my name.

I answered it, and I said the following, 'bring me fries and ketchup in the morning.' James Watkins said, 'what is going on with this guy? He's delirious.'

I slept, and I slept on my radio receiver Turned out they could hear me snoring for most of the night. I wake up, an I get a letter through the post.

A disgruntled Ryan Coleman. Wanting to fill me in for a mistake I had made. Turns out I had been keeping the whole force awake with my snoring.

He said, 'what the fuck is this shit?' - Not on the letter. The letter just said, to call him, so I did. I phoned him up. I said, 'what do you mean?'

He said, 'falling asleep on the job.'

I said, 'sir, I was not on call, the duty psychiatrist has given me lithium.' He was outraged. He said, 'lithium!?' I said, 'that's what it says there on the packet. I mean you have to take it.'

He said, 'are you high?' I said, 'not that I think of.' He said. 'You are pissing me off.'

I said, 'sir, with all due respect. I had

every right to see the doctor. I have some anxiety. I needed to sleep. These burglarys are fucking killing me.'

He said, 'someone has to respond to them.' I said, 'the last time I responded to one. SWAT gave me an ear full. I wasn't the same after that.'

He said, 'so I see what this is, this is rebellion.' I said, 'what the hell are you on about sir? Do you see me with any picket fences with slogans on? I literally am fed up of this whole routine. The sheer aggression of life has knocked me to a pulp. I can't let go. And I can't understand why you pull me into your office like this.'

He has me by the scruff of the neck, at his office. He said. 'One phone call to the IA.' He said in a way of making a threat. I said. 'Call them up. Phone up IA. See if I care. I am fed up of following your orders. Every single day sir. You think it's easy for me, living with you like this. This is supposed to be one big family. Yet you can't take your share of the responsibility. Which in my case. When you look at the record I am under. It was a different scenario all together in my world. I was a different person but I was fed up of sticking to the rule book. Fed up of waiting. Sick of waiting for the same spiel to come my way. Oh I am sorry for what I have done. I am sorry for this. Do you ever look in the mirror, and wander these things. Has it ever occurred to you that even though we have some fight. We are not some liberals on the picket fences. Protesting over some phony war done in the 80's. This is not liberation. This is assassination I am sick and tired of these games. You pull me into your bullshitting office again, and try to summon me out to be the bad guy. I will knock you right in the stomach.'

He said, 'wait here, you want to try it on, come on then, fight me. Be my guest. Let's have a tumble. Let's fight.' He rolls his sleeves up. I said, 'listen, I seriously doubt you would win in a fight with me.'
He said, 'well come try it.' I said, 'this is not working, you are not helping with these things. Everything you have spoken about. Sure it doesn't make sense. Not anymore. Times have changed.' He said. 'We are still police officers.' I said, 'of course we are. Yet I spent ages just babysitting that tumble dick, what ever his name was. Hemingway. Turns out the CCTV was fake.'

Ryan said, 'oh I get it, that case effected you. You could have bailed any second.' I said, 'then it would have been transferred straight back to the DA. We might have lost. It's not always bread and butter with you.'

Ryan said, 'it may have gone to a different police officer.' I said, 'no way, it doesn't work like that. It goes to the DA. Always has been that way. No wander all of these cases get thrown under the radar. We lose interest and you wander why it never makes sense anymore. All of this circle jerking, with the banks, with the teleport companies. With the fax machine. It never squared with you, so why all of this now?' He said. 'Just trying to make you understand.'

I said, 'sir, with all due respect. This whole department has been crumbling.'

He said, 'crumbling for what reason, and to what effect? We just want the best for you.'

I said, 'the best, you think it works like that. You can't just throw your weight around at every chance you get. That's not how it works. I was there sir, the last armed robbery. I was there. I had to take abuse off off SWAT.'

Ryan said, 'you know what. Pencil dicks. The lot of them, just ignore them. You can't handle some work place politics.'

I said, 'not really, not with all of this going on.'

He said, 'next time you go to sleep, don't lean on your receiver on your radio. Take your poxy stupid pills, and make sure you sleep well. Don't worry about us.'

I said, 'well sir, I am disliking the way you talk to me. My health is important. I am not a robot.' I left, and was walking towards the vending machine. I had to get away from this clown. Yet he was following me. Every inch I walked. He would walk. What was this? Some kind of mind game or something. I put my head in the drink fountain. I ordered the wrong pack of biscuits in the vending machine. I walked into the wrong office, disrupted a meeting.

I then, was able to find my office, and I sat down. He followed me. Pointing and said, 'one more word out of you, and you are fired. Next time you have a problem. You come and see me like a man.'

He walked away, down the stairs. I wasn't going to lose my job over a misunderstanding. Yet this dude was seriously impacting our professional working relationship.

I walked into my Jaguar. I drove off, which seemed to be the story of my life. I went home. Then it was time for day 2 of this madness. Lithium central. Very nice. 10Pm, and I pop the magic pill.

'All units, there is a fire on west thirty nine street. Female in her early 30's, burning in a building. All units.' Then I could hear Ryan shout, 'Lucas!' I thought, 'ah fuck this guy.' I turned my radio off, the pill knocked me out cold. I went to sleep, and that was my routine for that night.

Then came the third night. I had my radio on, I popped the lithium. I could hear James shout, 'all units, suspect armed.' I shouted, 'not interested.' I fell asleep.

The fourth night. 'All units, armed and dangerous robber in a car. The car's make is...' I switch off my radio.

I go up to the Police psych doctor. Who is laughing, and hissing with some real hysterics. I show him the pills and I said. 'This stuff is good.' He is pissing himself laughing and he said, 'of course it is. Why do you think I am in charge?'

I said, 'this is not funny. You do realise this.'

I walked out, feeling like my whole identity was threatened. I had been on the force for 33 years. Now these tumble dicks wanted to make me out to be the bad guy. Put me on meds. I slept like a baby for the last 4 days. It got to the point where I wouldn't even hear the radio.

Sleeping was difficult for me, and sometimes I just needed that nudge in the right direction. By the time I had returned to the world. James Watkins came in and shut the door. He was one of my best friends.

Detective James, said, 'look dude, I think Ryan overstepped the mark. I am going to have a word with him.' I said, 'don't bother.'

He said, 'he really upset you. All you were doing was taking prescribed meds by the psychiatric doctor over in the 12th court over there.' He pointed towards where the station was, in east direction.

I said, 'look I appreciate the help and all. Yet I don't know anymore. I can't stop thinking about Hemingway and Blakely.'

James looked concerned and he said, 'it was a slam dunk, the evidence was doctored We got the guy. He's behind bars.' I said, 'what if Hemingway did it, and Blakely is covering up for him.'

James, showing a bit of tough love, shouts, 'this is bullshit.' Even though shouting, he says it softly. I said, 'listen James, we are close, and I accept that. Yet the whole world seems to go around. Whilst some people remain still. I am not making any difference to the world.' James said, 'you are, and you have been. Don't take this blip as a way of just leaving. Either the force, or disconnecting emotionally. This isn't a holiday.'

I said, 'I couldn't, and I won't. Yet this whole thing has gone to shreds.' My rolex watch, not ticking, needing a new battery. My wide screen TV. Switched off. The

100

lights were dimmed and James looked very concerned, and angry that Ryan had been so menacing. James said, 'well I am going to have a word with Ryan, and that is the last thing I am going to say to him.' I said, 'by all means.'

I said, 'you don't mean that, he's part of the force.' James said, 'look dude, if I don't want to speak to him for a few days after. What's he going to do? Phone up IA? IA wouldn't be cruising around ground central right now. If only they could hear some of our bullets.' I said, 'I know what you are saying, and you can. It's just that case with Blakely.' James said, 'you are a god damn cop, not a god damn social worker. You do your job. You get out. No hugs, no story times. No kettles, no hot chocolate. No marsh fucking mellows.' I said, 'that's how it's always supposed to be.' He said, 'that is what it is. We are not social workers. Besides. If these prisoners behave themselves. They get their fare share of help from the guards. We shouldn't be babysitting them.'

I said, 'I don't know. I mean I joined the force to help people.' He interjected, and he said, 'you are helping people. Do you think this whole thing has happened for no reason. The reason we are talking in the first place. You worry too much.' I said, 'to be honest. I was able to deal with the press.' He said, 'there you go, but this whole self-pity thing has to stop. You are better than that.'

His tie was entangled in his shirt. His mean and kind expression, was radiating in his face. His sympathetic smile and sense of concern. Was a mere juxtaposition. His kindness and stability. Was a mere sense of calm in a storm I would not have had otherwise.

I was sat there, scotch in hand, looking over my blurry eyes. With the whole room around me spinning. My cornflower tie, and my empty glass of whiskey. Some left over prescription medication. The wife had just cleaned up the house. You could hear Alex upstairs, playing on that god damn Xbox, and I was stuck not knowing what to do anymore.

James said, 'is it that kid upstairs?' I said, 'sorry, what?' James said, 'Alex, dude, you took Hemingway to a barber, yet you don't take Alex to one.' I said, 'I have tried to get him to go to a barber. He won't listen.' James said, 'well you need to act fast, in a couple of years time. He's going to turn to dark magic, and smoke god damn crack. Sleep with prostitutes with no teeth.' I sighed and I said, 'I will get it sorted.' James said, 'god damn kids dude.' I said, 'it's a curse. You try to raise them well. He was kicked out of military school. He was there for 10 weeks. They couldn't stand him. He wanted to be a doctor. We signed his forms to go to a good school. He dropped out of that also.'

James, looking disinterested now said, 'I have a question.' I said, 'shoot.' James said, 'you know you look at things, our police force. Detroit. We barely have any cops with misconduct charges. IA haven't been sniffing around for years. I know you said you have trained the officers well. Yet, I just want to know, is it just down to you?' I said, 'what?' He said, 'the lack of misconduct charges.' I said, 'we are a tight force man. I know some forces can be a bit heavy handed. Yet we keep ourselves on a professional playing field.' James said, 'all down to you.' I said, 'I am not taking all of the credit, but I think I helped. I take all of the bullshit from SWAT, FBI, the powers that be. The powers that want us to be more ruthless. Yet, in my opinion, if we start over criminalising people..' James interrupted, and he said jokingly, 'you are a sociologist man. Disguised as a cop.' He said when joking, he continued, 'I told you, you are not a god damn psychologist, sociologist, or social worker. You're a cop.' I said. 'I know but we have to do things by the book.' James said, 'oh come on, seriously?' He continued, 'like

103

apprehending that suspect the other day in that store. He was shot dead, and nothing. No misconduct charges.' I said angrily, 'that guy was holding three people hostage. And had opened fire. I was allowed to use any force.' James said, 'it wasn't you who opened fire.' I said, 'no it was that deranged Jenson Davis. He likes to think he's SWAT. He likes to think he can work wanders but he isn't.'

James said, 'was he taken off the force?' I said, 'no.' James said, 'you are good.' I said, 'look, sir, with all honesty. I can respond to these bread and butter robberies every day of the week. Even when I am shoving my face full of Valium the doctor has me on. Yet we have to find out. This Blakely and Hemingway thing. Have we done the right thing?'

James said, 'well you visited Blakely once in prison. There is no obligation for you to visit him again. You have to let it go.'

I said, 'I know that.' I got the DVD out, and I put it on in the TV. The CCTV. I paused at Hemingway with a knife. I said. 'How did they manage to doctor that?' James said, 'Blakely used computer software.' I said, 'cut it out, this stuff looks realistic, he had us fooled.' I looked at the knife that Hemingway was holding.

James said, 'notice something changes.'

104

I forwarded the clip a bit. Blakey said, 'that is not Hemingway, that is Blakely. It looks nothing like Hemingway.'

I said, 'so maybe what they did, was, in actual fact. It was him.' James said, 'well look at the position of the knife. Look at the guy. Blakely was a stocky guy. Around 6 foot 3. An absolute monster. Hemingway was a short, scruffy guy, 5 foot 6 at best.'

I said, 'why would Blakely want to kill his own niece?' James said, 'power. It's all power with him. And craziness also. Something not right with that dude. You are going to start chewing over this. Nothing new has come. Then we talk about double jeopardy charges.' I said, 'bullshit, double jeopardy' He said, 'it makes sense. Can't do it, even with more evidence.'

I said, 'I am going to pull some strings, break some civil rights. Get in there and shake them up.' James scoffed and laughed, drank some whiskey. Snacked on some pretzels and said. 'Look man, you can rile them up for as long as you want to. It's not going to do any good.'

I said, 'I am going to visit Hemingway again. Question him.' James said, 'whilst your at it, make sure you find out exactly what happened. I mean this thing is a circus. Maybe you are right. Maybe things got heated. Yet putting Blakely out there to be an all time master, super mind. What if all of the time this was happening. It wasn't squaring with them. I didn't know which computer software they had. Hell if I know. Not that Hemingway had anything.'

I said, 'it's always very sweet with you. You understand people, and you get them. You understand them. Time and time again. Yet nothing like this adds up, and you know it.'

Chapter 18

I went to pay Giles Hemingway a visit. I didn't know how long it was going to take. I pulled up in my silver Chevron. His apartment was looking nice. He was well kept I said, 'nice place you have here.'

I said, 'is it okay if I sit down?' He said, 'of course it is.' His stocky but gentle built. His charisma. The fact he wasn't homeless anymore. The fact I still had a job to do. As cars were passing by outside. Road rage, and he had some scented candles. Some roses, and I wasn't going to stop looking there. He had a modest TV at best. Not a wide screen TV. I said, 'how have you been keeping?' He said. 'Fine'. I said. 'You are not talking much.'

He said, 'there is no need.' I said. 'I have

been discussing the case with James Watkins. We are still suspicious. Are you sure it was all Blakely. I mean, you stood up there and confessed.'

Giles said, 'Blakely threatened me on the day of the arrest. Said if I didn't confess, he would cut my throat.' I said, 'right, was that, at what time sorry?' Giles said, '3PM.' I said. 'That's an exact time.' Giles said, 'just roughly.' I said, 'you see Giles. What I don't understand. Is this. It stinks of a set up. We have the guy in prison. Yet we have anxious family members. We have mothers, sisters, aunts, uncles, and friends. Protesting. Rioting sometimes on the streets. Wanting justice. Now we feel like there is more to the story. They want you retried. I spoke to them at length and said because of double jeopardy charges. You can't get retried. Unless we find anything else to convict you for. Besides. I would like to think it wasn't your fault.'

Giles said. 'They are just looking for someone to blame. Why aren't they blaming Blakely? He is the one who is locked up.' I said. 'Blakely is a manipulative character. Plays the victim a lot. Likes to pretend he has a good life. Has all of this fake charisma. Even though he plead guilty in court. He's been spinning this whole opera music in prison. Getting people to do things for him. Scheming quite repetitively People saw him as a saint. He wasn't easy to read, and they look at you as...' Giles interrupted and he said, 'an easy target?' I said, 'yes, exactly. An easy target.' Giles said, 'so what's the plan now then?' I said, 'there is none. We keep everything secure. But we have to do some work together. I hate to tell you this, and this isn't the news anyone wants to hear. But I am going to have to tell you verbally. There is a Desmond warning notice against your name.'

Giles said, 'a Desmond?' I said, 'there is a Desmond warning notice, saying you are at threat of an arson attack. People have cottoned onto where you live.' Giles said, 'can't you rehouse me?' I said, 'we can, but these vigilantes, they are just going to find your new address. I highly recommend you take advantage of our witness protection scheme.' I hand him a number to ring on some card.

Giles said, 'how much is that going to cost you?' I said, '$10,000, to $100,000, and we will give you $80,000 to restart your life. Different passport, different part of the USA. You will be a completely different person. We will assign you a job as a banker, someone high profile. Someone nobody messes with. It's either that, or having you burnt alive.'

Giles said, 'so all I have to do is change my name and get moved?' I said, 'exactly.' Giles said, 'strip me of this identity.' I said, 'I know it's hard, and I know you associate with a Giles Hemingway right now. Yet, after time, you will get used to your new identity.' He said, 'what if they catch me with my new identity.' I said, 'they won't, we have FBI on this now. So many people are planning to burn your house down, your apartment. Even. We will get you a house. In New York, anywhere. If I have to pay some out of my own wallet. I will. It took convincing the DA for a few days to do this.' He said, 'a few days, is that all?' I said. 'Sir, let me level with you. I have seen victims of arson attacks. Dead, sometimes we can't even identify them. I am not trying to scare you, but it's never nice. You are sleeping in your bed, next thing you know. You are grilled alive. With no chance. The people after you are sophisticated. Friends with Blakely.'

He said, 'I thought SWAT killed Blakely's associates.' I said, 'I forgot to tell you this, but Blakely has more than 8 associates. He has around 100. He is very high profile. That's the problem. FBI are working hard to find them. Yet, it's going to take years. If we take you out the picture. Even though we spend money on witness protection. It's going to cost us more in the long run to safeguard you. Plus with the inevitable cost, of keeping you safe. Day in, day out. Preventing this attack.'

Giles said, 'what if I don't want to go.' I said. 'It's your decision, but you will get burnt to a pulp.'

He said, 'what's the likely hood?' I said, '100%'. Giles said, 'well let's get moving. Can I ask you questions in the car?' I said, 'you can ask me as many questions as you like.' I handcuff this guy as a ruse. Because there are angry protestors outside. People cheering that I have found him. He is kept in a custody block. We don't charge him, but we have to process him just like anyone else. The sad news is. Is that I found a charge to suit him. I charged him with public order. It was a piss weak charge and it would get dropped by the DA. Because I knew he had a row with the protestors. Yet it was the only way I could process him for witness protection.

Staff shortages were high. Very high, it was just me and him. Plus a female detective, called Lucy James, Coleman.

She was smiling sympathetically at him. I said, 'so we're sending you to New York.' Next thing I know. FBI agent Charles Paul Jenkins, joins us. Along with Rufus Clark.

110

FBI. It's 5 of us. In this interview room. I roll the CD. I said, 'Giles Hemingway, you are being cautioned. You have the right to remain silent. Anything you do say, may be used against you. You have the right to an attorney. If you can't afford one. One will be appointed to you. Do you understand your rights?' He nodded. I said, 'I am interviewing you under caution of a public order charge.' I smiled and said, 'you were shouting and swearing at these protestors.' Giles said, 'yes I was.' Rufus Clark, a big man, black guy. Very muscular. Very tall. He said, 'right. That's enough, cut the crap.' I paused the CD. I said, 'we are taking you to New York.' Lucy said, 'it will be a new start.' Charles Jenkins FBI. Big white dude. 6 foot 2, very broad shoulders. Musky light grey/light brown hair. He said, 'it's for the best.'

We escorted him into this limozine. This car. Lucy was driving. I was in the back with the FBI agents.

James was calling me, and I picked up, he said, 'you are with him?' I said, 'of course I am.' James said, 'good.' I then get a call from Ryan Coleman. The chief detective. He said, 'good work Lucas, well done. You really are helping.' He hung up, and I looked at Rufus Clark, and Charles Jenkins. Tough guys, but didn't look like they wanted to talk. I said, 'Lucy, have you got the new passport, the new social security number, and the new name?' She said, 'yes I have.'

I said, 'that's good.' Giles said, 'what's the name?' Before Lucy could reply. He bashed the window with his hand. Smashed the glass. He escaped through the shrapnel. He left, a van hit into Lucy. Looked orchestrated. We followed him and Lucy called for back up. He ran into a nearby field, and escaped. We drove to find him, but lost him. Lucy shouted, 'shit.' I said, 'it's okay, he's just scared.' I said, 'all units, all LAPD units. Giles Hemingway is on the run. He's not armed. Probably scared and vulnerable.' I get New York police shouting at me saying. 'Not my responsibility asshole.' Then a guy called Rufus Jenkins, LAPD detective, said, 'we will send a troop car over.'

We are following Hemingway, for ages. We finally meet up with him. He is in a field, by the lake. One of the only parks in New York, we didn't expect him to be there. He turns around, and he said, 'I don't want to do this.' I said, 'it's your only choice.'

Giles said, 'it will be like dying and starting again.' I said, 'you won't be able to do this with this name. People are blaming you.'

Giles said, 'I did nothing wrong. It was a

112

set up.' I said. 'I know it was, but I told you. Blakely, has contacts. The whole thing is a shirt storm. Plus even we had our doubts.'

Hemingway said, 'the CCTV was doctored It was fake.' I said, 'no shit, but other people won't realise that. People are scared. They are running around anxious. I don't think you understand. Blakely is a dangerous man. You are the victim. You are in danger. You need protecting.'

Rufus Clark of FBI said, 'look, sir, Giles. Look, let's get you settled into your house. We can talk over the paperwork, over some coffee. Some tea, some biscuits. It doesn't have to be rushed. Reluctantly, we see a disillusioned, and angry Hemingway, escorted back into the limozine. Which we had to change one of the tyres, as Lucy had served over a cork screw. We place him in his new house. In New York. A nice place, not in the Bronx. I will get to the address bit later, but it was very nice. His new identity was Charles Brown. He was a senior banking executive advisor for a Wall Street Bank. Named Ferguson and Henderson. A small banking and real estate firm. A top of the line stocks and shares company.

We sat him down, and I said, 'your new name is Charles Brown, you work for Henderson, a banking and equity shares firm.' We hand him his new driving licence. His passport. Social security number. His credit card score. His documents. It takes minutes, yet it took hours to calm him down.

I said, 'you are going to have to adjust the way you talk, walk, and your hair also. You are going to have to grow it out a bit. Gell it a bit differently. Your whole attitude has to change. From now on, you listen to punk rock. Your favourite band is the Sex Pistols. We had to do this for your own safety.' I hand him some hair gel, and tell hims to spike his hair up.

Rufus said, 'it's working.' I said, 'also, we want you to lose maybe, 6 pounds, maybe even a stone.' Charles said, 'this will take ages.' I said, 'no.' I hand him cocaine in a small jar. With some speed, some diet drinks. I said, 'this is going to shred you up.' Rufus Clark handed him some fat burners. A $400 state of the art, fat burner, waist system. We brought him a treadmill, already there. We did everything. We put up posters of The Sex Pistols. Kiss, and other punk rock and roll bands. We bought him a guitar. Several in fact.

I said, 'now, you are going to have to try to learn to play the guitar.' He said, 'won't it be suspicious if a high bank executive, plays guitar, listens to Kiss.' I said. 'Dude, everyone in Wall Street listens to music. Don't over think it. Only take the cocaine, or the speed, one at a time. We are bending a few rules to do this.'

Rufus said, 'no shit, it's come out of the evidence bag in custody. We didn't do shit.' He said arrogantly.

I said, 'well this is your new life. Your boulevard. You are a single man, right? Well that's not going to change. But we have given you some pictures. Of an actor. A random woman. One of our actors.'

Rufus Clark said, 'you are recently bereaved. You go to bereavement meetings.'

Charles Brown said, 'anything else?'

I said. 'That's it, but we want you on all the dating sites. We want you 're married', and we want you to have children.'

Charles Brown said, 'I understand.' I said. 'You are a family man now. Not a loner.'

Rufus Clark said, 'man you are going to go out there, meet some nice chicks..' I interjected and I said, 'that's enough.' I did a cut it out gesture with my hand.

I said, 'Charles Brown.' I winked, we are going to leave you.'

We left, the oak furniture, outside. It was different. A different world. We knew it was going to take time for him to adjust. We realised this but it wasn't easy for him.

115

Chapter 19

In the limo, on the way home. It wasn't a stretched limo, but it was a limo none the less. Lucy said, 'thank god that is over.' I said, 'no, not now, not with all of this going on. Blakely is more intelligent than you think.' Lucy said. 'How intelligent?' I said. 'Go figure, he's ex marines. He can smell a rat a mile off.' Lucy said. 'Charles is all set now.' I said, 'no, this is just the start. I am going to meet Blakely in prison when we get home.'

James Watkins calls me on speaker. Everyone listening. He said, 'well done. I heard the news.' I said. 'I can't talk now but rest assured. This is not over.' I hang up, as armed police escort us back to Detroit. It's time to meet Blakely in jail again. He's looking upset, and the house Hemingway had stayed in had been torched. With nobody inside. The army had carried a controlled explosion to demolish the house. As we weren't sure what material was used to destroy it. We also found a suspicious package inside. I said to Blakely. 'You think you are so smart. I want to know who you are speaking to. I will cut your visitations right down to zero. I have spoken to the prison staff. They have given me your phone call records on the pay phone.

CCTV. We have everything, we know who you are communicating with.'

He said. 'Then why are you here, if you know who I am talking to?' I said. 'Because I am trying to talk sense into you. You can't go around doing this. Hemingway was innocent.' He said, 'not in my book.' I laughed and I said. 'You are the one who set him up.'

Russel Blakely got aggressive, and he said, 'I was in the military. And this is how you treat me.'

I said, 'that's funny because I have spoken to your ex military crew mates. They found you really hard to work with. Very stubborn. They told me all about your exploits. Everything. Refused to do team work. I am not here to give you a drilling.'

He said, 'why are you here?' I said, 'I want you to let Hemingway go.'

Blakely said, 'he's dead isn't he.' I laughed and said, 'I can't confirm or deny that.' Blakely said, 'that means no, where are you keeping him.' I said, 'none of your business. I want to tell you something right now. Let it go.'

Blakely said, 'what if I don't want to.'

I said, 'then we add years onto your bit. Another 50.' Blakely laughed and said, 'you think I will see the light of day again anyway?' His big stubborn and husky demeanour Sprouting aggressively. His leather jacket. His toned but muscular physique. His arrogant look, etched onto his face.

I said, 'Blakely, let it go.' He said. 'This is not the end of this.' I smiled, because every time a suspect said, 'this is not the end.' It always is. Besides, we had Charles Brown in confines now. Nobody could trace him.

I walk back to more protestors. Acting up, I move in with a squad car. I go right up to this plump looking lady. In her 60's. A right wing extremist. I had met her once, when I was policing a Trump rally. She said, 'have you got the son of a bitch?' I nodded to Lucy from FBI. She said, 'Miss, Sarah, Jones. You are under arrest for disorderly conduct.' She was escorted into a cop car, and drove off by uniform. I grabbed my megaphone and shouted, 'everyone move away, and desist from this location.' It was a piss riot, so many people turning up. Looked like they were going to a barbecue, as some suburban middle class men. In khaki, light brown shorts, and sun burned, but brown faces. Were chanting amiably. 'We want to know what is happening.' I smiled, and put the megaphone down. I walked up-to one of them. John. I said. 'Show's over. Go back to your barbecue, and cut your hedge.'

He said, 'how do you know my schedule?' I said. 'I don't know, we are The Police. We're not exactly a laundry service here. Don't take that comment the wrong way. I just mean we are professionals.'

John said, 'We want to know where Hemingway is.' I said, 'no you do not.' I said firmly, as John walked towards his second hand Mercedes. Lucy said, 'nice job.' As Rufus Clark. Charles Jenkins, James Watkins and Ryan Coleman were with me.

Fiona, uniform, the same girl who used to run her mouth. All calm and tranquil. Alongside me as well. Was Chuck Jenkins, ironically the arresting officer of Charles Brown. Also known as Hemingway.

I said jokingly, 'it's a full house.' Most people laughed. Lucy said, 'next time that megaphone is mine.' I turned around and I said, 'maybe, maybe not.'

James turned towards me and he said, 'you couldn't make this up, could you.'

I said, 'what witness protection.' I whispered. I said, 'that happens all of the time. The only unusual thing as that Blakely guy. Passive aggressive, manipulative loser. Honourable discharge from the marine core. Up in Pennsylvania He was sent over seas. Afghanistan and Iraq mainly. Left and came back here.

119

Obviously had a chip on his shoulder as he couldn't make Police. Hence why he wanted to bother us, start this whole criminal gang.'

Lucy said, 'you mean organised crime gang.' I said, 'you say pota-to. I say po-ta-to.'

Chapter 20

Everyone regrouped. I returned to Detroit. One of the biggest cities in the world in Michigan.

I couldn't help but worry about Charles Brown. I wanted him to be okay. I knew it was going to be difficult for him to settle him. At least he was away from Russel Blakely. Things weren't the same anymore. Living my life. I couldn't understand.

I sat in my house. With everything just turned off. No calls, no phones were ringing. Nothing. We had to chalk out so much money on witness protection. So much.

All teary eyed and I wandered how much we could cope with this.

I had some digging to do. I didn't give a FUCK about double jeopardy I met up with a few people. The mother of Louise Grey. Charlotte Evans. I had my notepad, and pen. I was with Rufus Clark of FBI.

120

We were both taking notes.

Charlotte Evans was hunched over the table. In her house. Crying her eyes out. I grabbed her a tissue.

I said, 'how was the funeral?' She said, 'how is any funeral?'

I said, 'I know times are tough right now. I just have to ask you a few questions.'

She said, 'shoot'. I said, 'so the night of the incident. Louise Grey, was returning home from College. She was going straight to your house. Is that correct?' Charlotte said, 'yes.' I said, 'did you notice anything out of the ordinary on the day this whole thing happened.'

Charlotte Grey said, 'not that I know of. It was just a standard day. Just like any other day. She went with Sophie to the ice cream parlour. The chuck and cheese shop. They walked 12 blocks to college. They had lunch. I got a love you text. I wasn't expecting any of this.'

I said, 'but you knew who Giles was, and you knew there was an ongoing argument between Giles and Louise.'

Charlotte said, 'I was aware of this, yes.' I said, 'so did you ever try to intervene We checked our records. You hadn't phoned us up once. During the 12 months, this argument got heated.'

She said, 'I didn't think I could have any

121

influence.'

I said, 'but you could, and I am not trying to blame you mam. I know times are tough. I just wanna know. Do you think it was Blakely? Or Hemingway.'

Charlotte said, 'I know both of them, and both of them are deranged scum bags.'

I said, 'but, Blakely, he is part of your family. Your brother right?'

Charlotte said, 'blood isn't always more thicker than water.'

I said, 'but what I am getting at is you keep your family close. You would have kept tabs on him. Made sure he was okay. Made sure everything he was doing was correct. You knew about his military career. Leaving the military. Honourable discharge. Was allowed to keep some memorabilia. And some guns. To what effect I have no idea.'

She said bitterly, 'what's your point?'

I said, 'well correct me if I am wrong, but I don't know if you know this. But I was in the marines when I was 18, for four years. Left when I was 22. Went in straight after grad school. Then it was more homework before I got into this job.'

I pointed to my badge. I said, 'the point is, you never lose your training. I learnt some incredible things over the years. The training was ongoing. Yet you never lose it. It's like a bitter sweet after taste. Or some tangy chewing gum that you buy at some corner shop. That you can't get rid of the taste. Even after the Sprite. The Coke Zero.'

She said, 'he was well trained.' I said, 'he was, but he did more of a stretch than me. He was there for 8 years. In that time, he went from a reserve, to the navy. To a navy seal. He was highly respected. He learnt everything. He came back. He applied to join us, we turned him down. The references wouldn't check out. The cornel said that he left on bad terms.'

Charlotte said, 'there was an argument before he left. He belonged in that fucking job. Day in, day out. Night and day. He loved it. He was told if he wasn't discharged honourably. There was no guarantee they would keep him there. He was chucked out, they just gave him the honourable discharge. Because they wanted to have salt on their own reputation sir.'

I said, 'so you are talking about self preservation of the marine core. Correct me if I am wrong. But soldiers in there lose it all of the time. It gets documented. It gets sent over to the IRA. The CSA. The commanding bodies. I am not buying your story.'

Charlotte said, 'so you think I am a

123

suspect.' I said, 'I never said that.' I look over her white flower drape curtains. Cans and cans of spite on the oak table. The polished oak table. Her husband. Ray Charles. Standing over, like an over protective lab dog.

I am sat on this leather sofa, that looks like it's been bought from a second hand thrift store. Not that I minded whatsoever. I was fed up of going into these suburban middle class porcelain houses.

I said, 'Charlotte, anything else you want to say.'

She said, 'why are you still investigating this case?' Rufus of FBI command said, 'because there is someone else. Multiple people in fact. That are on this. They are working around the clock. It's an organised crime gang. Blakely led them on. Gave them some story. It's all one big surrogate family over there. Roses, wine, rose petals, and more god damn rose petals. It doesn't square with me.'

I said, 'the point he's trying to make is that Russel Blakely was a dangerous man.'

Charlotte burst out crying and said, 'he had some issues.' I said, 'what issues?' She said, 'depression, I don't know. Nothing too serious.' I said, 'I get depressed from time to time.' Rufus put his hand over mine gently, as if to tell me to stop talking.

124

He said, 'Charlotte, thanks for your help, it's much appreciate.' He placed our contact numbers, on a business car, on the oak table. We left in a hurry. I said, 'what do you think?' Rufus said, 'your gut was right. It is a set up. Yet we have to find out who the other gang members are. There's around a dozen of them.'

I said, 'do you have names, what's the name of the gang?'

Rufus laughed and said, 'it doesn't work like that. There is no name of the gang. That's what makes it so god damn hard to trace. These are organised criminals. Not some low life thugs.'

I said, 'yet they are low life thugs.' I shouted. He said, 'maybe, but they're not stupid.' I said, 'do you think they are still in Detroit?' He said, 'almost definitely We are going to get the fuckers.'

We got into his car. A black BMW, very nice, leather seats. He drove. I was in the passenger seat. We drove to the centre of Detroit. A lot of tourists. It was an unmarked police car but it still had a siren, and one of those single lights. That you could place on the top of the sun roof.

I said, 'so where do we start now then?' He said, 'with organised crime, we look at things that stand out. More than the usual criminals. Boats, ships, or anything like that.'

I said, 'what about cars?' He said, 'maybe, but we are not traffic division. We parked the car in a parking lot. We walked out, and between two trees. Was a man called Fred Walker. One of the organised crime gang members. He said, 'you want information about Blakely?'

Funnily enough he was a police informant also. He lead us onto this ship. We started talking to him for a bit. He said, 'I will tell you everything. I want a reduction in sentence.' I handcuff him and read him his rights. I said, 'it doesn't work like that, and you know it.' He said, 'come on now, I give you information.' Rufus slapped him and said, 'I have all of the information. Right with me. I have heard all about you. Domestic abuser. Used to beat on your wife.'

Fred Walker said, 'let's get to talking then.' I said, 'it's funny to have a cruise liner in Detroit. I will tell you that.'

I said, 'Fred, cut the crap. We know you have information here.' He was a 6 foot guy. Very deep voice. Leather jacket. He spoke very assertively. He said, 'oh yeah.' I said, 'I bet you if I had a look around this cruise liner you have here. Right in the middle of state Michigan. I would find something. Receipts Credit card bills. Paper trails.'

He said, 'maybe you would, maybe you

wouldn't.' I said, 'the point I am trying to make is you are looking at 50 years in jail at the least. You and your men, you have helping you.'

Fred Walker said, 'so what do you want to know?' I said, 'so telling me where they are. Would be a good start.' He laughed and he said, 'right on this cruise liner.' I said, 'no shit.' Rufus whispered in my ear and said, 'he's bullshitting us.' I said, 'no seriously, where are they?' Fred said, 'so why would I have to tell you?' I said, 'because we have discretion over what happens here.'

The cruise liner was an old, old liner. Just standing there in the docks. There was women and children passing on the street. We couldn't see anything but the ropes holding the boat together. That was moving with each wave.

Fred Walker was the type of guy, who you wouldn't want to meet in an alley way. Tough, assertive, big, bold, and brash. The type of guy nobody wanted to meet. He wasn't using, but he was carrying something. Weapons mostly. With him, even though he wasn't ex military. He would have been briefed by Blakely. Blakely would have explained everything. The whole murder trial we had of Charles Brown, also known as Hemingway. The whole thing stank. We couldn't get to the

bottom of it. I sure wasn't starting now.
Everyone wanted to pin Hemingway down
as the man responsible. Yet we had work
to do, and I was going to make Fred
Walker sweat.

I said, 'so once again, I will ask you.
Where are your men?' He laughed and
said, 'I am not telling you.'

Fred Walker punched him and said,
'right straight into custody.' We took him
into the black BMW. It was government
property. He was scratching at it like a
mouse trying to get out of a ferace wheel.
He kept scratching at the white leather
inside. I was laughing because it was kind
of taking away the new stench. Fresh car
interior. Someone had to break it up some
time.

Someone had to do it, and that was the
bottom line here. Fred Walker didn't seem
so impressed. Neither was Rufus Clark, as
it was his state vehicle. We got to Detroit
police station. We booked him in a
holding cell. No preferential treatment for
him. Full of low lives, this one massive
guy, with tattoos on his head. This one
schizophrenic woman who was banging
her head on the bar.

Some small dude, 5 foot 2, who was
arguing with the big man. A homeless guy
with no teeth just talking to himself.
Another homeless dude, with hair down

to his shoulders doing rock impressions. There was also a 19 year old female in there. Anorexic, pale thin, and was crying, and psychotic. Not literally Anorexic, but you get what I mean. Looked like a drug user. Lacerations everywhere.

Fred Walker laughed as he knew the drill. The custody Sargent. Tim Jones. Was there. A great guy who was swirling his keys around, like he owned the place. I mean, he did own the place. I said, 'Jones, this guy, this guy right there.' I point right to Fred Walker. I said, 'don't let him leave your sight.'

I said to Walker, 'I have my eyes on you asshole, one wrong move.'

He said, 'what you gonna' do?'

I said, 'lock you up in solitary confinement.'

He said, 'yeah, yeah, keep talking.' He looks angry, and bitter. The kind of look someone who give you, if you were walking your dog, and you let the dog crap on someone else's garden. Then refused to pick it up.

It was all play acting with him. The whole thing was a circus. Nothing washed between his ears and nobody was aware of the lengths he would take; To make the community in Detroit, some kind of crime wave. I didn't want to speak to him anymore. My gut was wrenching and I just wanted to go home. Rufus Clark was standing there, kind of oblivious to the amount of shit we had got ourselves into.

He said, 'time for a walk I guess.' I said, 'excuse me, sir, please. Can you let me digest all of this first.' He laughed, and said, 'what do you mean?'

I said, 'digest the amount of bullshit that Fred Walker was giving us.' Rufus Clark said, 'oh come on. It's just bravado. That's all it is. It's not serious. It's just an act. We will interview him in the morning.'

I said, 'is he sober?' Rufus Clark said, 'fuck if I know, but the treatment is the same. We keep him in there. Make him suffer. Interview him in the morning. Go back home to your lithium, and 10pm snoozes.'

I said, 'very funny, you heard about that. Funny that everything ends in 10pm doesn't it. Or everything starts with 10pm.'

Rufus Clark said, 'what, another conspiracy theory?' I said, 'the 10 o'clock news, the death of Louise Grey. The time I go to bed.' Rufus said, 'oh my god, you are in the wrong line of public service, if you are into crack pot conspiracy theories.'

I said, 'maybe I am. Maybe I am not.' He said, 'there is nothing unusual about these theories, yet it's best not to have them.' I said, 'I understand that. Yet it appears

130

that way. Everyone likes coming to me with their problems. If someone is having a bad day. I'm a nice guy. Yet things changed. Over the years I toughened up. I realised what I couldn't changed. I realised this. This gang is bullshit. The whole Blakely thing is a whole nightmare.'

Rufus got angry and said, 'no shit, but we can't stop there, and we can't leave any stone unturned. Even if what you are saying is correct. We stick by the rule book. Fred Walker, no preferential treatment. Because he didn't comply. Once he complies, then we give him some treatment. Small things at first. Reduction in sentence. Then if he's really good. We completely release that jack hole. Back into the wild where he belongs.'

I said, 'people like that don't change.' He said, 'you know what else doesn't change. The penal system. The prisons are over packed. That guy is a wolf.'

I said, 'just leave him there to suffer then.' He said, 'it's the same thing with you. Go home Lucas. We don't need your help.'

I said, 'you drove me to this custody suite. I don't have my car.' Rufus sighed and said, 'I feel like a baby sitter.' We got into the car. The back interior all scratched up. I said, 'babysitting me, and that criminal. You're lucky day.' He laughed. He dropped me home. Before I left, he gave me some wise words. He said, 'look, life is full of bullshit. What we learnt in the Beruea, and in our training. Life is full of jack offs. Moody and pissed off people. People with venom and shit to spray at you. Angry people, violent people. Piss heads, and ants that want to shit down your neck. I've had problems with custody suite officers, and uniform. Making jokes on my behalf. Look at me now. FBI. Earning over $80,000 a year. With the help of savings and other shares. Ignore other people. This is a god damn job. We are not babysitters. We are not social workers. The sooner you get that into your head. The sooner you will be able to chill with the big boys. The big men, not moan and groan with the nannies, and the wannabe carers. Looking after the elderly In some state home. Nothing against the carers. Yet this is Police work here. I don't mind doing welfares on compliant suspects. But non compliant ones, and jack offs like that Fred Walker guy. Can go piss up a tree. I am not interested.'

I said, 'okay, that's fine. Don't worry about it.'

Chapter 21

I didn't know what to think anymore

132

really. Things just went over in my head. A lot of the time. Sometimes you didn't want to talk, or you didn't want to explain things to people.

My life was not how it was, before this whole thing. It wasn't how it was after.

I wanted to find out the truth. I am sure everyone did at this stage. I am in my living room of all places. The white curtains. The feeling of confusion that rises over me. The feeling of anguish also. This was not a cut and dry case. We had idea of what had happened. I for one knew what may have happened. They were all in the same group. It had to be like that.

James Watkins turns up, in his jaguar. He walks in. He speaks. He said, 'chasing after these suspects non stop.' I said, 'I know and it doesn't really seem to help.' James said, 'I have no idea, this organised crime gang. It's like a fucking maze. Or rats, or mice or something. We catch one, and we get another, and another. All piling up.'

I said, 'that's life for you.' James said, 'with all due respect, I wanted to know the truth. I have done some digging. FBI are all over this. Won't let us touch a god damn thing anymore. We are left suffering here.'

I said, 'it's funny because I was with

Rufus Clark. You figure that out? All of the time I was with him. Then we nail some scum bag called Fred Walker. It's an insult that we even arrested him because he scratched the interior of the car. Made a real mess. Long finger nails. He's expecting me to interview him tomorrow. This guy makes the fucking hairs on my neck stand up.'

James said, 'well refer it to someone else. That's all you can do isn't it just?' I said, 'it doesn't always work like that. Not all of the time anyway. Besides. What if this scumbag has got information.'

James said, 'or he's just playing you. Just like everyone who we arrest does. I mean even Hemingway gave me the creeps man. It wasn't the same.'

I said, 'Hemingway was a good person.' James said, 'trying to sell me the hooker with the heart of gold. That story. Yeah well I understand what you are saying. Yet it doesn't wash.'

I said, 'well what does, we go around in circles here. Things change, all of the time. Once was okay, now this, then nothing. We run around in circles, and we get the same results. People are far to passive aggressive to review the facts.'

James said, 'well I will come with you, and add some extra beef to the interview then.' I said, 'you can if you wish. Yet if it

134

works out like that. The guy is going to be nervous. Three of him, one of him.'

James said, 'knowing that guy, he's going to have his heavy weight lawyer. Mr Thomas Oriely come and pay him a visit. It's going to be sweet and cosy. The sweet law society and everything. Man fuck Oriely.'

I said, 'yeah but we still got something to do. We go in there tomorrow. The interview starts at 11am. We go in there and we have words. We make sure we understand what the basic premise is.'

James said, 'blow the lid off the whole place. Just like we always wanted to do. Find the whole thing we were looking for. Now I wander. Now I think. Now I question. Everything. Wether MI5 might be onto this.'

I said, 'that's a stretch. MI5, and English Police onto this organised crime gang.' James said, 'you don't understand. This organised crime gang, shift their operations from the USA to UK. They hide their drugs in the chicken nuggets, and the chicken. It's laughable yet it happens.'

I said, 'sorry, just walk through what actually happens at the airports.'

James said, 'the organised crime group. This group. It's not just weapons, and perverting the course of justice. It's also drug dealing. It comes with the trade.

135

That is why Louise and her friends were high all of the time. Along with Sophie. In the same family as that fucked up dude. Blakely. Every month or so, they go over to the UK. They stash cocaine and heroine in hard to find places. Keyboards, laptops, and I spoke to customs, and border control. They even stash cocaine in food also. Don't believe me, speak to English Police.'

I said, 'this is bullshit, so MI5 are onto this.'

He said, 'no, they are not, you are missing the point. Anything that happens in overseas. England, Spain, or anything like that. Is out of our fucking jurisdiction It doesn't wash and it doesn't make sense. MI5 aren't digging around in some god damn treasure hunt over in the USA. What do you think this is? This is now how it works. The secret service won't get involved, because this is nowhere near Washington. Maybe I am clutching at straws.'

I said, 'so all I have to do is phone up MI5, and speak to them. Tell them we are working on catching these organised crime gangs.'

He said, 'they already fucking know everything, they don't need us speaking to them. I am just explaining to you the customs side of things. How the drug trade fucking works. We do things in our own time. We consult the FBI.'

I said, 'with all due respect. The FBI hate our guts. I have seen how Rufus looks at me. Like I am some kind of insect or something.'

James said, 'nah that's just their training. Because of the beruea training they get. It's all federal stuff. We just get what the academy has given us. Plus our detective training.'

James said, 'nah, it's not like that. They actually think they are above us.'

I said, 'it's because they are above us. They call the shots. We just pick up the pieces.'

James said, 'well don't think like that. We go in tomorrow and sort this whole thing out. Everything will be square. People will find out the truth. Of what these organised crime gangs are doing.'

I said, 'James, don't you understand. This isn't to do with organised crime. This is about putting Blakely in his place.'

James said, 'bullshit. How's Hemingway now?' I said, 'probably in New York, dipping into some salad dressing and dating some ladies. How the fuck should I know?'

James said, 'tomorrow, 11 o'clock Lucas. Don't fuck this up.'

I said, 'I won't.'

137

11am, we walk into the custody suite. Here he is. Fred Walker. Looking like a plum. All red and swollen from where the big guy in the holding cell has beaten him up.

I ignore it, and I look at the black leather chairs, and I said, 'look, are you going to talk or not?' He said, 'what have I got to say?'

I said, 'why don't you start with the truth?' Fred Walker said, 'you are not going to believe the truth.'

Rufus chimed in and said, 'look, I have been working with the FBI now for 20 years. I know full well your operation, and I know full well that you know. Stuff, that we know.'

Rufus paused, and continued, he said, 'we have a lot of information, and informants. We can put you away for 50 years. With your co-operation. If you help us bring the other men to justice. We can exonerate you. On one condition. We put you on a tag. Indefinitely. Until you can show you can behave yourself.'

Fred said, 'okay I will bite. That sounds like a good deal. There are 7 other men, not including me obviously. It's all on that cruise liner, near where the Atlantic ocean is. That is where it's all going down. We have seven guys running the place. Slaving people and sweating 100's. Forced labour.'

I said, 'human trafficking.' He said, 'yeah, it's all shitty, and I regret signing in for that shit.' I said, 'why continue.' He said, 'because it was how it was at the time. We were working around the clock and the money was good. It was tight, but then you used to look at the pale faces. Of some of those slaves. Almost like I was in World War 2 all over again. Not that I have ever been in the first place. It's like living in a god damn documentary. I tried to escape, but Blakely said, oh Blakely said if I quit. He would slice my lips off. He threatened me.'

I said, 'and if you spoke to us.'

Fred Walker said, 'if I spoke to you, the same thing. I felt powerless. So I kept working. In a way I am glad that are talking to me.'

I said, 'how about some names, to get us going.' Fred Walker said, 'wow, okay. Gavin Newman. Steve Price. James Smith. Tom Jenkins. Gary Newman. Charles Enderson. And Gavin Pierce'

I said, 'anyone else?' He said, 'no, that's them. And of course me. But you said you will exonerate me now.' I said, 'we will file in the paperwork.' I said, 'come here.' I got this electronic tag. I clipped it around his ankle after loosening up the sock. I dangled the remote in front of him. Built in GPS. I said, 'if you take that tag off, an alarm sounds. When that alarm goes, we are there looking for you within 3 minutes. If you take this off. You will go to jail for a very long time.'

Fred said, 'can I go now please?'

Rufus Clark said, 'just sign this release form. You have been a good help.' He signed the release form. This was all done, without any lawyer, even though Oriely was just staring in the background. Almost smiling that his legal advice had paid credence. He didn't want to enter the room. I had no idea why. Fred Walker was our new informant. Every week, or every month. We would get a phone call. We figured he wanted to get that tag off, and being an informant was his way of relinquishing it. We were going to take it off eventually.

We went back to the centre of Detroit, and we entered the cruise liner. The seven man that had been grassed up. As they say in the criminal underworld. All staring there. Completely unarmed as we had used the element of surprise.

Chapter 23

Gavin Newman was a real piece of work.

He was the guy in front. Kept running his mouth. We had a swarm of FBI and SWAT arrest all of them. Gavin said, 'why are you getting SWAT involved?' I pointed the truck load of weapons on the cruise liner and I said, 'for this reason alone. You are going to spend decades, and centuries behind bars. Come on ladies.'

They all walked slowly like cattle. Into these police vans. That said LAPD on them. They were all interview. They all served a 350 years between them. It was a sweet deal. I return to Fred Walker. I look at his apartment. I walk in. Still wearing the tag.

I said, 'I was wrong about you.' He said, 'well there you go. No more talks about Russel Blakely. No more talks about Giles Hemingway.'

I said, 'we always talk about those two. Because they are always causing trouble.' He said, 'bullshit, where is Hemingway anyway, it's like he's disapeared.'

I said, 'keep your nose out of other peoples business. You should be worrying about yourself. Yourself only.'

Fred Walker said, 'if you say so, then you think this is easy.' I said, 'it's an electronic tag. It's not going to bite you.' Fred Walker said, 'no, I mean this whole scenario we are in. I have $100 dollars in my pocket. I have two grocery stores, either side of my house. I have to walk 3 blocks just to get essentials, as those two stores don't sell what I am looking for.'

I said, 'you gotta be fucking joking me, haven't you? A convenience store is a convenience store. What have you got to worry about. You trying to break your tag conditions.'

I get the wire clippers. I am fed up of this mans games. I look at him and I said, 'I can do two things with these wire clippers. I can cut your fucking toes off. Or I can release that tag I put on you.' He said, 'which option.'

I said, 'it depends on how much you piss me off. Which right now. I am kind of taking both options. You behave yourself. You don't talk to anyone. You don't go out of your little nest you are in. To talk to the dregs of society.'

He said, 'what do you mean?' I said, '2 blocks for a convenience store. That means you are dealing again?'

He said, 'no I am not dealing again.' I said, 'bullshit, we have seen you on TV.'

He said, 'look, I have given you lots of information.' I said, 'hand it over.' He was complying. I reached for my radio. I threw the clippers on the sofa. I said, 'hand it over, don't play games with me.'

He threw me some heroine, and I said, 'all of it'. He gave me the cocaine also. I said, 'that wasn't hard was it now?'

I put my radio on the table, I handcuffed him, and I sat down. I said, 'I am going to search you.' I searched him, nothing else. Released the cuffs. Sat back down. I said, 'seriously, you are testing my patience. Don't do it again.' He said, 'am I under arrest?' I said, 'what, dealing to some junkies, with your little bit of personal use. Come on, don't be daft. I'm a police officer, I have big fish to fry. You were once a big fish. Now you are nothing but a little gold fish in a big fucking pond. You are old news.'

He said, 'that is how it is.' I slammed him to the ground. I said, 'listen, you don't call the shots anymore.' He said, 'what if I have changed. We can do something. Make some arrangement, anything.'

I said, 'you give us the tip offs. We take a blind eye to your disgusting drug habit, and your occasional visits to those slums.'

He said, 'is that all?' I said, 'no, I am pissed off with you.' I radioed into speak to Rufus, I said, 'look, can we arrest this guy again.' I hear lots of laughter over the phone. At first it was nothing, but then it kept going up and up. Rufus said, 'you high?'

I said, 'no'. Rufus said, 'write him a fucking citation. Make it quick.' I said, 'you heard the bloke.'

143

I reach for my pocket. I write him a $80 fine citation for possession of narcotics.' I said, 'if you don't pay within 14 days, it doubles.' He said, 'yeah yeah. I know the drill.' I walk towards the door. I said, 'you are really testing us. Keep bouncing on that grey line. The line between law abiding, and seriously messing up. See how far that takes you.'

He said, 'thanks for being fair with me.' As soon as he said that. The door was slammed shut. I walked down the stairs, and away from the apartment. I kept leaving my car, so I ordered a taxi. The driver wouldn't fucking shut up and he was doing my head in. Some big man, caucasian. Talking about the trips to San Fran, then talking about his bowling trips. His chips and dips. His long walks in the park, and everything else. It was upsetting me, so I said, 'listen, I don't want to hear about this anymore.'

He said, 'are you a cop, a nark, what are you?' I said, 'I am a detective' I throw him $20 and walk out, and I walk inside my house. I take some Vitacin, and I sleep like a baby.

I wake up to the sun shining from my windows. My breakfast on the table. I start afresh, regretting even talking to that asshole Fred Walker. Regretting even doing this god damn job in the first place.

144

Yet 'someone has to do it'. So I am carrying on. Regretfully speaking, even though tensions were high. It was my time again to have a rest day. Which meant not taking any calls. Yet you knew how long that lasted. Nothing I could do to speed up the process of the calls. The red alert system, the code red. Everything else in-between All of the operations we had been serving. So some jack hole could get arrested for sentencing

I was sick and tired of the burglarys, the armed robberies and everything else in-between I worked with the FBI closely. Even though this whole thing with those brothers, and the Barkley's was coming to a swift end. I still had my suspicions about Giles Hemingway, and our new status we had given him as Charles Brown. We spent lots of money on him.

I felt like he was hiding something, yet I didn't know if that was wishful thinking or not. I had to wait. I had to figure out what was so god damn special about him. I paid him a visit, yet, I was regretting even doing that. The trips to New York were lonely. Boring. One flight one minute. One lonely car drive the next. Going from state to state. Eating the same food. Going out of my way to speak to the same people. Blakely was a piece of work, but Hemingway was just as frustrating.

145

It kind of felt like a tennis game, like as soon as I had pinged a ball over. The ball had come over to my side of the court. I kind of didn't realise what I could do to fix this. Yet every energy I had given on anything, had been disrupted. Yet I didn't want to sweat this guy too much. Yet any more information he had. Would help me hugely with finding out exactly *what was going on. If anything.*

Chapter 24

Time stood still at one point. I was tired of the same games. The same gossip. I had my radio on me. This day was going to be annoying for me.

I went to pay Giles a visit. New York, took the early morning flight. I went to see him. I said, 'Giles. I know it's early, but can I come in and speak to you?' He said, 'sure.'

I said, 'we have arrested all of Russel Blakely's men, all 7 of them, one on bail.'

He said, 'well done.' I said, 'do you feel relieve?' He said, 'of course.' I said. 'This isn't the end of it, you do realise that. This case has been lingering in my head like a bad dream. FBI are all over this. All over you also. Think you had something to do with the murder. Even though we have exonerated you, and they tried burning your old condo down. They were

146

successful.'

Hemingway, said, 'I have told you everything, everything I knew. Every small detail. The CCTV was doctored It was fake.' I said, 'maybe, but I just don't know anymore. Why did people hate you so bad anyway?' I looked at his beige sweatshirt. His nice tie. His sense of character. His new sense of importance. Knowing this was indeed Charles Brown. Not someone you wanted to really question too much.

He said, 'I have told you everything.' I said, 'even so, that confession in court. Really realistic. You had been doing something. Now is the time to talk.' He said, 'I have told you everything.'

I said, 'bullshit, how about we run the night of the murder back in our heads. On more time. Louise, at 10pm. Was stabbed, fatally. You look nothing like Blakely. Yet Blakely was able to frame you. Without your help whatsoever. Still doesn't explain the murder weapon.'

Hemingway said, 'you trying to indict me on the fact I had that murder weapon?' I said, 'well I know Louise Grey sold it to you. I also spoke to Charlotte, a mother figure of the Blakely's It just doesn't sound like the whole story was adding up. Why take the knife, knowing you were going to be set up.'

147

Hemingway said, 'I had no choice. I felt vulnerable.' I said, 'every time we booked you. We took you into custody. Every time you had a chance to rat on Blakely. So let me guess. He threatened you. He said that if you said anything he would slice you open.'

Giles said, 'yes he did.' I said, 'you know. When I did the 4 year bit in the military. Before all of this. Detective work. The training we had there. Was nothing like what we were doing here. One slip, one mistake. And you were on watch, another mistake. You were gone.'

I cleared my throat and continued, 'we will look at everything, and if we find out you have been lying to us. It's straight into cuffs, and straight to prison. Perverting the course of justice, perjury, we throw the book at you. Co-operate with us now, and we won't do anything. Giles, let me help you.'

Giles said, 'I have told you everything I know.' I said, 'the night of the murder Charles. The night of the murder. You were sleeping rough. Louise comes up to you, and asks you for a light. You wanted cocaine, she couldn't score you any. You were then met by Blakely. He took the knife off you. Holding gloves. Before that he covered the CCTV. He stabbed her. He then swapped the tapes in the sorting

148

office. It doesn't make sense.'

Giles said, 'no, he taped a doctored video over the CCTV camera.' I said, 'it just doesn't make sense, even if he did, where's the switch over.' I had the DVD in my hand. I waved it. I said, 'oh don't worry we have copies of this.'

Charles said, 'I don't know, play it.' I played the DVD. Giles said, 'and pause at 0:35. Do you see that?'

I saw it. A hand, a man's hand, covers the CCTV. Then I played it. I said, 'it's like two videos played into one.'

He said, 'rewind from 0:35, can you see Blakely.' I said, 'yes.' He said, 'well that was him covering the CCTV. Now afterwards, it's different. Same kind of lighting, but different day, from a year ago in spring. That's a previous altercation.'

I said, 'but you are holding the murder weapon.' He said, 'that is Blakely, stabbing Louise.' I said, 'that knife, that fucking knife, and a big man appears. It's switched over. First your pushing her. Then he appears, for a split second. It doesn't make sense. This guy is playing us.'

Giles said, 'he has all of the state of the art computer software, editing software, he took this down to a T. Everything was made up to fix this narrative. Of me being the bad guy.'

149

I said, 'the only thing I don't understand. Is if they wanted rid of you. Why didn't they just give you $100 dollars. To go on a bus. Give you some money to go out of county. Why this?'

Giles said, 'they hated me. They saw me as a bad influence.' I said, 'with no disrespect. You were just trivial to them. Just some bum sleeping on the streets. I am not buying this.'

Giles said, 'well re arrest me then.' I said, 'I can't because of double jepordy. Even if you have been bullshitting me.'

Giles said, 'I haven't.' I said, 'this whole thing stinks. That Blakely is one son of a bitch.'

Giles said, 'there's more to the story also. They saw me as a threat. They knew I was intelligent.' I said, 'oh this is not making any sense. None of this is.'

Giles said, 'that's the whole point, he's playing mind games with you.'

I said, 'true, and it's working but I just can't believe this. The CCTV. Yeah it looks like it's been staged. Yet you didn't come forward. I know you were being threatened. But you had to stop it. You had to be a man and stop that.'

Giles said, 'never crossed my mind.' I said, 'oh come on, this life, this existence you lead. You were nothing important to them. Absolutely nothing.'

Giles said, 'it makes perfect sense.' I said, 'unless there is something you are not telling me.' Giles said, 'I have told you everything.'

I said, 'you feel safe under witness protection do you?' He said, 'sure I do. I don't have to worry about being burnt alive?'

I said, 'you found a girlfriend yet?' He said, 'I have been on a couple of dates.' I said, 'man this whole thing stinks. I believe you, but this Russel Blakely is one nasty son of a bitch.'

Giles said, 'no visitation, nothing. No rights to see him. All of his men in different prisons. All of those slaves set free. Nothing more to investigate'

I laughed and I said, 'I have been a detective for 32 years or so. Lost count. There is always something to investigate.'

I said, 'this isn't over, every shred of evidence of this case is being screened by the FBI. We don't even know if we have caught all of his men. Besides, even if we have. We don't know if there are going to be copycat versions. It's made all over the news. People will be hunting this down like a circus. There will be people copying this for fuck sake.'

Giles seemed agitated and he said, 'oh please, please don't start with this. Are you serious? Do you seriously know how unwell I have been recently.' I said, 'I feel for you, but at the same time. Do you see me most nights. Swallowing some pills, what is it now? Lithium pills. Every night. Trying to make ends meet. Trying to do something positive with my life. Trying to do the right thing. Being a cop isn't always a good thing, and once you reach detective. People think you have all of the answers. It sucks, you know it. I know it.'

Giles said, 'everything sucks nowadays, you just have to grin and bare it. Not saying it's easy or anything. I wish I could help you. Yet it's law abiding people like me, that have bad ills. Despite the priors I have. Misdemeanours. Come on, you are not serious. These are felony charges you are looking at, and you paint Louise Grey to be a fucking angel. She was the antichrist.'

I said, 'she didn't deserve to die so young. Not her, not in that way. Never her. She was 21 fucking years old for fuck sake. With her whole life ahead of her. I am sick of you making excuses.'

Giles gulped. I said, 'look, emotions, my emotions on this case. I have three children. Things are getting out of hand. My emotions. I want to find out. Any more killers, anyone. Anyone who has had anything to do with this. Yet I don't know anymore. You look around, and the police work I have done. We sure fucked up.'

Giles said, 'what do you mean?'

I said, 'we should have spotted this was a set up all along. We wasted a lot of your time, and energy. On that bogus court case. We owed you one. Hence the favours with witness protection.' Giles said, 'well thanks, but it's not exactly heaven out here. Can't talk, can't explain myself too much. It's like I am a fucking ghost.'

I said, 'that's the point, ghosts, organised crime. You were the victim. Now this. Us here. Like two bad people. Which we are not. We are not looking at child abduction or murders. We are not looking at anything like that. Yet all I can think about is this fucking job.'

Giles said, 'what has child abductions got to do with any of this?"

I said, 'when I first joined the force. There were lots of child abductions. Pedophiles with priors. Used to befriend children. Put them in their fucking cars.'

Giles said, 'and you were doing your job to catch them right.' I said, 'I was chasing this one pedophile. He had a teenage boy in the front seat. I was chasing, had my blue lights, sirens. Everything. I got there before the boy was hurt. I knocked two shillings out of the pedophile.'

Giles said, 'you did the right thing.' I said, 'bullshit did I? I got a disciplinary IA

153

were choking down my neck. Thinking I had no right doing this. The pedophile gets put under witness protection. For fuck sake.'

Giles said, 'sorry, when we are talking about modern day slavery. The Blakely's. Do you think they are in some ring, some child abduction ring.'

I said, 'almost definitely That's why it doesn't make sense. Yet I wasn't sure, so I thought about it. I have reviewed the case of Louise Grey. So many times. We have thousands of missing children every day in Detroit. Hundreds of thousands of missing children in Michigan.'

Giles, 'what's your point, it's not all related to Blakely, and his men.'

I said, 'no it's not, but it got me thinking. What is they were prostituting Louise Grey.'

Giles said, 'well you tell me. What did the forensics report say?' I said, 'I will read it to you.'

I take out this piece of paper. I read it. 'Louise Grey, found dead. West Avenue street, 35th. Severe and fatal wound to the heart. Severe loss of blood. Pronounced dead at the scene.'

Giles said, 'go on'. I said, 'it reads that no sexual misconduct was present. It wasn't sexually motivated. There was no rape, or attempted rape.'

154

Giles said, 'well this is bullshit, carry on.'

I said, 'there was a man's DNA on her right thigh. The DNA matched Russel Blakely.'

Giles said, 'carry on.' I said, 'it was originally thought that Russel Blakely had sexually assaulted Louise Grey. Yet there is lack of evidence to support this.'

Giles said, 'that stupid son of a bitch.' I said, 'there is lack of evidence.'

Giles said, 'cut it out, that dude wasn't a pedophile. He was just fucking weird.' I said, 'well there's lack of evidence. The DNA report was in. They did swabs and it says here, 'Blakely's DNA, was found, present, on one of the swabs.' Giles said, 'don't read anymore. I am fucking angry now.' Giles started crying and I said, 'he raped her.'

I said, 'no fucking way, not now, not with all of this happening. He didn't have the guts, the coward.' Giles said, 'listen, before we get involved in this. Let me explain something to you. If this is true. It changes everything. It means it explains why all of those children are missing, and it explains that Blakely was running some trafficking scam.'

I said, 'I already knew he was doing a human trafficking ring. Yet, I just thought he had those women working on the boats. There were men as well.'

Giles said, 'oh come on, you seriously expect me to believe it was just forced labour. I wouldn't put anything passed that guy.'

I said, 'the DNA ruled lack of evidence. DNA can get anywhere. I can touch a lamp post. Someone else can touch the same one. Touch their mouth.'

Giles said, 'cut it out man, you are in denial. You seriously expect me to believe this is one coincidence.'

I slammed Giles to the wall, breaking the wall, and I said, 'it's lack of fucking evidence. Don't you understand?' He said, 'no.' I was exasperated. I shouted, 'we know he did it, but we don't have the evidence to convict him.'

Giles said, 'well get a confession then. Find out who else he is hiring.'

I said, 'this is some bullshit. I am not believing anything to do with this anymore. This guy is deranged.' Giles said, 'you walk over there. You go to the jail cell. You speak to him. You get a confession.' I said, 'the guy is smart. He will know what's coming to him. He will realise what we are doing.'

Giles said, 'secretly record your conversation with him.' I said, 'not admissible in court if I do that.' I continued, 'we are going to have to interview him. Again. Bring him in, talk to him, and then find out what is going on.

I said, 'Giles, thank you for your help, and enjoy your home made pasta Bolognese'

Giles was digging into this penne pasta. This bolognese, with cheese. It was to die for. It was really. I grabbed a fork, and took a shovel in my mouth. I said, 'hey, you son of a bitch. Big portions. I am a greedy man.' He laughed and he said, 'go and get your killer.'

I said, 'already have, the son of a bitch.' I walk out, drive to the airport. Hand in my rental car. Go back, get my real car from the airport in Michigan. Go all the way to Detroit.

Go to the prison that Russel Blakely is staying in. I said, 'Russel Blakely. I am arresting you on one count of rape, you have the right to remain silent. Anything you say, will be used against you. You have the right to an attorney. If you can't afford one. One will be appointed to you.'

You could hear people jeering in the background. Rufus was with me, and we escorted him to the police car. Straight into the custody suite and interviewed on the second floor.

I said, 'right Mr Blakely. We have found evidence. Your DNA, matches a swab we took of Louise Grey. There's evidence to say you have raped her.'

He said, 'that never happened.' I said, 'what, are you going to tell me there was a struggle, what about the bruise mark on her thigh. She wouldn't have gone near you.' He said, 'she did, and it was consensual'

Rufus said, 'what the fuck are you doing, a 50 year old man, doing with a 21 year old in the first place. Even if it was consensual It's still weird. Find someone your own age.'

Rufus said, 'tell us the truth, what happened?' Russel Blakely said, 'the night of the murder. She went over to my apartment. We had sex. What else is there to say.'

I was shocked and I said, 'right, that's it. I am calling of the prelim. This is sick what you did to her.'

Blakely, said, 'what evidence have you got to suggest I raped her?' I said, 'the fact we found the DNA. At the crime scene. Linking you to the time she was murdered. The DA wants you charged.' He said, 'well charge me' I said, 'admit it.' He said, 'fine, I raped Louise Grey.' I said, 'well that was good for you to confess. Enjoy 60 years, another 10 years.' He said, 'when's the hearing?' I said, 'I will speak to the DA. I will send a cover officer over. I don't know how many more years you will serve. With your prior history. I wouldn't expect anything less than ten years. Though if you co-operate, which you have. Maybe 4 years. I don't know. But your chances of parole are slowly slipping beneath your feet.'

He nodded. I said, 'can I ask you something?' He said, 'shoot.' I said, 'why is your family so dysfunctional. Nothing makes sense. We know you weren't blood related to Louise. Yet Sophie. This whole over controlling, almost petrifying sense of controlling attitude you have. With anyone, weaker than you, female. Anyone. Anything. Plus all of these charges. You just want to do everything you can to corrupt people.'

He said, 'only the judge can give those speeches.' Rufus said, 'listen here. I will tell you something. I have worked for the FBI for 20 years now. We don't investigate many rapes. Not as much as these clowns on the third floor. Yet we do investigate some. If it's involved in organised crime we do. You stupid son of a bitch. What do you expect? I am sick of this, and we have to return to our police work now.'

Rufus carried on and said, 'get a woman your own age.' I said, 'right that's enough, this isn't ladies coffee time. I have had enough of this. Send him back to the cells.'

Rufus whispered, 'we dealt with that very smoothly. I can't believe you had to re read the autopsy report. Then get a confession. You did due diligence.' I said. 'we knew this all along, we just needed a confession. The DA wouldn't press without one.'

Rufus said, 'those tumble dicks. You speak to the DA a lot and I don't know why. What they do is just what we do. The file the paperwork, no motions to suppress Goes straight to court. Then that is the end of it. Evidence goes to the judge.'

I said, 'anyone who says the DA's office has it easy, they sure don't.'

Rufus, all big, and big chested. Very assertive, but deep down you could see some kind of tranquility. Like maybe he wanted to talk. He wanted to say something outside of the policing work. I beat him to it. I said, 'look, this is a stressful job and I don't want to keep you. You care to join me and James for a few beers tonight. I know it's short notice. I just, I could do with some company.'

He said, 'ah you are feeling lonely.' I said, 'not at all.' He looked at me again. I said, 'look do you want to come over or not.' He said, 'sure.' He came over. It was us three. Eating pretzels and watching the game. The red socks were playing

Michigan. Baseball caps. Football stickers. We were having a good time watching the game. With one thing in mind. Our radios were buzzing.

I said, 'James, you have met Rufus. Rufus works with the FBI.'

Chapter 25

We are enjoying our evening. It's very good, very nice. Everything is still. Everything is tranquil. The radio going ten to a dozen. Sure never squared with me, but I could understand it. I could know what was happening as I looked outside. It's like the world didn't make sense anymore. Everything stood still.

Everything in it's own merits. Being in the police, too cautious, too this. Too that. In my own experience, just spending time with my colleagues On a social basis, was worth all of the time in the world. We weren't called to any incidents. We had the whole night to ourselves.

Just three men enjoying the baseball. Rufus said, 'look, let me level with you guys. Being in the FBI. I mean, what I am saying. It's hard work sometimes.' I said, 'oh cry me a river.' He said, 'I am serious. We arrested this jack off, a couple of weeks ago for fraud. Wall street fraud. Federal department all over him, like a rash. He walked. His defence lawyer was spinning this whole record player. About him being a 'confused but overriding law abiding guy.' It completely threw me off balance. It shocked me and I have never been the same since.'

I said, 'this all happened a week ago, you have been in the job 20 years. It will get better. Some people walk. Go figure.'

James said, 'I caught this one guy who tried robbing this bank. His defence lawyer tried claiming self defence. It was a bank robbery. He grabbed the murder weapon. Close range. Shot the clerk dead. We arrived in. For some reason SWAT took pity on him. Fired him with rubber bullets. It went to trial. Then he started saying the clerk was rude to him.'

Rufus said, 'then what happened?'

James said, 'the lawyer claimed self defence. It wasn't washing, but it was agonising. He didn't get away. Then that was dismissed by the judge. They pulled the magical mental health card.' I said, 'which is valid for all criminals.' Rufus said, 'I know, mental health, and the sentence goes down dramatically. Yet I know when I see a real mental health crisis.'

I said, 'which doesn't always involve crime. But sometimes it does. Mental Health Cases are unpredictable.' Rufus said, 'no they're not. They are simple.' I said, 'really?' Rufus said, 'yeah, the dude

162

or the girl. They have mental health. It's bread and butter. I met this one homeless woman living on the pavement. People handed her money. We gave her a citation because she refused to leave. She was causing a disturbance. Then the media tried blaming us, and criticised us. Span this web of lies, claiming 'police harassment' Even though we were doing our damn job. Wasn't even a fine. She was just asked to leave. Paperwork is standard.'

I said, 'so what people don't realise is that we are not nurses. We treat people as we find them.'

Rufus grabbed some chips. His sweaty and big muscular hands all over them. Eating them wildly with every gulp. James was more cautious. Digging in very slowly. I took some chips also. James said, 'who cares, lack of work ethic. These homeless people.'

I said, 'lack of work ethic, or nobody has had the chance to give them some work.'

Rufus said, 'doesn't make sense, we would like to think we can house them all. Yet I have met uber drivers who are homeless.'

I said, 'so, can I cast everyone's mind back to Blakely verses the state. Or in fact. Hemingway and Blakely verses the state. It doesn't add up.'

163

Rufus said, 'what doesn't add up?' I said, 'I trust Giles Hemingway. I trust him. I just think Blakely has made him out to be a right fool.'

Rufus said, 'that's exactly what has happened?' Rufus continued, 'it doesn't add up.'

I said, 'I don't know what else to say. I really don't. We can talk all of the time about right verses wrong. The CCTV footage.'

Rufus said, 'that is all it was, the dude duped us. Or tried to. Now he is in jail. Nothing more we can do.'

I said, 'I want justice for Louise Grey. I am going to speak to the mother again.'

Rufus said, 'why? What good is that going to do? She's in a hell of a lot of pain. Grieving all of the time. You show up. She claims police harassment' I said, 'no, I will phone her before hand.' Rufus said, 'or you let me handle in. I go in there.' I said, 'yeah because you're FBI, she'll take you more seriously.' I hand Rufus over the memos, the logs. The autopsy report.

He said, 'I am doing this alone, well, me and Charles Jenkins.' I said, 'is Charles Jenkins your twin or something? You look just like him.' He said, 'aha very funny. I have light brown hair. He has dark hair. I can lift more kilos than him. He is less broad shouldered than me. Easily upset.

164

More smaller. 5 foot 11.' I said, 'bullshit, he's 6.' Rufus said, 'no he's not. Just bullshit he made up to get into the academy. Did you know that dude has only been in the FBI now for 4 years. 4 fucking years. I am sweating my ballsack off doing 20.' I said, 'were you in LAPD before all of this?' He said, 'I was, for 2 years. I moved ranks. Did an on-the job degree. I was not settling for average. Bullied my way to the top.' He joked. I said, 'I better hope you are joking, because I thought your resume checked out to the IA. Everything we do is above board.'

He said, 'The IA keep tabs on us, every wrong move. Straight back to the drawing board. Every wrong move. They always treat us with suspicion. They investigated us, for this time, we raided this warehouse. Illegal drugs, massive corrupt organisation. Organised crime. We seized heroine. I was put on suspension for 10 days. Because I forgot to declare all of the boxes of heroine.' I said. 'that is quite funny.' He said, 'how is it?' I said, 'well, you have to file the report with how many drugs you seized Otherwise it becomes lost property.' He said, 'what, you think I snorted, and smoked/injected it all?'

I said, 'Charlotte. Louise's mother. Next on the to do list.' Rufus said, 'go in there and speak to her. Me and Charles Jenkins.

165

You rookies can just eat more chips, and watch more baseball.' I laughed, as me and Fred Watkins turned our radios down.

I said, 'you know, that's life isn't it, turning our radios down, waiting for people to respond. Waiting for anything but it's always the same. Always the same feeling we have. If we mess up, it's on us. If we do anything wrong. It's on us. All of the time.'

Rufus said, 'we are the police, we are not invincible. The amount of bullshit paperwork I have to sign, just to get the powers that be off my case. IA, and all of that.'

James said, whilst wiping a happy tear from his face, he said, 'look boys, you don't realise what is happening here. These slam and dunk cases. Then all of a sudden we are back to square one. How many man hours is wasted on Blakely and co? How many man hours is wasted on that son of a bitch Hemingway. Both are guilty in my eyes. Even Hemingway. Something stinks about him, and I am not sure what. You expect me to believe the *whole thing was a set up? You expect me to believe that?* You expect me to believe that whilst he was just there, with a 10 inch butchers knife. That Blakely was able to manipulate and control the whole

166

thing. Hemingway was naïve, but he wasn't fucking stupid. He knew what he was doing. He was in on it. Now I don't know the ins and outs of this case, because I wasn't involved in it up to the end. Yet part of me feels he is guilty. Yet, he plays the sadness card. You see through his teary eyes, and you expect time to stand still for him. It just keeps on moving forward. First this, and now silence. Nothing else. Like we have no idea the level of corruption that is going on.'

I said, 'Hemingway's story checks out. He had nothing to do with it.' James said, 'oh come on, he had the murder weapon, he had history with Louise.' I said, 'well what do you want me to do?' James said, 'send the CCTV in for more analysis. Send it to a crime expert. I mean, a videography crime psychologist, or forensics. Or a video forensics?'

I said, 'clutching at straws.' James said, 'cut it out, it might work. The whole thing will.'

I said, 'how many more man hours is this going to waste?'

James said, 'do you want to get to the truth, or do you want to keep painting this dude as the victim. In all of this. He had a part to play in the abduction and killing. If you want to call it an abduction. Yet, we look at the big picture here. Something has happened. He is just playing dumb.'

I said, 'okay, I will send the DVD off to a video forensic expert. Yet I am not sure what else we can do. I will let FBI speak to Charlotte.'

Rufus said, 'yeah, and me and Charles Jenkins will use our FBI training and our handsome good looks to get the information' I said, 'you're kidding me, you truly are. This whole thing is turning out to be a nightmare.' I said, 'one condition.' James said, 'what's that?'

I said, 'I want to be there, me and James. Outside. FBI can wear a wire.'

Rufus said, 'okay, but that's it.'

Chapter 26

We had the whole thing set up. Me and James. In an unmarked police van. I mean it wasn't even a van. It was disguised as a run of the mill campervan. We were listening into everything. Wires, speakers. The whole thing was a very good set up. FBI came in, in an unmarked Mercedes, Police car. All courtesy of the state. Detroit and Michigan. The two lads roam in, and ask questions.

Rufus said, 'Charlotte. I am Rufus, I am with the FBI. This is Charles Jenkins. He is FBI. We are both investigating the murder of your daughter. Louise Jenkins.'

Charlotte said, 'I thought that was done and dusted.' Rufus said, 'there is more evidence.' Charlotte said, 'what is that?' Rufus said, 'Louise Grey, on the night of the murder. Was sadly sexually assaulted by Russel Blakely.'

Charlotte said, 'raped?' Rufus said, 'we have him on one charge of rape. He has plead guilty. The verdict is tomorrow.'

Charlotte said, 'all this time, you boys just came here to rub salt in the wound.' Rufus said, 'no, we had to tell you. FBI rarely gets involved in these cases. Yet this whole thing is linked to a drug, and human trafficking ring. We want you to find closure. Yet you will be unable to do this. With the likes of Sophie and the others roaming the streets. Vulnerable young ladies. Yet with all of Blakely's crew behind bars. You should be safe. We are worried about copycat versions.'

Charlotte said, '*copy cat versions?*' She said in shock. I said, 'yes, we are worried that people may copy what Russel Blakely and his crew have done. It has been all over the press. The New York Times. The Washington post. CNS, CBS, and all of the news channels. It's just a precaution. Yet we will put them all on a vulnerable victims database. Technically, that is all we can do. Stretching it here. We don't usually get involved in these matters. Yet it helps us trace these organised crime groups.'

Charlotte said, 'what else do you need to know?' Rufus said, 'look, we want to help you through the grieving process. As much as possible. Yet it isn't going to be easy. I have an excellent psychologist called Andrew James. He works pro bono cases. He's a real smart guy. He wants to give you his services for free. He feels that is the least he can do.'

Rufus handed the card, to Charlotte.

Charles Jenkins said, 'you know, us FBI folk. We just want to help. We just want to help victims of crime. Yet that isn't all we do. We deal with everything. Every single thing and it works like that. I mean top secret stuff. We don't dabble with the secret service. Can't remember the last time I was in Washington.'

Rufus said, 'the secret service aren't interested in our case with these gangs. They have to protect Washington. Yet that isn't the reason we want to talk to you.'

Charlotte said, 'look, I have told you everything. I am grieving, please. Officers. I don't know what else to say. It's a scary world out there.'

Rufus said, 'it's scary, but we will get to a point in time when it makes sense. Injustices happen all of the time. When I was a kid. I was told I was Dyslexic. Couldn't read, couldn't write. Look at me now. Earning nearly 100k dollars a year, catching the biggest criminals in the USA. You know? Just because you are in pain now. Just because you feel helpless now. Doesn't mean you can't recover.'

Charlotte said, 'you reckon.' Rufus said, 'I know how much Louise meant to you. I really do, and we will do everything we can to support you. I just want to let you know we will keep you informed. It's a strange case because usually when someone goes to jail. Everyone is safe. Yet, the thing with organised crime is things happen without us realising. We have the outside world to protect. This guy was getting his boys to commit offences. Whilst he was in prison.'

Rufus said. 'Charlotte, can I ask you another question?'

Charlotte said, 'of course.' I said, 'you know in my lifetime. When I work closely with agents. We make something work. Doesn't always work all of the time. Sometimes we mess up. We want to do the perfect job. Yet sometimes it's not working. I keep the stove on some nights. Get so angry with myself. Always messing up. Always doing the wrong thing. Always getting myself in trouble.'

Charlotte said, 'I know, it's tough for you

171

right now.'

Rufus pointed and said, 'we will do the best we can. Just realise this. Another day for us now.'

I was in the van and so was Fred. I couldn't believe what I was hearing. We were getting results. Slowly but surely.

Chapter 27

The next day was different. I wasn't feeling myself and people were changing. Not straight away but it was happening. I felt kind of powerless at first. As it everything I had known would rain down on me. I would feel clueless as to what our next objective was.

I woke up on Tuesday, just feeling like life was almost, taking a shit down my neck. I wasn't happy with the investigation work. It was like getting blood out of stone. Deep down. I wanted to carry on trying to work things out.

No, not Hemingway after all of those times I had spoken to him. Put him in witness protection. It just didn't make sense. Blakely fitted the profile but this guy was who I knew. Very quick to blame other people. I just couldn't shake my head off off this CCTV.

I headed over to the video forensic psychologist. Handed the DVD in. I returned, her name was Barbara White. I said, 'so tell me something, what is going on in this tape?' She said, 'well your gut instinct is right, he's definitely used a video editing software.' I said, 'Blakely. I know, what about Hemingway. Is he involved in this?'

Barbara said, 'probably, through coercion You can't fake these things. It's impossible that Blakely stabbed her.' I said, 'we have this guy locked up and so you think it was Hemingway.' She nodded and said, 'no computer software can alter that.'

I said, 'what about the change in patterns, the video shifts?' Barbara said, 'the most likely scenario is they were both involved. Hemingway gave you the slip. This whole editing thing. Deep down it's realistic, but the two were up to no good. It's a double bluff.' I said, 'the screw heads.'

Barbara said, 'excuse me?' I said, 'I am not sure if you are aware of this or not. But Hemingway is in witness protection.' She had blonde curly hair. Quite a nice lady actually. She said, 'well take him out then. Get him tried again.' I said, 'double jeopardy, can't do it, he was exonerated.'

Barbara said, 'ain't that a bitch.' I said, 'you keep the copy of this DVD. I will do some digging.'

Barbara said, 'listen, I have been involved in these cases before. They don't go away. They never do. I know the CCTV was altered. Yet your compassion for Hemingway. It's impeding your judgement.' I said, 'Blakely is more guilty in my eyes.' She said, 'maybe so, but you have to think clearly about scenarios here. You're a god damn detective. Do your job.'

I said, 'I will have a word with Hemingway.' I smiled and she got defensive. She said, 'what's the smile about?' I said, 'nervousness. Frustration.'

She said, 'can't just take it on board, can you? I know people like you. Always wanting to over sympathise.' I said, 'hey, this was a clear cut case. Blakely was setting the whole thing up.' She said, 'maybe, I don't know.' I grabbed the DVD and walked out unconvinced. Down the stairs. In the car, with James Watkins.

James said, 'oh come on now, why the long face?' I said, 'she's telling me to look at Giles Hemingway again. Figured that he's responsible, some way.'

James said, 'it's just not possible. That guy was exonerated. I know that psychologist. They are not always right.' I said, 'it's like everything I am doing isn't working.'

We are sat inside the Mercedes. I am feeling angry, and we have no alternatives now. James Watkins said, 'listen, something has to happen. Some kind of corruption. Something.'

James said, 'listen here. Don't go getting any ideas. It's not going to work like that. We all know that is the case. We have been working this job for ages. The same thing happens over and over like a tape. We don't quite agree on anything. Do you know the state of the world at the moment?'

I said, 'no I don't. I really don't and don't want to get into it. That female we booked the other day. Homeless lady.'

James said, 'the one we fined for jay walking on the side walk.'

I said, 'yeah, but she was done for obstruction. I knew Giles very well and still do. He's not the typical guy, you just book and leave out in the open like that. With no flies. Nothing.'

James said, 'oh come on, you see one psychologist, and now you want to implicate him in this again. I am not sure if you understand what is happening here.'

I said, 'and if I pay Hemingway a visit, I don't know what's going to happen next. Just more conversations.'

James said, 'how long were you in the army? You said 4 years, but did you go to army school before then?'

I said, 'I did indeed for the full year the school provided.' He said, 'so you did 5 years?' I said, 'being an army cadet doesn't really count as being in the army. Yet if you want to be technical I guess I did.'

He said, 'so you would realise this whole thing stinks of a set up. Maybe a bigger set up then what we are looking at here. What if the FBI are in on this?'

I said, 'oh come on, you can't be serious. We are going over this. What would the FBI want to do with all of this?'

He said, 'I don't know, and I don't want to know. I am fed up of having this conversation. Everytime we involve IA. Or we try to. Everytime we think of something. It all comes back to what we are thinking about now.'

I said, 'this one time. I was in the federal reserve. Once. Looking over my shoulder. Moved to the army, the helicopters whizzing by. The blood on my shirt, as I was shooting. The dizziness around me. The long distance travel. The apartment we stayed in. As we moved onto bunkers, and dirt tracks were my home. We set up tents, and I was sitting there. You had a flask of water. People stood around smoking. It wasn't like a vacation, like some of the guys say it was.'

He said, 'it was war.' I said, 'yeah it was

war. Back then, you know when I joke, and I say, it was Afghanistan. It wasn't. 32 years ago boss. The cold war. You can't handle the logistics here. I just can't seem to shake it out of my head. The gun in my hand, and then, nothing. Things evaporate I look around me, and I realise this job is different. The one I am doing now. I just can't seem to want to blame anyone. Not Hemingway. Nobody. Doing this job is different. Yet, it's more than that. If Giles is guilty. I will arrest him. Get my cuffs out and do it. Yet, we don't have solid evidence, just some psychologist.'

James said, 'so you are saying the psychologist isn't credible?'

We were sat in the Mercedes The wind going through my hair. The glass on the door. The people driving passed. Honking their horns. It was a busy city.

I said to James, 'I spoke to the psychologist. We have seen people get involved in this case. The sheer light. The grey scale musk around her face. The lighting in the room. The smell of coffee downstairs. The smell of cigarette smoke on her breath. As she eats a mint. Then nothing.'

James said, 'she is only human, you know that. I knew this quack up in South Central. Took me ages to figure out what

177

she was doing. Spoke to her all of the time at one point. Trying to nail this guy for Fraud. It was how we were going. It was stupid really. Every day he would change his story. Then some quack comes in, starts saying it's okay to leave it. Went out for a smoke. Came back and that was it.'

I said, 'oh come on, you can't compare this to a fraud case. We are looking all around for answers here. Anything we can do to kind of separate ourselves. From any of this.'

James said, 'we have to move onto other cases. But I know you, and I know you well. You want to get to the bottom of everything. I don't care what we have to do. Louise had her whole life ahead of her.'

I said, 'Sophie, and the friends, are on a victim's database now. We have them protected.'

James said, 'good, because that gang Blakely had. It wasn't going away. We see copycat versions in Ohio yesterday.'

He spread open the evening times from the day before. There was a woman, shot dead. The guy who did it was a religious nut. Said, 'I love Blakely.' Over his shirt. He was arrested, and put into a quack house.'

James said, 'people idolise this guy and he's a fucking psychopath.'

178

I said, 'I realise that. Flip over to page 4.'
He flipped the evening standard over.
There was more news.' I said, 'I don't
want to see anymore. I get what you are
trying to say.'

James said, 'everyone does. Yet going
back to basics now.' I said, 'oh right. So I
will talk to Giles, I will try and make sense
of this. Yet these trips to New York are
killing me.'

He said, 'you've gone this far, would be
unfair to take you off the case now. I am
not buying your theory that FBI are on in
this. Or MI5.'

I said, 'no, and you never will know. The
guys do their job by the book. It ain't a
conspiracy. We speak to them all of the
time. We would know if they had any
undue influence. Yet it's just how it is. You
look around. You look at the cigarette
smoke. You look at everything. Every bit
of detail.'

James said, 'yet the smoke alludes you.
We speak to people all of the time and this
is all you come up with. What exactly have
you been smoking?'

I said, 'absolutely nothing, you know
that. We speak to this psychologist again?'

James said, 'if we need to, I will come
with you to speak to Hemingway.'

We both drove over. It was a two day
drive. I was getting disorientated at this

point. Wanted the whole thing to come to a conclusion. Wanted to find out who this guy really was. I never really knew him as much as I wanted to. Not after all of this.'

We sat down with him, James said, 'look, we want to know more. That CCTV was analysed by a forensic psychologist. She said that you may have had some undue influence.'

Giles said, 'never would I do that. It was all Blakely.'

I said, 'if so, why is that quack in our division saying you had some influence.'

Giles said, 'why don't you ask her. I am seriously getting fed up of this. All of the time. You try and blame me.' I said, 'this is not what we are doing. We just want to know the truth.'

Giles said, 'it was a set up. I wasn't involved. I was framed.' I said, 'that is your story, but originally in court. It was different. You admitted to stabbing Louise. Now you say you were threatened into doing it. Doesn't really make sense. I mean on the surface, but when you look underneath.'

I was looking around at his apartment. He was wearing his suede jacket. You could see punk rock bands up on the walls. The walls were a crystal colour. Almost like a pastel-grey colour. The room looked dim, and looked kind of tranquil. I looked around and saw the sun shining through. Almost a vacant reminder of the sun caressing the interior of the sofas. The three of them all combined. The pastel colour walls. The stairs, leading up into the bedrooms. The kitchen and the insulation of the building.

I looked at the carpet. A very delicate green colour. The one you would expect in a place like this. Yet it was dug up, and looked un furnished. I was expecting him to get it changed. Live in a proper house. Do something unique with his time.

The stairs were wooden, and full of oak, varnish. As I looked outside, at cars driving passed. All of the time. They never stopped. Like they did in Michigan. When he was living in Detroit. They always used to stop. You would get an elderly woman glaring through the window, and driving on. In New York, nothing. Car drove passed. After car, after car. A Chevron, a Merc, a Ford, a Chevy, a broken down BMW, with plates hanging off. A Honda, the kind of cars you would expect in a city. That it's suburban nightmare was a whisper away from the same kind of concurrent thoughts you would have. That the pastel colour of the house would give off a vibe of encouragement. As if we had been there and seen it. All of the time.

The walls, and the posters Giles had put

up. Was what I could see around me. I looked around, as the sun caressed my face. As I grabbed a coffee. I didn't even need to ask, as the pale green kettle, on the whistle. Was boiling, as I poured right into a quenched state of coffee beans. My hair was flourishing, as I sat down. It wasn't the type of city to send you into a whirlwind. It was the type of place to almost make you want to sleep. Buffalo New York. A place of dreams, and for me. A place where we could sit this guy down. In his nice semi detached house. A whole apartment block in his name. Even the next door part where other people could stay all turned into one house for him. Downstairs, a little garden terrace some trees. We wanted to create the image of someone hard working. As the witness protection programme. I didn't people cottoning onto the same guy. The same dude. The same loner. The same loner with the grey shirt. With the apple grey tie. Who lived in a random apartment block. On the 4th floor. Who would get harassed, choked and beaten at every opportunity. Then I start getting bitter, and I think. That this psychologist, and the nerve to involve him again. As if the guy hadn't had a rough life was it was. It just got better and bitter, and with resentment and irony into the whole

182

equation. I had not really thought very hard about this. It had all washed over me like a dream. I choked on my coffee, as I could see James chatting idly to Giles.

I fell asleep in the bedroom, as James had handed me my lithium. I slept like a baby, and I woke up. With everything around me that I needed. We got a contractor in to fix the carpet. Yet this is where it got interesting. I am not even knowing the full state of affairs that happened. We got rid of the green, and added a more beige colour.

The contractor was called Sam, a nice amiable guy. He had a beard and used to talk very enthusiastically. He said he was in the navy, and we used to bond over that. Even though he was loud, as subtle paradox. He could be quiet. I bit into this cake, some kind of salted cake. Wasn't quite sure of the name. Some kind of assortment The contractor changed the carpet. Absolutely nothing underneath. Just empty floor boards, piece of dust. Nothing. Nothing to implicate Hemingway in anything.

Not that I would know how it was. In this kind of cold morning. I felt like I had closure. I felt like I had known everything I had known. Even though I was replaying it over and over in my head. The night of the incident. The night of the attack. I could feel that Louise was safe.

Sam said, 'right, that carpet change comes to $300.' He whispered. I said, 'is that all?' He said, 'well just for this one.' He got his calculator out. He started adding things up. I was too distant at this point. Everything was in a whirlwind. I let James take care of the rest.

The opaque tiles underneath the carpet. The long days not knowing what was going to happen. The care free attitudes. The long faces. The wind in my hair. The overriding memory we always had. The psychologist in my head, over and over again. Like a tape, replaying, and replaying. James had slept easy that night. It was one big sleep over. He woke up, and poured on the coffee machine. He woke up, napped, woke up, napped. Over and over again.

He wasn't a smoker, but the occasional one. I could see this cigarette in his hand. A small straight one, as the match stick he was holding. Was attached to this box he struck. He opened the window, and grabbed the remote to deactivate the smoke alarm. I laughed and I said, 'remember to put it on after you finish.' He said, 'of course.' I said, 'yet we look at things differently now. Summer is near, which means you look at those parties we had to break up. The spring break parties.

Where you shouted at that college girl who wasn't going home.'

He said, 'oh it's different now, yeah we broke them up for smoking cannabis, and breaking and entering this guy's home. That wasn't spring break. That was idiocy.'

I said, 'you know what I mean. Summer is a busier time of the year. Things happen. Buffalo New York seems almost silent. It's a good place. We look around, and we see nothing. Nothing to suspect anyone of doing anything wrong. Nothing to suspect that anyone has given anyone any hope. That was our life. The desperation of summer would quench the aspirations and depression of Spring. The deep slumber of winter, seemed to juxtapose. The fact we are now here.'

James said, 'it's poetry. That is all it is. Poetry. Nothing more. Nothing less. We get someone. We book them. We get someone. We book them. None of this pity party, or feeling sorry for certain people.'

Chapter 28

There was something about James. He was a nice man, and everything he did was by the book. Yet his attitude was how it always was. He was a calm bloke, and he didn't have much of a temper. If he had a temper whatsoever. Yeah we knew, that

185

we were staying in Buffalo for a while.

Yet I couldn't shake certain things. Not now, now after all of this. Not that I could anyway. The long distance drive had killed us. We sure knew this. Yet the silence of the present time. As we looked over. We just wanted some conclusion. I wasn't going to go on any witch hunts. Not anymore. Not now. Not that I wanted to implicate Giles. Yet if evidence precluded to his involvement. I would have to arrest him.

We were still in the apartment block, and James was coming up of new theories. New people. New ideas as to who helped kill Louise.

He said, 'it wasn't all Blakely.' I said, 'yes it was.' He said, 'cut it out, it would never be all him. Not after everything we have been through. He walked over. He pulled that knife. Anything else wouldn't make sense by the DA.'

I said, 'you are missing the point. He had people helping him. The guy was a lunatic. He wasn't, and is not to be trusted.'

James said, 'so this whole witch hunt, yet someone has to be blamed. I refuse to think it's all Blakely.'

I said, 'well which names have you got?' James said, 'what about Sophie?' I said, 'cut it out, those people were young and dumb.' He said, 'exactly what I was thinking.' I said, 'I didn't mean it in that respect. You really want us to talk to Sophie Anderson again. After all we have been through. She's on a victim database. Vulnerable. Not some murderer.'

He said, 'okay, so what about Fred Oniel?' I said, 'what about him? He was an abusive alcoholic on the west thirty fourth street. Fred Oniel had nothing. He had nothing to do with this. What, some homeless guy? On another kind of story.'

He said, 'we are speaking to Sophie. We are going to get to the bottom of this.' I sipped my coffee and I said, 'if what she is saying is true. She had no part to play in this.'

He said, 'well, what about getting Giles to talk to us.' I said, 'we have outsourced every avenue here. We have spoken to people time and time again. We have conversed. We have tried to make happy mediums. It doesn't seem to be working. The same things happen. The same mistakes. This was no coincidence. Besides. Giles isn't a homeless guy. Not anymore. Not after all of this. No sir. Wouldn't make sense.'

James said, 'FBI are still on this.' I said, 'I don't blame them but we have limited time.' James laughed and seemed angry, he said, 'we have all of the time in the world. Just because you can't stand the travel. Doesn't mean you can't take the pressure. I am going to make sure of that.'

I laughed, and I said, 'me and my wife, we don't talk as much as we used to. All the children are grown up. Thinking about it. Now wasn't the time to make snap decisions. Now wasn't the time to act like I was God's gift. Now wasn't the time to go around in circles. Look at everything I had accomplished with the force. Like there was nothing left anymore.'

James said, 'we have done everything we can. Every paperwork signed. Every I has been dotted. Every t has been crossed. I can't take anymore conspiracy theories. We have to get back to interviewing people. Sophie, and then we move on. Then we speak. Then we get moving. Giles is a friendly man, don't get me wrong. Yet we need to speak to the DA and legal council.'

I said, 'you have it, and in the mean time. Watch this poor guy suffer. He's all alone here, no wife. Nothing.'

James said, 'he's making do with what he has. You look over Buffalo New York.'

I did look over Buffalo New York. The snow from the winter, had been long shifted. The sun was caressing the bricks, the silence. Everything we could see. Every bit of hope. Every landmark. People came here to dream. People came here to have long nights. Long pauses in conversations. People came here to relive the same dreams they had.

I could spend ages here, and I could have lots of naps, and lots of rests. In this city. In this district. It wasn't like Detroit. In Detroit you would get busted just for looking at someone the wrong way. A cop car would swarm passed if you had stolen a bagel. A doughnut, anything. Buffalo New York, had some calm about it. Almost like the buildings were more firmer also. More kind of solid. With everything going around. The same brick temples, and freedom you would have. All corresponded with my lack of guilt, and sense of self compassion. Everything was a home for me, but this seemed more homely than ever. Seemed to have this sense of independence. Nobody else could shake. We look at the taxis, the long walks. The senses of confidence. I only had been here from time to time. It was the only time I could properly relax. I could get a transfer here. Realistically it wasn't going to happen.

I had work I had to do in Detroit. I had work I had to do in Michigan. There were more cruise liners filled to the rim of narcotics. There were more copycat versions of that asshole Blakely. We

189

needed to find, and there were more feathers to ruffle up. Which I had no qualms with doing. Yet I look over, and I look at the people walking passed. New York, when some people came here, they wouldn't like it. Yet I admired the business of the city. Mixed with the apprehension, that even though people were cutting each other off. Arguments, and the same bagel shops on any counter. The sense of tranquility and ambience was a different kind of silence. You wouldn't always get in Detroit. Yet my heart was in Detroit. So I couldn't stop. I couldn't stop working.

I couldn't shake what James was saying, yet deep down I knew he was right. We had more people to interview.

Chapter 29

I was back in Detroit. Back trying to make ends meet. Back trying to do something to help myself, and others. Back trying to go out of my way to help.

I had met up with Sophie, all teary eyed, but she had told me she had got into law school. I sighed and spoke to her. I said, 'Sophie, so how's university. Law school?' She said, 'I am going to Harvard.' I was pleased for her, truly. I said, 'congratulations.' She said, 'really.' I said. 'When you pass the bar, what's your desired specialty?' She said 'criminal law.' I said, 'wow, so if I ever have a suspect in, you will make sure I dot my i's and cross my t's.' She smiled, and she said, 'almost certainly.'

I said, 'Sophie, the reason I am here, is I have more questions regarding Louise Grey.' She said, 'fire away.' I said, 'look, I know this may be a difficult time. Yet I just want to know. Do you think the murderer was definitely Blakely. We have tried Hemingway. Yet absolutely nothing.'

Sophie said, 'sure it was. He was a dirty old man. He was perverted. The attack was sexually motivated.' I said, 'but is there anything else. Any inclination Giles could have conducted this? Also, the fact Louise gave Giles the murder weapon. A butchers knife. A couple of blocks of the street she was killed.'

Sophie said, 'Louise was a complex person. She wasn't all that bad. She was young and dumb. She didn't deserve to die so early.' A tear shed down Sophie's cheek, but for some reason. She stayed smiling.

I said. 'I think we can both agree with this, but I want to know more. I want to know who else helped. I want closure for Charlotte. I look at the memories. All of the times we spoke.'

Sophie said, 'Giles was a strange dude.' I

191

said, 'what do you mean?' Sophie said, 'I don't know, just complex I guess. He kept complaining about the loss of his postal work job. That's all he spoke about. His regret. He hated his life. The whole year he was homeless, was like a cardinal sin for him.'

I laughed and said, 'oh come on, homelessness isn't a crime.' She said, 'technically it is.' I said, 'yeah, but if we enforced every crime, we wouldn't have the man power to do that. He has misdemeanours. That's it. Plus the felony charge was dropped.'

Sophie said, 'look, life hasn't been easy for me. Not for you or anyone else involved in this case. For anyone who says life is easy. They are lying. We just have to make it as comfortable as possible. Which means facing up to the cold realities of the situations here. Looking for what we can't see.'

I said, 'I have looked everywhere with Giles. Underneath his floor boards. Everywhere.' Sophie said, 'maybe he's sophisticated, he's hiding things. He's organised.'

I said, 'you think he's lying?' She said, 'almost definitely That CCTV footage was altered. In some way or another, but I know there was an altercation between Hemingway and Blakely. On the night of the murder.'

I said. 'tell me more.' She said, 'what happened is, Russel Blakely, was accusing Hemingway, on being on his turf. Hemingway as an ego maniac. Didn't want anyone lying around on the block. Was very, and is very protective of me. I will admit he is an asshole. Yet that doesn't pay to the credence of the fact. There was a scuffle.'

I said, 'okay, carry on.'

Sophie said, 'the butchers knife. It was getting passed around a lot.' I said, 'we only have Gile's fingerprints on there.' Sophie said, 'everyone was wearing gloves. Blakely has his men involved. Kept saying, 'stab him'. To Giles.'

I said, 'this still doesn't make sense. Why would Giles be lying? We know Blakely's history. We don't know anything Giles could have done. He wasn't a violent man.' Sophie said, 'he was pushed into it. He dug the knife deep into Louise's chest. It could have been him who changed the CCTV.'

I said, 'look, I have been a detective for 32 years. Barely in the case of organised crime, and doctored CCTV footage. Do we get cases, where we can't decide. Which murderer we are dealing with here. Blakely will get life. Irrespective of how much prerogative or intent he had on the killing. Irrespective of if he was entirely him who killed Louise Grey. It was the same guy we all knew. The organised crime. The cruise liner ships. The human trafficking Irrespective of wether it was entirely him or not. He's not going to see the light of day again. Well not until he is 72, and his parole hearing arrives.'

Sophie said, 'look I know all of this. You came to me for information. I have given you info, and my honest opinion. Do what you want with it.'

I smiled and I said, 'hey, good luck at Harvard.' She smiled and said, 'I will be seeing you in custody one day.' She pointed in a jokey way.

I said, 'hopefully as a criminal defence lawyer, and not a suspect.' I said jokingly. She smiled. I left.

I got in the car. I slammed on the horn. James and Rufus in the back. Just looking star struck. Ryan Coleman was there also. I said, 'boys, now we are officially fucked. No recourse. Nothing. No idea. Sophie thinks Giles is hiding something. Hell, she said she saw him kill Louise. We have no choice but to arrest him.'

Ryan said, 'what about double jeopardy' I said, 'doesn't apply, this is a double homicide It's plausible that Blakely and Giles worked together.'

James said, 'so we call him.' James

switched on the phone. We could hear the phone ringing. He answered. He picked up. 'Giles speaking.'

I said, 'what the hell is wrong with you?' He said, 'what do you mean?' I said, 'how did you know it was me. Charles Brown.' He said, 'caller ID.' I said. 'right no time to hold your hand anymore. I have spoken to a cooberating witness. She said she saw you stab Lucy.' He said, 'who told you that?' I said. 'I can't say, she's on a vulnerable victim's database.' He said, 'this is bullshit. I didn't do anything.' I said, 'that's what I reckon. What's confusing me is everyone's fucking story is different.' Rufus was laughing, grunting, he was FBI, and even he was getting annoyed. He said, 'look, Giles, we are going to have to interview you under caution. The DA have already approved it. Hell, we can even do it in your house, providing you let us record. But we need to get to the bottom of this. ASAP.'

Giles said, 'sure.' He said, 'tomorrow 8:30am.' He hung up. I said. 'Strange.' Rufus said, 'man this is annoying me. It really is. I look at the whole thing now.' I said, 'nah it's not annoying. It's just weird is all. We fly over. We are not driving.' We checked in on a business flight, straight away. Stayed in a hotel. We knew it was going to get dicy. We arrived. Giles was

195

angry. Upset. We put him in cuffs. All of the floor boards had been broken. Everything.'

I said, 'what is it with you and those floorboards. We just had those detailed.' Rufus looked suspicious, and did a full search of the house. We had LAPD search the house. With a forensics officer, finding a stash of knives. Covered in blood.' I took a photo on my phone, as I walked in. I said, 'Giles, is there something you are not telling us?' I showed him the picture on my phone.

He said, 'no fucking way, I can't tell you.' Rufus said, 'cut it out man, we have found your secret stash. What are you using these things for?' He pointed to the weapons as they went into evidence.

He said, 'one of the most cardinal sins. It was me who stabbed Louise. I had a fight with Blakely. You believed the CCTV was doctored You bunch of hypocrites All I did was change the lighting. Switched one of the main beams off. There was no doctoring involved. You think that Blakely is some kind of expert, in videography, he's a low life son of a bitch.'

We place Giles in cuffs, and we drive him, with sirens, and lights. To the New York office. Everyone is around him, as he is interviewed more cautiously there. In an interview room. Recording everything.

As I left FBI handle this as I need to take a breather.

Rufus said. 'Look sir, you have sent us on a wild trip here. I have spoke to DA. We are charging you with one count of first degree murder. Attempted murder, yeah, because double jeopardy isn't going to wash with you. Possession of weapons. Possession with intent to inflict grievous bodily harm. As they say. Possession of narcotics.'

He was read his rights. At this time. The old Giles Hemingway seemed to flood away. I hadn't had any luck trying to reason with him anymore. That all that was left was the new guy. The same deranged monster I had laid eyes on. The same guy, I had never seen before.

That all of the money that was wasted on him. Now here is with us. In some suite. Where we interview him. As we can see is character change. We break him down, until he's crumbling. He turns into a wretched soul. Yet the monster he is. With nothing to do but appear very abusive. Looking drunk, even though I knew that wasn't his fault.

I could feel the room go dizzy. My feet went numb. I couldn't see properly. I was having a migraine and a panic attack all rolled into one. I opened the door, and sat down. As the light was shining in my eyes.

I couldn't forgive myself for believing that son of a bitch. Now we had Blakely in jail for a crime he didn't commit. The whole thing was getting intense. I kind of walked forward a bit. Walked into this room. A kind of broken kind of room. Where the floor boards were aching underneath my feet.

I sat there for a bit. And looked in the mirror. My grey suit, and my demeanour It changed. I was the same guy. I was stuck in New York, with a murderer. With all of those knives.

I walked back into the room, and I said, 'so what the fuck is it with you and those knives. Have you been self mutilating or something?' He showed me this whole ray of scars over his legs. Where he had cut his legs, from head to toe. One big mark. I had never seen anything like this.' I said, 'ah Giles'. I said sympathetically. I said, 'we could have dealt with this differently. Now I know what the knives are for.' He said, 'but you wouldn't listen.' I said, 'I am getting you a doctor.' He said, 'you wouldn't listen, and you still are not listening now.'

I said, 'I am listening sir, it's just we have to book everything into evidence. And get you a psych.'

He said, 'that's all you are going to do.' He opened his mouth. A missing tooth was present. With blood, looked like he had punched himself repeatedly in front of the mirror. He swallowed a tooth in front of me. As two fell down his mouth.'

I radioed into control. I said. 'We need a doctor to go in and sort this out please. Giles Hemingway, east branch of north twenty two street. Lacerations to face, neck, arms, and legs.'

I am feeling sick. I said, 'you piece of shit. First Louise, and now this. You can't live with yourself or something?' He said. 'That's right.' A doctor came in and was sending him away for stitches. The CD was paused. I looked over at all of the Police I had with me. I said, 'wow.'

Rufus said. 'that's enough work for one day. He will be in the infirmary for several weeks.'

I said, 'all part of the tax payers investment.'

New York, more sophisticated, than the cell block we had. Even though it was pretty much the same. We had an infirmary on the custody suite. Wasn't as good as a prison infirmary. Was more a remand cell infirmary. With several doctors, and nurses. So they were going to put him on an IV drip, and he could be there for weeks. Even months. Before he's deemed fit to stand trial. I just wanted him to be better. He was handcuffed to the hospital bed, and an armed police guard. With two guns. Was there with him. A pistol in the holster. Then on the arm. A glock 39, semi automatic. Looked like a little Yacuzzi gun. The Police officer looked ex military. His training amounted to what he was saying.

I nodded at him, as he put his thumb up to me. I walked over to the block. I drove home, and I knew that this night's rest. Was going to be different. Yet home wasn't in Detroit anymore. Home was New York. The FBI had paid for me to stay in an apartment near the custody block. They wanted me on the case. I couldn't see my wife or kids for ages. Not that I minded. I knew I had work to do here. I was living in Buffalo New York. For all I know. I could have been there forever. I felt sick.

I couldn't stomach what had happened. I couldn't even comprehend it. I regret blaming myself, and I packed into some crisps. Ironically I was living on the same block. The same street. As Hemingway was. I knew I could do some work here. Some sting operations and maybe even do a stake out. My binoculars at the ready. Yet all I saw, from day in and day out. Was prostitutes. People getting into cars with hookers. If I called that in, I would get ignored on the radio. Maybe even laughed at. Yet I still took an interest. As this one prostitute walked in with these one business man. He was looking arrogant. As he short skirt, and her skimpy outfit. Her handbag, looked posh. Fancy leather. Could have been Gucci. I could see inside the handbag. Two condoms. Blue. The packet was shiny. Inside her handbag was some crisps. Some cheese and onion crisps to be in fact. I had a birds eye view. Of her handbag, and I could see it all. The tampons, the over sized biscuits. The cell phone, two in fact Some more biscuits. Some kind of phone directory book. Looked morel like a note diary. Could have been both. I lost interest in the book, and the whole thing. As the car whizzed off, and the business man eloquently drove away.

I felt like I was going to vomit. I went to the toilet. No sick came out. I looked in the sink. I looked at my face in the mirror. I sat down, and I was worried. Scared. Frightened, and I felt alone. Alone that this whole thing was going to happen. Frightened that I had to even comprehend why I was here. Buffalo New York. The finest city. Where not one building was the same colour.

The small kind of district, over shredded my self doubt. I was not alone yet it felt that way. My own company alluded me. My own sense of opportunity. Kind of felt like a walk in the park. I knew life was what you make of it. That the mind was everything and you had to be positive. Yet it was stuck with nothing, and I was stuck with nothing. Just some monster of a man called Hemingway. In some infirmary. Under arrest I had to make calls. I had to do the right things.

He had been playing us from the beginning. Yet the cruise liner ship and everything inside there had happened. I got text messages from the DA. The prison office. FBI. Even internal affairs were involved now. It was shitty, as a letter from internal affairs comes through the post. Warning me if I don't sort this mess out. I am up for review.

I felt kind of isolated, and stuck. I didn't want to be under review. It wasn't my fault he had lied to us. I phoned IA up, and argued the toss with them. Told them it wasn't my fault I was lied to. I spoke to a guy called Tom Franks. He said the letter was accurate, however, it could have been an error somewhere in the paperwork. Tom Franks came over to my apartment. We spoke for a bit. He cleared me of any wrong doing there and then. I have been vindicated. As he could see around me.

202

I was a hard working professional. I was doing everything I could to help. I showed him the pictures The lacerations we had seen. The images we had seen of Giles Hemingway. He took notes and gasped.

He said 'that little fucker.' I said, 'nature of the world. It's how it is.'

I said, 'no it doesn't work like that. Him, in that position. Just gutted. Thought he had changed his life around.' He didn't change his life around. Now we had to wait until he was out of the infirmary. Which was going to take ages. He was in casts, blankets, operations, and we had to speak to him. To get the doctors to heal his wounds. Blisters on his legs.

I spoke with forensics the next day, and they were very concerned. They were looking into the knives. Turns out they weren't sure if these knives had been used on anyone else. Yet we were looking into it. They looked up every past homicide in the USA. In the last 30 days, and tried to match the DNA of the blood. To any victims in that time period. Absolutely no match whatsoever. Either this guy is so smart, or he's just been self harming.

Louise, the forensics officer, medical doctor. Felt like he had used the knives on other victims. Wiped them off. Then the self harm thing was a cover up. That was was too psychopathic to feel remorse I kind of was tending to agree. Yet with no trace. We couldn't do anything.

Louise said, 'hang on, there is a match.' I said, 'bullshit, I don't believe you.' The computer read the following and I read, 'girl, in her, early twenties, stabbed in the leg. Wasn't killed. Grievous bodily harm. Needed stitches. No sexual motivation. Man left scene...' I stopped reading. I said, 'I have read enough of this. Who is the girl involved?' She said, 'I don't know, some law graduate called Beth Giles.

I said, 'what is it with this guy and students and law graduates. Law students and straight A students.'

Louise said, 'he's a psychopath, he thrives off impulse, and what ever inclination he has. He picks on people, who are over conscientious People who try to understand him. These people are the targets he goes for.' I was scratching my chin at this point. I said, 'what about another match?'

Louise said, 'man in his 40's, knifed in the stomach, minor injury.' I said, 'so he's not just targetting students. He's a fucking nutcase. He just goes after anyone.'

Louise said, 'the other theory is that he is just a psychopath, and he comes close to anyone he can.' I said, 'I spoke with

Sophie. I spoke with the rest of them. I had to go to the autopsy slab. Now you are spinning me this pack of lies that he's going after intelligent people. He could be going after anyone.'

Another match came up. 'Ryan Smith. 40. Major stab wound to the leg. GBH.' I said, 'so it's not premeditated. He's going in the nut house. It's not just students.' Louise said, 'I have no idea, unless he's just a psychopath.' I said. 'Sounds like it.' Louise said, 'oh let me guess. He's been giving you all of this superficial charm. Spinning you the victim sob story. Or playing the victim almost.'

I said, 'yeah pretty much, but this wasn't the end of it. Sociopath or psychopath. Please don't tell me it's the same thing. Because I knew those students used to harass him.'

Louise said, 'Sociopath, psychopath. It's the same thing. It means the same thing on paper. He attacks anyone who gets near to him. People can be cruel.' I said, 'but the older people?' Louise said, 'probably had been jerks and probably had been mouthing off to him.' I said, 'yet he never talks, people just harass him, even when he's off the streets. In a house. It doesn't add up.'

Louise said, 'look pal, this is literally all I have right now. Looks like he's going in a nut house. I don't have time for this.' I turned my back as Louise said, 'rude'. I dialled James, his pager. I said to Louise, 'thanks for your help, doctor.' I left, and I met James down the tavern. A double whiskey for me and him. He was looking at me in disbelief. Almost as if he was worried and bewildered. As to why I was so emotionally involved in a cut and dry case.

He said, 'listen, we can talk all day about motive. What is right. What is wrong. What the law society are going to do once this guy is stitched up. How much of a sob story he's going to play in court. Like some fucking fictional narrative. We have nothing. It's just a pack of lies, and I am in the middle of this.'

James said, 'are you listening?'

I said, 'yeah I hear you.' James said, 'you are disassociating, you tune out. In the academy, this is a sign of depression. That's why we would remind you to look at the cracked ceilings and tiles. So you have something to get out of this fucking state of depression. FUCK.' He shouted, very loudly.

The whole bar gasped. The owner said. 'look, I know you are cops and all. So I will let you off, but please tone it down. Should you be drinking on the job?' I spluttered, 'we're both off duty.' Then this large woman said, 'oh I thought a cop is never off duty.' I said, 'we have finished out god damn shifts.' I slammed the table. I smashed a glass, and it ricocheted on the woman's face. She reached for her phone, going to phone up 911. I said, 'don't bother. I have dispatch around my little finger.' James was unapologetic, and said, 'hey fuck you, sit down with that phone. It's not a mince pie.' We both walked out, and got into the Chevy, and drove off. Both over the limit. I smashed the chevy glass with my handcuffs. I kept smashing it, as we drove on.

I kept smashing the god damn glass. My hands were bleeding. My mind was racing. My heart was aching. I shouted at James, 'where the fuck are you taking me?' James said, 'home, of all places. Sleep it off.'

He parked outside my house. We both walked in. The wife Louisiana, was moaning at me, saying, 'where have you been? You are drunk.' I said, 'don't start.' James ushered me up to the spare bedroom. I shouted, 'yeah Louisiana, I am not sleeping in our bed tonight, you're pissing me off.'

James said, 'he's drunk.' Louisiana said, 'well no shit, what's happening.' James turned around and said, 'we are having a bad time with a suspect right now.'

Louisiana said, 'well get over it, that's life. What's happening?' James said, 'it's fucking Giles Hemingway.' Louisiana said, 'who the fuck is that?' I said, 'you been living in a cave?' James said, 'ignore him, you switch on the 10 o'clock news.'

James sat with Louisiana, as the TV reporter from CNN news said, 'so Giles Hemingway. A 45 year old, ex homeless man. Who was under secret witness protection.'

I shouted from the spare bedroom. 'oh god damn it.' The reporter said, 'on witness protection, and was caught, in his secret house. Arrested by Police. For the murder of Louise Grey. The trial soon awaits. Back to the studio.'

There was a photo of him, and there were protests outside the news studio. Outside the police station in New York, down town Manhattan Every cop in the district was getting an earful of what was happening here.

James said, 'Lucas, Davis, my man. He went over to the old Oak tavern. Some broad decides to give him beef. We left impromptu style. That is why we are back here. Talking. Just talking. He's having a nervous breakdown.'

Louisiana said, 'we have children.' James said, 'oh grow up, they are all adults, and that douchebag Alex. Got his hair cut, sent him straight to the marines next week. It's a cut and dry case.'

Louisiana said, 'I know you are upset, but this is my son you are talking about.'

James said, 'yeah, and it's my county I am fucking policing here. Forgive me if I am wrong. But I am doing the best I can with the fucking resources I have. Do you think I am a magician? Do you?!'

Louisiana said, 'no I do not.' James said, 'so butt out of my affairs. I am calling a pizza restaurant' He dials the number, and at this point I am fast asleep. He has dialled for pizzas, and he is eating them with Louisiana I slept, really weirdly. I didn't like it. I kept waking up. I kept feeling anxious. I kept feeling sick. I forgot that god damn lithium pill also.

Chapter 30

Adjusting wasn't easy. Never was for me. Not for the first time either. Thoughts went spinning around in my head. My second temp home in New York. Became some kind of blessing and a curse. I tried to wrap my head around what had happened. I tried to think clearly. I just felt sick. It wasn't supposed to be like this. I wanted everyone happy in their beds. Sleeping softly.

As soon as Giles Hemingway started

attacking people, and we find out. Louise Grey had been the victim. Yet he was at this point still stuck in the infirmary. I didn't want to disturb him. I just look all around. I look at everything. I mean you had to work at your happiness. Sure wasn't handed to you on a plate. Not anymore. Born into a rich family, everything but a silver spoon.

I had to realise what my alternatives were. I had to think about what I could do. What my objectives were. I was tired of going around to the cell block. Just to find out we can't charge this guy until the doctor say's he's fit enough to be charged.

The days turned into weeks, turned into months. I just wasn't having it. Not on my watch, and this wasn't supposed to be like this.

It took some considerable time to know what the facts were. As soon as we see this figure. Giles Hemingway. Appearing half normal from all of the work. In chains and looking better. I said, 'right, Giles Hemingway, I am charging you with attempted murder, murder, and the grievous bodily harm of 5 people.' I read him his rights. He was escorted to the remand cell.

James was with me, and he chortled, 'that dude, seriously. Been fed up of even dealing with him now.'

I said, 'we do are damn job.' He said, 'oh yeah which means, we don't know what else to say on the matter. I have seen this guy. Very manipulative' I said, 'even so, it just doesn't make sense. Not anymore anyway. This guy is a user. A mass manipulator. I regret giving him sympathy. I am going to have to be in court.' James laughed and said, 'well get over yourself. It doesn't make the slightest bit of difference. I will be there.'

I said, 'for once in my life. I couldn't feel like this pain, it trickled down me. What do you call that?' He said, 'fuck if I know. You want to know what I think. I think if it wasn't for us. This jerk off wouldn't be behind bars. Too many uniform cops chasing after super light offences. Like prostitution. Hell, leave that up to God. I don't want to write citations for those.'

I said, 'uniform, traffic, citations. It's what uniform do. They write citations.' James said, 'yeah, and us detectives. We are not in that position. Not belonging to uniform.'

I said, 'I knew this guy in uniform, who would always leave the office. Always bragging about issuing citation. This homeless lady. Fined. I told you about that already. For obstruction. Where is she going to find that money?'

James said, 'prostitution. That is how

they find the money for their fines. They get from us, for obstruction.' I said, 'you are harsh. I will give you that.' He said, 'you think this was an accident we were assigned to this case?' I said, 'oh come on, don't start me on any of your wild conspiracy theories It's just luck of the draw.' He said, 'oh come on, and you wander why the FBI had so many times to transfer us..' I said, 'because we do a good job.'

He said, 'yeah right, and you have seen the size of Charles and Rufus. Massive people. That's if Ryan Coleman is in on the juice.'

I said, 'I spoke to Ryan the other day. He knew nothing about this magical kind of conspiracy theory you have. We were all just given pot luck things to do. It's like leaving your god damn radio on. You always get called.'

He said, 'yeah, law of averages.' I said, 'that is what we are talking about.'

At this point. Outside the office. Our radio is going. '4-5, units, all units in the area. Can you please respond to a traffic violation up on west thirty nine street.' I said, 'this has to be some kind of joke right?'

James put an assertive gesture out with his hand and said, 'no wait'. The radio said, 'female, in her early twenties.

Injured. Stabbed in the back of the car. We have a male in custody.'

I shouted, 'bullshit.' James said, 'what is this? Some kind of revenge attack?'

The sun was shining in my eyes. I got tinnitus at this point. The whole world was swarming around me. I had a panic attack. Right there, right at this time. Voices became slower. James was talking to me, but it was an echo. One word. Then one syllable.

The lights were shining in my eyes. Making me feel uncomfortable. The sounds of cars around me screeching I sat down on the little wall behind me. I sat down. And I dripped a small amount of mineral water over my head. James sat down next to me. Looking concerned.

I said, 'fuck,' He said, 'it's okay, FBI are taking this call anyway.' He said gently. I said, 'I don't understand. It's a copy cat attack.'

James said, 'yeah and that is what it is. Some nut case with no life. I don't fucking understand it.' I said, 'we work hard all of the time. We press people for answers. When those answers aren't there. We have more to press. We go around just thinking of things to say. The sunlight, this whole American Dream thing we have here. And for what?' I shouted.

James said, 'for the purpose of we do

our damn job. We don't listen to dispatch if we don't want to. And we don't listen to the press.'

I said, 'you are out of your mind, we do respond to dispatch, we do talk to the press. This Hemingway case. Is going to destroy me.' He said, 'I am taking you off that case, if I feel you can't cope with it.'

I said, 'yeah right, and Ryan Coleman just blowing smoke down my neck. It doesn't make sense James. We did everything we could for that guy. We did everything we can to make sure he was safe. Now this happens.'

James said, 'some people are just sick and perverted. We meet all kinds of characters all over the place. Show pays no credence to us.'

I said, 'well I am stumped.' James said, 'that's how it is.' New York, in this kind of street. Made me wander. I was asking myself all of the questions about my life. How life was treating me. Even though deep down. I didn't want to know. I knew I had to. The life of a cop wasn't easy. Yet I have to figure out things along the way.

Things that seemed easy at first. The things I had no control over. I was wearing a lot of grey that day. My blue tie just draped over me. My grey trousers. I felt lost, you know. My second hand rolex watch. The Mercedes parked outside.

214

The radio dispatch kept going and I wasn't sure what to do anymore. Everything I knew hadn't made sense this far. Turned out the stabbing was a copy cat version. Me and James hit the Tavern. Not banned from the previous escapade, and we sat down. I said, 'a double whiskey.' James nodded, 'same.' A big lady comes out and said, 'I want no more trouble. How have you boys been doing?' She laughed.

I said, 'Sarah!' She said, 'a friendly face and all.' James smiled. She was wearing cornflower blue with a white apron. I said, 'Sarah, Sarah, Sarah, the day I have had.'

Sarah said, 'turns out I know what is happening. Time and time again.' I said, 'what do you mean?' She said, 'this case you been working on. It's stressing you.'

I said, 'no shit, that has always been the way.' James said, 'we are all on edge right now.' Sarah said, 'just wait until trial. You are going to be more on edge then.' I said, 'no way would we ever get to that point. We are fine. Relaxed. It's not going to phase us. FBI are on this anyway.' She said, 'and IA'. I said, 'yeah, they just checking in on us, just making sure everything is alright.'

I said, 'turn up the TV.' A reporter in New York was saying, 'so, the trial. Giles Hemingway vs the state. We will get to that soon.'

I said, 'I don't want to watch this.' James said, 'shh.' The reported said, 'Giles Hemingway, an ex homeless man, fatally stabbed Louise Grey. Outside a liquor store the other month. Giles Hemingway. Already cleared of charges, the state now has new evidence. On the case, and it's moving to trial again. What's your opinion on this. Desmond Brown, our political correspondent.'

Des said, 'well it's a very interesting case. This guy, is very evil, very sick. We will keep you updated. The court case is going to be interesting.'

Then he was rambling on about it for ages. I blurred it out. I had to. I could feel some things getting to me. Some minor things at first. Like the light. Or the sound of trucks. I needed a shrink. I needed someone. Yet there was nobody there. Just me and James. Just in this bar. Just sipping our drinks. Just eating our pretzels. Doing what any other men would do once shift has finished. Some young punks behind us. Some big chested, big guy. Pointing his fingers, with tattoos. Shouting, 'hey come here. I sae you on TV.' A skinny punk guy shouting the same. 'Hey!' He shouted. Me and James walked towards them. They backed off a bit.

216

I spoke to the big guy. By the pool table. I said, 'what gives you the fucking right, to come to our bar. Of all places, and pull a stunt like this.' I showed him my badge. 'We own this place.' The dude said, 'no you don't.' I said, 'want to fight it out.' James shouted at them, 'go home losers.' They both left, and walked off. I shouted, 'and don't come back until you're sober.' James said, 'never off duty.' I said, 'never off duty, but I am going to watch them leave.'

Which was a cardinal sin or something because then they were showing off, as they were leaving. The one dude was shouting, 'this is police harassment' The big dude. His name was big Mikey. He had his nipples pierced He had been in custody before. He had tattoos all around him. I said, 'go the fuck home.' I shouted again.'

Big Mikey said, 'what if I don't want to.' I said, 'then I call in LAPD'. The streets were almost evaporating this guy's sense of compulsion to argue. The streets were clear, and it was a quiet night. With cars driving passed. I felt kind of annoyed. As the fresh air had passed me on separate occasions. I felt whole again. As the rain was trickling down. This was New York, this was Manhattan This was where we were going. The overriding sense of comfort we had. It all made sense.

The rain trickling down, yet, I had to return to the bar. As big Mikey, was talking ways I would never personally understand. The more abuse I got. The more I kind of switched off from it. Me and James walked inside. To find Sarah, just picking up the broken pool cue. She said, 'those jack asses.' I said, 'I know.' She said, 'it turns out, every asshole who comes into this bar wants to fight.'

The TV was still going in the background. I said, 'you know what. Everyone does want to fight. Everyone does want to have arguments. Everyone does do that. Because in New York. I mean everything is a big deal. Everything. Even the smallest things. We look around.'

We look around at the tranquil nature of things. The subtle differences. The wide eyes. The broken promises. It just was not the kind of life I had wanted.

I had felt kind of stuck, in this sense of vision I had. As the bar we were staying in. was leaving us in whirlwinds. Time and time again. We would look around and understand our own premise here. As far as I knew. I would know where life was. A dream. Some kind of fairy tale or some shit. No this was reality. It wasn't like some hocus pocus law we had. We

218

had rights, and so did the people.

James was sitting there casually. His slim figure. Leaning over a glass of whiskey. Couldn't sure what he was thinking. He looked closed off, as his light 'LAPD' shirt, kind of reflected in the distance. His grey jacked hung over him. His grey trousers. His black socks. His sense of coolness and dryness. He was clean shaven, he had a very many look about him. Yet he was calm, very astute, and kept a youthful figure. Being the same age as me. Just his attitude.

I looked at Sarah, and I said, 'look, I know you get people come into this bar and talk to you. All of the time. Sob story, after sob story. Like I don't want to do that. You know. We are seasoned professionals. So this is what I am thinking of saying. We come in here. Some asshole out the back starts causing some problems. So we put him in his place.'

Sarah said, 'no shit, it's part of the work we do here also. Every time, every time I am not thinking straight. The amount of times there has been pool cues smashed. We keep them behind lock and key now.'

I said to Sarah, 'did you ever meet Hemingway?' She said, 'just once.' She looked tearful, as she was looking back in hindsight.

219

She continued, 'I met hime once. A long time ago, 4 years ago to be precise I was in Michigan. Visiting an elderly relative. There he was. In his postal gear. Just putting post in the mail box.'

I said, 'did he say anything to you?' She said, 'it was such a long time ago.' I said, 'well you must remember something. Anything.' She said, 'he looked me up and down. He said, 'have a nice day mam.' He left.'

I said, 'that's all he said?' She said, 'yeah, as far as I can remember.' I said, 'it's just strange how some people lead double lives. You know. One minute, they are calm, no problems. Go to work. Now this shit storm.'

Sarah said, 'look, it's just how it is. That guy gives me the creeps.' I said, 'you told me you only met him once.' She stuttered and said, 'no I mean, I have seen him on TV, so many times. Hairs on my neck stand up.'

I said, 'why?' She said, 'you know you watch those horror movies. Where you watch the vilian. And he's out to get the victim. He's the typical psychopath.' I said, 'I have known this guy for ages. At first, I was fooled. Thought he was innocent. Not going to believe he had a violent bone in his body. Now for example. He is, at large. One of the biggest fucking psychopaths on the east. '

Sarah was looking around. I had never seen a big woman so happy. So happy to see me. So happy to see James. Even though he was wandering in the distance. So happy to see cops, maybe it was her sweet little protection she needed. We had a drink, she said it was on the house. In exchange, we made sure things were sweet for her. In reality. I don't think it worked like that. Not anymore anyway.

It doesn't matter how much of a tough life you have had. You always get to know what's beneath the surface. Every time someone blows kisses at you, frowns at you, says something to you. As a cop you have to make sure you know what to do. What avenue to go down. Every small detail is relevant. Every small detail adds up and stacks up.

I was sick of just wandering what to do, and I was sick of myself sometimes. I would see myself in the mirror. Was sick of my grey jumper. Or how my hair never changed. I was sick of how I was treated by some civilians. I was sick of the stress this job gave me. Every time I experienced something new. Every time I put on my shirt in the morning. Everytime I just wandered around, in my temporary apartment. I was someone. Yet I was not stupid and I was clever.

221

No long was I going to wear that jumper, or keep doing stuff that pissed me off. It was back to the drawing board. It was back to being my own man. It was back to finding out which things to buy. Which textures. I didn't need a new wardrobe. I needed a new attitude. I didn't need another drink. I needed a good state of mind.

Yet looking over Sarah. With her hair tied back. Her apron on. You could hear her doing the dishes out the back. I was suspicious of her. It just seemed weird is all. How nice she was being. I mean, I know we were cops and all. But, we didn't want the drinks free. Until she insisted, and she seemed like the type of woman who could handle her own beef. I said to James, whilst whispering. I said, 'look around.' James looked shocked, as I had woken him up from a short nap. He said, 'what, are you at of your god damn mind?'

I said, 'no tired of your god damn lies. Look around.' He said, 'without the attitude.' He looked around, and at first. Nothing. No inclination of where we were going. Checked under the floor boards. Nothing. He said, 'seriously, this is a witch hunt.' I laughed. He said, 'no stop laughing.'

I then found a note underneath the seat. It said, 'Dear Sarah, it's Giles here.

Adjusting to this new life is difficult. I think The Police are onto me. Speak to you soon. Love, Giles.' Handwritten note.

Sarah comes out of the kitchen, she lets Dave, the kitchen assistant. Who is just as big as her, and listening to an iPod Finish the washing. She turns to me and said, 'are you fucking serious, searching my place without a warrant.'

I held up the note. I said, 'care to explain what this is about huh?' I said, 'barely knew him huh, did you?' I kept saying, whilst gently showing her the note. Out of her way so she couldn't grasp it. The look of guilt in her face. I couldn't describe.

She said, 'it's not what it looks like.' I said. 'It is, and we can arrest you right now. You start talking to us. Properly.' She said, 'okay'. We sat down with some stools. She said, 'I took pity on the guy.' I said, 'you knew what he did, but you didn't do anything about it. You didn't phone us up.' She said, 'I was scared.' I said, 'you will go on the witness stand.' James said, 'cut it out.' I said, 'seriously, we are going to take you there. We can do you for perverting the cause of justice.' Sarah said, 'oh that's funny, I will just feed them a pack of lies. Saying you knew about this note.'

James said, 'right you two, cool it down a bit. Maybe we don't need to do

223

anything.'

Sarah started crying. I said, 'look , Sarah, I forgive you. I really do. I know you regret not telling us. But we need to find out everything we know about Giles. Everything. We need him locked up and away from all of the victims he has injured, hurt. The family of Louise Grey, need closure. So do the other victims. We have to protect the public.'

Sarah said, 'you got him home and dry.' I slammed the table, and the whiskey shot. Well one of them went flying. I said, 'double jeopardy' She laughed and she said, 'the other charges.' I said, 'it's the murder charge we want him on.' She said, 'do I look like the DA? I am a bar tender for christ sake. I am not a lawyer.' I said, 'I have gathered that.'

She said, 'look, we need to find out what to do moving forward.' I said, 'it's just this double jeopardy charge.'

James laughed and he said, 'look, I will talk with the FBI and the DA.'

Sarah said, 'that would be a good start.' I said, 'I don't think you realise how serious this is Sarah. I am not going to be too harsh on you. Yet you give us everything you know. Or we are taking you into custody.'

James said, 'you are running a bar for christ sakes. You are not an agony aunt.' I

224

said, 'it's true.' Sarah said, 'but people look up to me.' I slammed the table. 'He was in here wasn't he. That is why you are talking as you are. That is why you grew a relationship with him. Hence the note. He used to drink in here.' Sarah said, 'yeah he did.' I said, 'right, I want the CCTV footage' Sarah said, 'excuse me if I am wrong, but all you are going to see is some jerk off just sitting down on the stool. Talking to me.'

I said, 'oh I see how it is, you defend him. You call him a jerk off. You defend him again. You refuse to give CCTV. One phone call to the DA, and we can prosecute you.'

James said, 'I think what my colleague is trying to say is that we need that CCTV. We need those tapes.' He continued, 'what the hell are you doing with VCR in 2020 anyway?' Sarah said, 'I am old school.' I said, 'we need these exported to DVD.'

Sarah said, 'listen, all of you, that's enough. I am not going to do this. You want to fuck up this whole operation. You do it on your own terms.' I said, 'we are trying to help. This shows motive. He has a letter. He has written to you.' She said, 'it shows shit. All it shows, all it fucking shows is he went in here a few times.'

I said, 'maybe so, but why the apprehension' She said, 'what?' I said, 'oh

225

come on Sarah. You have never been in one of these cases or trials before?' She said, 'I have.' I said, 'explain it to us then.' She said, 'ten years ago. Me and my husband were arguing. I went home to take out the trash. I walked along the side walk. I saw a woman. Young, early twenties. Getting harassed by a male. 40, couldn't see his face. It was dark. He shot her. Once. She was dead within seconds. I reach for the payphone. I dial up 911. I can hear, the operator say. '911 what's your emergency?'. I said, 'I have just seen a man shoot a woman dead.' The Police were there within seconds, patrol units, canines. The guy was arrested I didn't even have to do a citizens arrest He was so shocked he fainted. So a year later, after some convincing. Some arguing also. Because his trial was being argued all of the state. The final verdict arrived. He was found guilty and sent to life.'

I said, 'did you testify in court?' She said, 'yes, I told them everything. I had to.' I said, 'so what else? Besides testifying in court. So you don't want to go through something like this again. That is why you took pity on Giles.'

She said, 'partially and yes, that case destroyed me.' James said, 'with all due respect Sarah. This case, has been nagging us. And nagging us, and nagging us. We

226

have IA, the DA, the DEA, FBI, and we have even had talks with SWAT. Even MI5 were in on this when that asshole Blakely went over to England to see his cocaine. Exporting them in his human slavery ring.'

Sarah said, 'what's your point?' James slammed the table and he said, 'it will take zero time, we have this guy nailed.' She said, 'what about double jeopardy' He slammed the table again, he said, 'I don't give a toss about double jeopardy I will make sure of it.'

I said, 'to be honest, the judge could dismiss it.' James said, 'and he will do time for the other offences.' I said, 'it's not enough for the family involved. Charlotte also.'

Chapter 31

The next day. I walked over to the DA's office. I spoke to Mark Obrien. A heavy weight attorney. I showed him all of the evidence. I was alone. Just me and Mark. He was wearing braces. A pin striped shirt. Shoes. Nice trousers.

He said, 'well, so you want to know where he stands with this double jeopardy charge?' I said, 'yes.'

Mark said, 'technically the judge could over rule it. Your only option then is to

227

say you have new evidence for the murder. Yet the judge is still going to overrule it. On the other hand. You change the plea from 3rd degree, from what it was. To 1st degree. You say you have new evidence. We get him in there. Different charge.'

I said, 'so it's solid then.' He said, 'nothing is solid, the judge is going to take convincing.' He was a big muscular bloke. Short hair. He said, 'good luck.' I said, 'oh wait, have you spoke to Giles?' Mark said, 'of course, I am the one prosecuting him.' I said, 'so what is he saying.' Mark said, 'he's telling the truth, for once in his fucking life.' I said. 'Ah no shit, you have this thing down to a T. Don't you.' He said, 'it's not that, it's not the way we are looking at this now. The whole thing. Government ops. The whole sidetracked version of events. The reason we are talking. It makes perfect sense to me. The guy is a deranged lunatic.'

I said, 'maybe so, but we will put him behind bars.' He said, 'maybe, maybe not.' I said, 'who is the judge?' He said, 'Alan, Joseph Carter.'

I said, 'it's going to take some convincing.' He said, 'it always is. It is always the same. With anyone. This is what is happening. This is where we are going.'

228

'All rise', Alan Joseph Carter shouted. Everyone arose. Samuel Davidson defending.

I was on the witness stand again. Out came a bible. I said, 'I swear to tell the truth. The whole truth, so help me god.'

Mark Hoffman said, 'so, the judge has already explained, how she is taking heed. Of the fact. That double jeopardy does not apply here. Because what we are seeing is new charges. What was third degree murder. Is now first degree murder.'

He continued, 'so we see we have more evidence. I am going to ask you Lucas Davis. What is that new evidence?' I laughed and I said, 'well I am not prosecuting him.'

Mark smiled and said, 'but you knew two different sides to him.'

I said, 'when I first met Giles Hemingway. He was misunderstood, knew him for 11 years. I just feel like I have been lied to. He spun a web of deceit around me. In the last case also. He took advantage of witness protection. Paid by state. He tried manipulating the system. Now here we are. Talking. Talking about how my professional life. Has been strung up in balance, by the IA. It was soon sorted out.'

Mr Hoffman said, 'back to Hemingway. Is he a grievous person to you?' I said, 'well yeah sure.' Mr Hoffman said, 'how?' I said, 'what he did showed intent. He would have killed again. If we had let him go. On arrest He became violent. He has lacerations on the legs.'

You could see, a spec of the man. Mr Giles Hemingway. In a wheelchair. On the front row.

Mr Hoffman said, 'this man here. This man, not seen a barber for 3 months. In the infirmary for three months.' I said, 'yeah that man.' He said, 'no further questions.'

Next talking to me, was indeed. Kyle. Defence lawyer. Short guy. Slim, bit of podge on his belly. He said, 'Lucas, what do you want to tell me about this new evidence?' I said, 'well, we found knives, underneath the floor boards.' Kyle said, 'but he was self mutilating' I said, 'yes, but he was also attacking other people with these knives.'

Alan chuckled and said, 'forgive me if I am wrong, but is self mutilation Is that a sign of depression?' I said, 'it can be in some cases.'

Kyle said, 'so do you think, that this shows remorse He has pleads guilty. He doesn't need the third degree. We have him now.'

I said, 'I have spoken with Forensic psychologists, they have all said that. The self harm, is a deliberate attempt to distract away from the grievous nature.'

Kyle said, 'so why did he self harm?' I said, 'I just told you.' Alan said, 'but he could of committed those crimes anyway?'

I said, 'possibly so, but if he did, without self mutilating.' Alan interrupted and said, 'this is a load of baloney and you know it. He could have committed the crimes, with or without mutilation. It's not always a defence, or a reason to persecute.'

I said, 'with all due respect. He self harmed to distract away from what he was doing.'

Kyle said, 'what was he doing?' I said, 'he was maiming and torturing innocent people. He was spinning a web of deceit over the fact that he had killed Louise Grey.'

Kyle said, 'so you think the self harm is a distraction method? Do you think he wanted to be in the infirmary for 3 months?' I said, 'no, and I would like to think, that it may have crossed his mind.'

Kyle said, 'is there any chance, this guy, might have depression.' I said, 'it's possible, yes.' Alan said, 'what has the psychologist diagnosed him with?' I said, 'Anti Social Personality Disorder.' He said, 'explain what that is?'

I said, 'well sir, I am no expert. But it

just means lack of remorse for crimes. It means impulsivity. Reckless behaviour. Willingness to manipulate others.'

He said, 'but it is a psychiatric disorder?'

I said, 'yes, and he is on medication for it as we speak.'

Kyle said, 'what is the name of this medication?'

I said, 'Risperidone Anti Psychotics, Clonazepam, Citalopram.'

Kyle said, 'that's one hell of a cocktail. Of drugs, for a psychopath. What you originally had said.'

I said, 'he is using this mental health issue, to abuse his way through. He is holding onto it sir. The guy is deranged. Maybe he does have mental health issues.'

Kyle said, 'he does have mental health issues.'

I said, 'can you let me finish sir. You talk over me. He does have mental health. But there is no excuse for what he has done.'

Kyle said, 'but doesn't it lessen intent?' I said, 'no it does not. If this guy wants to act like an animal. There are play parks for that. Activity centres. He had the whole world at his feet. Instead of abiding by state law. He ran a mockery out of us Police.'

Kyle said, 'so you were angry with him.' I said, 'yes, I was, he lied to me.' Alan said, 'so angry, that you wanted to bring him here. On some more false charges.'

Mark Hoffman said, 'objection, argumentative.'

Alan said, 'overruled.' He continued. 'Courts now in recess.' He slammed on the hammer. We got to talking outside.

Kyle Davis, defending, said, 'nice try asshole.' He said to me, as he left the building. I said to James, 'no I don't agree with how that was handled.'

James said, 'screw that guy, just came out of Harvard Law School and now thinks he's god's gift.'

I said, 'with all due respect. I think you are right.' I walked over. I spoke to people along the way. I spoke to Kyle. I said, 'you go to Harvard, right?' He said, 'sure'. I said, 'next time I would appreciate it if you toned down that bitchy temper you have on you.'

He said, 'it's a court room, not a tea party. I can saw what I want.' I said, 'prick'. He walked off, and I could hear him laughing.

James said, 'just ignore that guy, thinks he can rile up the court. We are in recess now. Now is not the time to be playing hard ball with that creep.' I said, 'it's weird, it's fucking weird.' James said, 'I am angry too.'

I said, 'you know, sometimes life is okay you know.' James said, 'I know.' I said, 'I

233

look over at the trees. I look over at everything I had been through. I look over at life. How I wanted to be the person people go to. Time and time again. Then nothing. Not a sound.'

James said, 'it's lonely being a cop.' I said, 'it's not, it's a rewarding job. You look at the resume. You look at the pictures. Yet everything else, it just doesn't make sense. Everything else doesn't add up. We are just catching butterflies here. Just waiting. Waiting for the sun to shine on this disgrace that has happened. Government ops, or not. Or maybe it's genuine. Yet we do something. No, not this time. Not right now. Not with this hanging over our head. We do something positive.'

James said, 'to hell with that. That is what is happening here. You look outside your window. Nothing. No word of a lie. Nothing you can see. I am tired of playing around with these clowns.'

Rufus Clark arrives, we all laugh. Rufus said, 'oh right, so you have the big boys now.' I said, 'Rufus, nice to meet you.' James walks to the canteen. I whistled, I said, 'the canteens that way.' I pointed assertively. I said to Rufus, 'look dude, this whole thing is messed up.' He laughed and said, 'we have our boys all over that guy. He doesn't stand a chance.'

234

I said, 'no fucking way it doesn't.' He said, 'time to ruffle some feathers.'

Chapter 32

'All rise.' Alan Joseph Carter shouted. I walked into the court room. The oak furnishings. The off colours. The way everything was looking. My mind was distant. I sat down. Second row, next to James. Feeling like, the court had swallowed us whole. Yet James was taking a more relaxed approach. Members of the jury, 11 of them. A black woman with frizzy hair. A blonde woman, with whitish blonde hair.

A man, glasses. They all looked stoic. They all looked okay. I looked at the judge. Alan Joseph Carter. A very sensible man. No wigs this time. It was too hot. He had reading glasses. Mature face. Around 55 to 60. You could tell that he would dye his hair with just for men. Get rid of the grey bits.

A bit of stubble, as he was taking notes. Sat on high above everyone else. Kyle Davis, a short guy. 5 foot 5, straight out of Harvard Law School. 35. Appearing mean, menacing, and bitchy. Not that I could have said that to him. I was feeling frustrated and my frustration grey. As I looked around. Nothing seemed to be working like it used to.

I couldn't be getting all emotional again. I always used to think a court room looked like a church. A church yard or a church room or something. The light pale windows, and the expression of the jury. All stoic. Yet I wasn't feeling the same notion. I felt confused. I felt lost. We all had to hand our personal phones and bccpcrs in. They let us keep our radios for emergencies, but it was in my briefcase. I was wearing a suit. Tie. I felt kind of lost. Kind of distant.

I felt kind of distracted. Kind of upset. I looked at everyone. I looked at people as I would look at them anyway. The angry faces. The determination to bring this case over.

One of our forensic psychologists. Gill James. Was stood there. Sat on the witness stand actually. I knew this was going to turn into a circus. Just like last time.

Kyle Davis was first to ask questions. He said. 'Gill, how many times have you spoken with Giles Hemingway?' He is wheeled in slowly in his wheelchair by one of the guards. He whispered. 'Thank you.' Kyle Davis said, 'how many times?' Gill James said, 'lots of times, around 20, whilst he was in the infirmary.'

Kyle said, 'was it you who diagnosed him with Anti Social Personality Disorder?' Gill said, 'yes it was.' Gill was a middle aged woman. Kyle said, 'so in your opinion, what are the major signs of this disorder.' Gill said, 'impulse control, self harm, eagerness to manipulate. Short temper. Confusion.'

Kyle said, 'it's a mental health disorder, so surely this man has self harmed. Would you say this personality disorder was a contributing factor?'

Gill said, 'oh definitely I wouldn't say it wasn't.' Kyle said, 'do you believe the attack was done in malice?'

Gill laughed and said, 'well, I don't know. I mean, I have only spoken to him..' Kyle said, 'what? Only spoken to him 20 times. Must be a lot if you ask me.'

Gill said, 'I have gotten to know him. It's possible he committed those crimes. But he's still human. He is suffering inside.'

Kyle said, 'so would you say his mental illness mitigated what he had done?' Gill said, 'almost definitely'

Mr Hoffman, from the DA. Prosecuting. Was next, he said, 'Gill, how long have you been a psychologist?" Gill said, '10 years.' I said, 'Mr Hoffman said, 'is your specialty criminal psychology?' She said, 'yes.' Mr Hoffman said, 'would you say he was a criminal?' Gill laughed and said, 'well isn't

237

that up to the jury and the judge to decide?'

Mr Hoffman said, 'look, could you see any motive?' Gill said, 'well, to be honest with you. I think he did it. But I think he was emotional. Upset. He blanked out. He was confused. He was being taunted by Louise Grey.'

Mr Hoffman said, 'or so you say, but he could have done something else. Phoned up 911, pushed her away.'

Gill said, 'but it was Louise Grey who bought him, encouraged him to have the murder weapon. A 10 inch butchers knife. She got from the butchers. She wanted him in jail.'

Mr Hoffman said, 'but she didn't want to be dead. It was a childish prank.'

Gill said, 'what trying to falsify evidence, and handing someone a butchers knife. Is a prank? This girl had felony charges against here. She had a long history of harassing this man.'

Mr Hoffman said, 'ok, so now you claim. But it's not going to end there. You have to know what exactly is happening here.'

Gill said, 'look, I am confused. The guy is depressed. He has mental health issues. If you are trying to paint him as a monster. I am not going to do that for you.'

Mr Hoffman said, 'do you think this guy,

killed, Louise Grey.'

Gill said, 'yes'.

Mr Hoffman said, 'no further questions your honour.' Alan Joseph Carter spoke. He said, 'right, another recess. I want James, and Lucas in my chamber. This is turning wild.'

We followed the judge into the chamber He was laughing and smoking some kind of fat cigar. He was in hysterics, and he said, 'you two jokers.' I said, 'wait, what, what are you saying?' He said, 'this whole court room thing. Bringing everyone in here. Trying to indict him. It's not going easy with us. Not sat in this office. Pushing papers Monday morning. Trying to chase god damn seagulls away from us. Come on boys. Tell me what is happening.'

I said, 'well, your honour. This guy, Giles. Is a massive manipulative person. He has done everything he can to try to pull the wool over ur eyes.' James said, 'it succeeded, and is succeeding sir.'

Alan said, 'but, what do you want me to do? Just sit here. On my chair. And not intervene' I said, 'no.' Alan Carter said, 'I have been a judge for 30 years. I know how this works.' I said, 'explain.' He said, 'I don't want any politics in my court room. That psychologist was bordering on contempt of court.' I said, 'so bring her in

239

then.'

He said, 'she's your god damn psychologist. I don't need to. You see me arguing the toss here.'

I said, 'not really, but she's a good psychologist.' He said, 'she is, is she? *She's a good psychologist. Well I am not sure about that.'*

I said, 'your honour. With all due respect. She is a great psychologist.'

He said, 'I don't know about this anymore. I doubt I would hire her to cut my grass.' I said, 'wow.' James said, 'oh come on, you can't just blow the whistle on this whole thing and say it's stupid. Blame the whole testimony down to a T. Play safe, or not. This thing is a slam dunk. I know it is. Yet walk in here.'

Alan said. 'listen, we will carry on as planned. I am just saying. Proceed with caution. I am not fining you boys.' He clapped his hands.

We both left. He remained in his office. James said, 'what the hell was that all about?' I said, 'shaking us up, asserting his authority. Fuck if I know.' James said, 'but it's working, the judge seems on our side.' I said, 'maybe, but the jury have to decide. It's going to take ages.' He said, 'bullshit, only will take several hours.' I said, 'several hours we don't have. Do you know how stretched and stressed I am?'

He said, 'I know, the cuts are getting to you, but do you seriously think you can blame everything on them?' I said, 'we have a great investigation department. We have a great team. We don't always see eye to eye. Yet we try our best to. We look for solutions all of the time. Yet that is all I can think of here.'

James said, 'I don't know. I joined the force because I wanted to help people. I didn't know of anything else to do. Been in this job for a while. Then for what I know. Nothing makes sense anymore.'

Me and James went outside, it was scorching hot. Traffic was whizzing passed. I said, 'I am tired of this. I really am.' James said, 'oh come on, it's just a case of dotting the i's and crossing the t's.'

I said, 'you know what I don't get.' James said, 'no.' I said, 'we come here every day. We talk to uniform all of the time. I just feel like, I don't know. The officers around our place are chilled. That is the way it has to be. You know? Being chilled, and doing the right thing. Going after what you believe in. Being your own man. Wearing those sun glasses. Going out there and doing what you can. Letting people off for citations you could write on a bad day. Hell when a bad day comes along. You don't write them either. It's discretion. It's right in our faces. It's what

241

makes our force unique. Now I get transferred all the way over to NYC. For a bullshit trial, just because I couldn't cope with his god damn lies.'

James said, 'we all work the same under pressure. It was lie after lie. I appreciate that. Yet I don't know what else I can do.'

I said, 'I don't know what else can be said either. It just carries on. Like a bad dream or something.'

James said, 'we go in there. That courtroom. We do everything we can to make sure life is working out. I mean that was the whole point. Nothing else could be credited, as there was nothing else I could do. You look around for answers. You look around for clues. It's the same as has always been. Yet this doesn't add up. The amount of resources spent on this guy.'

James pulls out a smoke. I said, 'look boss. I know what you are saying, and I know what is happening here. We have the best legal defence in the county. Yet it just doesn't work. It goes on and on, like a train wreck. Or a bad memory. We have lost sight of our values. As men. We just have. I don't know what the god damn answer is. Hell if I know. I just want to know where we are going to go with this.'

James said, 'look sir, what I want to know is the following. If we do the things we are supposed to do. No signs of arguing. We get to the bottom of life. That's fine. That's what we plan to do. We make sure our i's are dotted, and our t's are crossed.'

I have never seen New York City so beautiful before. The sun was out. The sky was blue. The cars were whizzing past. The cars were zooming passed. I felt happy. I felt happy because for once. The sun, and the blue, was echoing over my face.

This kind of ambience we always had. As the traffic went passed. The arguments happening. This is what happens. The same kind of things. We had seen life for what it was. For what it was. For what it was. Even though I am kind of lost here. Looking at this one minicab driver. Who kind of looks lost. The female driver. Some lawyer walks out without paying. Some blonde lady. The man chases her up the road.

I said, 'what on earth do you think you are doing, not paying that cabbie?' She said, 'sorry. I am late. I don't have any money.' I said, 'you are an attorney for crying out loud.' She said, 'not a good one.' I said, 'look here's $30 dollars. Go back and pay the cabbie.' She said, 'I am not your bitch, you pay him.' She walked into the court room. Her luxurious blonde

hair. Her sassiness. She was a fox. I think
she knew she was also. I went over to the
taxi guy.

I said, 'sir, here's your money.' He said,
'tell your lady friend to wind it in.' He got
in the cab, all hot and heated. He drove
off, honking and swerving in and out of
traffic.

I said to James, 'who is that lady?' He
said, 'she's a defence attorney on another
case. Linda Charles Reed.' I said, 'she's
fiery' James said, 'most defence attorneys
are. That's what you get. That's the kind of
attitude you get.'

I said, 'so you know what I am saying.
About peace, about preservation. About
hope. Everything we have learnt from
this. Everything we have done to go out of
our way. To try and make sense of why
these things are happening. We don't
quite understand it. Yet we are okay. We
haven't quite found it, yet we are
comfortable. We know how life is. The
same kind of scenario we would see.'

I could feel kind of still. As Linda
ventured out again. Looking very still.
Kind of calm. She said to me, 'look, do you
have a light I need a smoke.' I said, 'don't
you have trial?' I handed her a lighter.'
She said, 'I got the wrong day.' James was
pissing himself laughing and he said,
'seriously?'

244

I said, 'you got the wrong day?'

She said, 'what, did I stutter before. Yeah, I got the wrong fucking day. Now pass me the light.' The light was handed over. She was smoking some mental smoke. She sat down with us, and we didn't mind. I said, 'typical blonde moment then.' I said as a joke, as James leaned in and said. 'You know, if you go into that court room a minute late. They don't let you in.'

Linda said, 'I know that.' She said in a jokey/bossy way.

James said, 'so what's your backstory?' She said, 'criminal defence lawyer. Harvard. I am representing a vehicular manslaughter case.'

I said, 'defending.' She said, 'yeah sure.' I said, 'well did it involve a vehicle?' She pointed at me, and she said, 'what is this guy five?' James said, 'he's just joking. So go back to your story. The vehicular manslaughter charge.'

Linda said, 'he killed a girl, she was 14, he was driving in his car. Intoxicated. He's looking at 3-10 years. I will try to get him 3.' I said, 'wow, tough break.' Linda pointed at me. She said, 'I have seen you on the TV. You are prosecuting that Giles Hemingway.'

James said, 'trying to.' He said. Linda said, 'so how's it going?' James said, 'let's just say we are making small progress. Small progress all of the time. One step forward. Three steps back.'

Linda said, 'well that is perfectly okay.' She said sarcastically. I said, 'look, I know you got the wrong day and all, but we are in the middle of something here. Trying to get this case unravelled Wait in the canteen. We will drive you home.'

I handed her $10 bucks. She said, 'thanks.' She was texting on her blackberry and walked inside.

James said, 'why are you being so nice to her?' I said, 'I don't know, why not?' He said, 'is it because she's a smoking hot blonde. You have a wife for christ sakes.'

I said, 'no, it's nothing to do with that. It's just how it is. I will drive her home.'

James said, 'oh let me guess. You didn't have your fair share of the ladies in your younger years. You didn't have any of them. Now you come here. We are sat here like two bad apples.' I said, 'yeah well, you know what I mean. With all due respect. It's how it is.'

James said, 'but you don't make your suspects take poly's or something?'

I said, 'I have done in the past.'

James said, 'Giles Hemingway has refused to take a polygraph. Even though it's not an admission of guilt. We know he's done it.'

I said, 'of course. Of course we know he has done it.'

James said. 'It's just how it is. Us cops. Get blamed. For everything. Linda, yeah she's a sweetheart. But you look at everything so still. So silent. Almost like you can't recognise things anymore. It's a fact that we messed up. In some times.'

I said, 'bullshit, Giles was spinning a web around this whole thing.' James said, 'and we took the bait.'

I said, 'don't go blaming yourself, this is not your responsibility here. Not mine. To take that burden on our shoulders.'

James said, 'well it's how it is. We live and we succeed. We conquer, we do the right thing. We work hard. We make the right judgement call.'

I said. 'Yeah, but deep down, nothing like this is working. We can talk all day about human rights. Or the pack of lies the defence can pluck out of the sky. It doesn't even make us seem like bad people. Yet it is how it is. It's funny how this world works. It's strange how we are just stuck here. With nothing to do. Because the court is in recess.'

I said, 'it has to. Imagine no breaks. Nothing. No fines yet, and the judge seems like a decent character.'

James said, 'but we will get there. We will understand. We will get to the bottom of all of this. We will try to make ends meet. But NYC is a stretch from home. They got me staying in one of those estates also. As temporary accommodation The FBI and IA must love us.'

I said, 'we are being rewarded, punished. It depends which side of the coin you want to look at it.'

James said, 'yeah, but they couldn't pluck charges out of the sky. They needed us here. New York, the city of dreams. We had to make ends meet. We had to do the right thing. We had to talk about this now.'

I said, 'go figure. Yet it's how you look at it. I knew in my whole life time what this world meant. Any small fucking mistake. You were shredded. Yet it didn't work like that anymore. This court room. Anything we set ourselves up on. Or even the shitty misdemeanour charges that were fast approaching us. We had to work hard. To do the right thing.'

The sun set on the boulevard. I was kind of relieved we were talking. I said to James, 'look, for what I know. I want the right things to happen. We are just going to baby sit Linda now. Fuck. She's 40 years old.'

He said, 'no, we are not going to do that. Just drive her home.'

248

I said, 'we go back in that court room, and we talk. We talk about all kinds of things. Yet we talk. We try to make sense of what happens. We have conversations. Yet the bottom line is we talk.'

The sun was shining over the boulevard. James was attempting to chain smoke. I plugged the smoke out of his mouth. I said, 'in the court house. The court room. It's about to begin again.

Chapter 33

Judge Alan Joseph Carter shouted, 'all rise.' Everyone rose. Alan was smiling and he said, 'I have enjoyed, this. So far. I want to make one thing straight, play by the rules of this court. Last time someone was in breach of contempt of court. I held them accountable and fined them $10,000. This is my court room.'

We had the usual things. A typographer was typing everything that was being stated. There was an audience at the back. Due to the grievous nature of the incident. Press were barred from coming near the court. It was going on and on like this for a while.

The trembling sense of light, that overshadowed the fore-caught outside. The sense of promiscuity in the fields. The wild kind of adventures in the furnishings.

This was a moment. To know. How life was. The bushes outside. Rose petals. An orchard. Grass. Greener then what I had ever seen. Rose petals out stretching the garden. Then some more. All for what I had seen. Freshly cut grass. Nice trimmed hedges. Bushes very neat.

You would look on to the forecourt. You would look on passed what we knew. You would oversee what life foreshadowed Then we would see kind of like these birds outside.

Alan Joseph Carter, the judge, with anger etched on his face. Yet the more I thought about it. The more I realised it was just determination. Determination to get the whole trial finished. Determination to get things resolved I was in no position to blame him for this. I was in no position to.

Then you would look at the jury once again. Pens in hand. Ready to take notes. Ready to see what they had. Ready to understand what was beneath that shiny white paper. They were making notes on.

The pearl curtains. The smiling remarks. The long and distant echoes of charisma, echoing down from the court. The oak furnishings, and the long court. In some kind of memory. Almost like an opaque figure. Sat behind were two guards. The same height. Guarding the door, that was

250

one of the fire exits. Another guard, guarding the door we went out for recess. The chairs were nicely stacked, and nicely seated.

I looked at the people around me. Then again. I looked at the floor. The janitor had cleaned. Looking fresh. Looking nice. Looking like we had done what we had expected.

This court house was how it was. Due to particular reason and due to particular influence. It was the kind of courtroom people would fantasise about. In so many ways. I don't know why. It just seems like it makes perfect sense. Moving forward to see everything we can see. To see everything we wanted to know.

Maybe I was the one who was the problem. Maybe my pedantic nature got in the way of the work I was doing. We had to do the right thing. We had to. Yet it was other stuff also. Like knowing where you stood in all of this. Knowing what we could speak about. What we couldn't. Knowing how long the judge could drag things out.

We looked at the witness box, and we could see Giles Hemingway, not in a wheelchair this time. In crutches. I looked at him, in pity. As he sat down, as every bone in his body. Seemed emaciated. He had lost a lot of weight. For reasons that were beyond me. I didn't know if he was starving himself, or not. I guess he might have been. His thin face. He was a wretched man. He had a wretched temper. He wasn't the person I knew.

I wasn't sure of life anymore. It didn't make sense. Next on the stand. Was Giles himself. Kyle, defending said. 'Giles, how long have you known Lucas?' Giles said, 'a long time.' Kyle said, 'so it's fair to say that you two, got on very well.' Giles said, 'yes.' Kyle said, 'did you intend to kill Louise?' He said, 'no, I just blanked out.' He said, 'was she antagonising you?' He said, 'yes'. He said, 'how much was she antagonising you?'

Giles said, 'wouldn't leave me alone. She bought me the murder weapon.' Some people in the court room sounded shocked. As Alan Joseph Carter was slamming his hammer on the table. Saying, 'calm down. Quiet in my court.' Kyle said, 'so, do you agree with the analysis..? Do you think you do have a personality disorder?'

Giles froze for a minute. He was barely able to stumble onto the witness box. He was frail. Almost like an old man in a 45 year olds body. He was shaking. Upset.

Kyle said, 'Answer the question please.' Giles said, 'I believe I do have Anti Social Personality Disorder.'

252

Kyle said, 'so, is it fair to presume, that that would limit your capacity.' Kyle did a little bit of shrugging and non nonchalance with his hands. Arms, torso.

Giles said, 'capacity for what?' Kyle said, 'capacity to kill. Does this personality disorder impede you from killing people?'

Giles said, 'yes, I was provoked.'

Kyle said, 'so, as you say 'provoked'. What lengths did Louise Grey go to, to provoke you?'

Giles said, 'she spat at me, abused me. Bought me the murder weapon. There was always a glow in her eyes. Like she wanted revenge. Like she wanted to exact revenge. I was surprised this would even go to trial.'

Kyle said, 'so how vindictive was this lady?'

Giles said, 'extremely Wouldn't leave me alone. Always blamed me for things. I am on the straight and narrow now. Yet I don't know anymore. Everyone has their own problems. You know. They can't face others. Not in my light of respect. Yet I never meant to hurt her.'

Kyle said, 'no further questions.'

Mark Hoffman, DA attorney, and prosecutor at law. Two jobs. Approached the bench. He said, 'Giles, come on, let's be honest here. You were out for revenge. You hated, absolutely loathed this woman.

She made your life a misery. Louise Grey. Targetted you, and you wanted to seek revenge. This is exactly what you did.'

Kyle shouted, 'objection opinionated.'

Judge Carter yelled. 'Sustained. Please rephrase the question.'

Kyle said, 'okay, I will rephrase.' He paused. Drinking some water. He said, 'there had been some history with you two?'

Giles said, 'history, yeah sure. I mean who doesn't have history?' Hoffman said, 'well you tell me, because where I am coming from. It seemed like there was a lot of history. She provoked you.'

Giles said, 'and what? What is your point? Of course she provoked me. So did every asshole on the street when I was homeless. Still wouldn't give me justification, to do, what I have allegedly done.'

Hoffman said, 'but you did do, what you had 'allegedly' done?'

Judge Alan Joseph Carter, was looking over the court room cautiously. He said, 'I will let this continue.' He said softly. Insinuating there was some sensitivity to come.

Giles said, 'I didn't kill her.'

Hoffman said, 'hang on a minute. Your statement says 'you stabbed her once in the stomach.''

Giles said, 'I panicked. I mean, I didn't mean to kill her. Surely that's self defence.'

Hoffman said, 'you have plead guilty.'

Giles said, 'I don't have a choice. Okay. I took that blade. I stabbed her. But *I didn't intend to kill her.*'

Hoffman said, 'oh so you didn't intend to kill her. So if I punch someone in the face. Can I say, I would not intend to kill them. If later, they were found dead?'

Giles said, 'possibly.'

Hoffman said, 'if I cut someone off in traffic, can I say I didn't intend to do it. And I was late?'

Kyle shouted, 'objection, irrelevant to the case.'

Judge Carter smiled and he said, 'no, I think I will let Hoffman proceed with caution. I think it's relative to the case.'

Giles said, 'to answer your question sir. It was a mitigating circumstance.'

Hoffman said. 'So what about all of the other people you have named, caused grievous bodily harm to. Did they provoke you also?'

Giles said, 'yes, and I have a problem with impulse. Part of my personality disorder.'

Hoffman said, 'this is one lie, after another lie, after another lie.'

Judge carter was banging on the table

255

with the hammer. He shouted, 'right, that's it. That's enough. Continue your questions. Sensibly. That wasn't a question.' He said assertively.

Hoffman said, 'okay, so let me ask you one last question.'

Judge Carter said, 'one last question..Don't turn it into any more than that please.'

Hoffman was cautious, composed, and ready to strike. He said, 'Giles, did you kill Louise, irrespective of intent?'

Giles said, 'yes'.

Hoffman smiled and said, 'no further questions.'

The judge was hitting the hammer so hard. I am surprised the whole hammer hadn't fallen off. People were bickering. Arguing. Paperwork was being flung everywhere. This woman in the back fainted. We had to turn on the air conditioning and open the windows. The paramedics arrived to take her away. Everything was unsettled. Everything was. So Alan Joseph Carter. In good faith, could not avoid a recess. Yet he said the following.

'I was going to have a little recess, then continue this session a little bit. However, this is damning evidence. Go home, get some rest. Come back in a couple of days. We will talk then.'

He then shouted, 'you are all dismissed.' He was doing waving gestures with his hands and arms, and shouted. 'Go, fireflies, you are all dismissed.' He said sarcastically.

I said, 'what the hell was that about?'

Alan said, 'emotions are running high, what the fuck do you think was happening?'

I said, 'I understand emotions are running high but we are on limited time here.' I said aggressively.

He said, 'not really, if you think about it logically. We are not on limited time.'

I said, 'so call in the prelim, do some work, do anything you can. But I am not in favour of any of this. If you want to turn this into a circus, be my guest.'

He said, 'it's not a circus. We have to follow protocol. Forgot you had your foot out the door. Wanting to get out. Forgetting we had a job to do. Your only motives are money, and I don't know what else. Then you start blaming people. Saying it's government ops. Or it's something planned. It would never make sense like that. Or we wouldn't see it like that.'

I said, 'government ops. What I said was MI5. When we were tracing the organised crime group of Blakely and his men. They shifted the heroine in bags. Left the cruise

257

liners. Flew over to the UK and back. MI5 were on it. Everyone was. Everything is above board.'

He said, 'maybe so, but I don't understand why you keep bringing up Blakely. He's away in jail is he not?' I said. 'Yeah, but what I am trying to say is he's always there to speak to. I don't want to sound anything other than shy of what I had said. It turns out nobody else would know. The whole narrative of twisting someone's arm. To get what you want. That isn't why this court was in recess in the first place. We talk to people, we help people understand their motives. Yet I had no idea. Of any of this.'

Judge Carter said, 'it seems like you are emotional. You had every time to request a transfer.' I said. 'Then we might have lost. I am a good police officer.'

He said, 'detective.'

I said, 'I am a good detective. I belong on this case.'

He said, 'yet you keep turning my court room, into a circus.'

I said, 'it's emotional for a lot of people. Right now, that is all we can say. You talk about government ops.'

Alan said, 'no, you brought up the subject of government ops. I didn't.'

I said, 'don't you see what is happening here. You look out in the twilight zone.

258

The whole picture alludes you. You try so hard to make things work. You try so hard to make life work. Now this. Now nothing. Now all of these people around us. For NOTHING.'

I shouted.

He said, 'I know you are angry.'

I said, 'but that is all you are going to say. You work hard. It pays credence to this fact. Nobody's head is out any door.'

He said, 'go home.'

I said, 'I am.' I walked out of his aggressive face. Mind you I was just as nasty. I walked out, and saw James. Who was looking all mellow and quiet. For some reason that was beyond me. I said, 'time to drive that broad home. Forget her name already. Oh yeah. Linda.'

He said, 'you have a way of words.'

Linda was sipping a latte in the canteen. I went over and I said, 'right pose petal. Time to go. Time to go home. No, before you ask. I am not ordering you a taxi. Those men are going to kill you one day. The way they drive.'

I shook my keys in my pocket, and dangled them.

She smiled and she said, 'you have a Mercedes'

I said, 'of course I have a Mercedes. So I am going to drive you home. Me and my friend here. You've met James.'

259

She shook his hand, she said, 'yes, nice to meet you.' She said.

James said, 'likewise'.

We walked towards the open door, a guard opened the door. We walked into a parking lot. I put Linda in the front seat. James was in the back laughing. I don't know why. He was wearing a grey over haul jacket. Kind of the type a lawyer would wear. Hell I wouldn't be surprised if he got it from the law society. He was clean shaven. His hair was waxed back. He was giggling, as I spoke to Linda.

I said, 'so Linda, tell me about your profession. Criminal defence law. What's your conviction rate?'

She said, '95%'. I said, 'impressive.' She said, 'it would be higher, but some of my clients lie to me.'

I said, 'everyone lies, it's just the good liars who get away with it.' I said jokingly. She didn't find it funny.

She said, 'this is not the kind of remark I would expect.'

I said, 'so what is going on, criminal defence lawyer. 40 years old. You did time at Harvard. Went out. Studied for 5 years again. Whilst doing pro bono cases.'

She said, 'have you read any of my profiles online?'

I said, 'no'. I laughed. I said, 'I am a detective. It's my job.'

She said, 'what your job to stalk people.'

I laughed and said. 'No, it's my job to dot the i's. Cross the t's. Fill in the blanks.'

She said, 'give me an example.'

I said, 'a real example or a made up example?'

She said, 'doesn't matter, your choice.'

I said, 'right. I will tell you a real life example. We were working night shifts. Back home. Back in Detroit. This robber, was claiming that he was locked out of his 'convenience store'. He wanted a hand going back in.'

I coughed and continued, 'I knew he was a robber, but I wanted to do some more digging.'

I said. Linda said, 'what did you find, and how did you go about it?'

I said, 'well I started talking to him. I wasn't going to arrest him for attempted burglary. I mean that shit is weak. So I pressed him and pressed him. Yet I did it in a way, of making a conversation. So he likes the hockey. He likes the ball games. He likes the nice cars. Yet he likes the pay phone visits. The long night drives. He likes his post apocalyptic movies. Where zombies go and attack him whilst he's at a payphone.'

Linda said, 'so what did you manage to get out of him?'

I said, 'we spoke for ages, and he started

confessing. After I told him I wasn't going to arrest him. I then span him some lies, that I was off duty. Which wasn't true. But it wouldn't get me in trouble with the IA. I mean night shifts are a fucking doddle anyway. He was high on some kind of drug. He ends up confessing to the fact. That he did indeed. Kill, a 4 year old boy. In cold blood. Outside a motel. On Christmas Eve. '

Linda said. 'so you are a good detective. You know. I commend you. I really do. That's great.' She said with no sarcasm in her voice. She said, 'how do you get the truth out of people?'

I said, 'well, you'd have to join the police, if you wanted to know what our training involves?'

She said, 'oh come on, cut the wise cracks. What are you getting up to.'

I said, 'i'll be honest here. We don't use, anything other than. What we have been trained to do. Is talk to people. Open up a dialogue If someone is a victim. We will know, that they will tell us. If someone is a suspect. That will come out of the conversation. We don't try to deceive'

She said. 'But you lied about being off duty, when you were on duty.'

I said, 'a white lie, because being on the night shift. Is being like off duty. It's a piece of pie.'

262

James in the back, said, 'making me hungry already. Can we go to Mcdonalds or something?' I said, 'I don't know. I am more concerned with dropping off Linda here.'

Linda said, 'look, don't worry about it. I fancy some fries.'

We pulled into this Mcdonalds. We got out, and we were sitting around the table. I had spoken to Linda for ages. She even told me she used to be a cop. In her twenties. Whilst she was saving up to become a mature student at Harvard. She worked 4 years in traffic division. Writing people tickets.

I said, 'they didn't teach you any detective skills in the traffic division?' I asked Linda. She laughed, and she said, 'no, it's all paperwork.'

Chapter 34

Mcdonalds was a doddle. It really was. We were just sitting around. Just eating. We were going to take Linda home. I mean it was a matter of time. Our radios kept buzzing off. I got a radio call from this one gentleman in dispatch. Who said, 'calling all units. Fire, in progress.' I turned it down, and I said. 'right, we get down to brass tax here. This whole thing is just stupid you know. Everything. The court case.'

Linda said, 'for the record. I am not part of the same court case you guys are on.'

I said, 'maybe not, but you have to be living in a cave, not to hear about Hemingway.'

She said, 'I have heard about that guy yes.'

She continued, she said, 'he's a monster.'

I said, 'I know, but would you defend him?' She said, 'definitely not.'

I said, 'yet you are defending, a manslaughter?'

She said, 'that's different.' I said, 'depends, which county you are in.'

She said, 'it's the same thing, the same rules apply. Yet the man I am defending is elderly.' I said. 'Oh it gets better. If someone is elderly. Do they get a get out of jail free card?'

She said, 'no they don't. Yet manslaughter is less sinister than murder. Besides. That douchebag had been maiming people. Causing grievous bodily harm. To lots of people. The guy belongs in a whack house.'

I said, 'that guy, in my humble opinion is insane. Yet I am not sure if prison can help him.'

Linda said, 'most people in prison are insane.'

264

I said. 'Is that the quote on your resume. Look at the big picture here. The guy is not going to walk. I will make sure of it.'

She said, 'you put me on the case then.'

I said, 'no shit, you have a lot of time on your hands. To go and defend this elderly vehicular manslaughter mystery charge.' I said.

She said, 'maybe so, but I bet I could help.'

James retorted, 'forget it, the trials almost done. The judge is just nit picking. He tried grilling us with a contempt of court fine. Didn't work out. Don't sweat it.'

Linda said, 'so, do you attend every call on your radio?'

I said, 'you were in The Police for 4 years.' She said, 'yeah but things have changed. It's not the same now. It seems like more of a dynamic unit.'

I said, 'no, it's stayed the same. I have been doing this job for a long time. Nothing like a good old snack. Just after a court case. Yet, remember, there are so many characters in this world. So many stories as well. That I would love to tell you.'

She said, 'cut it out, not interested. You think paying for my taxi, is going to help?'

I said, 'well I don't know. What do you think?'

265

She said, 'I think you are fishing for information.'

I said, 'so what good is that going to do. The case is almost over.'

Chapter 35

Linda said. 'You are trying to grill me over something.' I said, 'are you guilty of any crimes?' She said, 'no'. I said, 'you had to think about it.' She said, 'maybe.'

I said, 'let me guess. You defrauded the government out of $14,000 dollars, and you forgot to enclose the cheque to the IRS?'

She said, 'no, nothing like that?'

I said, 'you have missing papers to the IRS?'

She smiled and she said, 'no'.

I said, 'oh come on, we are just three people having a conversation here. I want to know.'

She said, 'I stole a pack of smokes. I was desperate.'

Me and James start laughing, and it's just hurting my guts.

I said, 'seriously, is that your deadly crime?' I said in a sinister voice.

She said, 'I regret doing it.'

I said, 'oh come on, are you in debt?'
She said, 'yes.' I said, 'by how much?'
She said. '100,000 dollars.' I said, 'so,

it's the Harvard university. You still owe. You have unfinished student loans?'

She said, 'I am behind on my mortgage also. Also my husband just left me.'

I said, 'you rack up that kind of debt. No wander you are worried. How can I help you out?'

She said, 'I really don't want your money.'

I said, 'well maybe you don't, but I can clear things.'

She said, 'well, I live on west avenue block.'

We got into the car, and we drove to west avenue, on first, and third street. Just up the road from the Chucky Cheese, and the Frosty Mountain store. There was a Walgreens on the left. A Wallmart had just passed us.

I said, 'so here you are. There you go. Your humble abode.'

We saw her walk inside a modest, semi detached house.' We drove off.

I said to James, 'do you think she is bullshitting?' James laughed and said, 'a hundred percent, up to no good. I haven't heard so much baloney in my life.'

I said, 'what do you think's going on?' James said, 'fuck knows, a whole lot of crime by the looks of it. Probably defrauding the government. IRS on her back. I don't know.'

I said. 'No it's not the IRS. It's nothing to do with them. She's in debt.'

James said, 'the debt and smokes stealing was a ruse to someone or something else.'

I said, 'do you think she knows Giles?'

James said, 'with all due respect, everyone knows him.'

I said, 'no, but do you think she knew. Or knows him personally?'

James said, 'who the fuck knows? Or cares for that matter.'

I slammed on the brakes at the red light. I said, 'I fucking care. I care about this, I care about it.'

He said, 'well we'll do some background research then.'

I said, 'this isn't personal.'

We get a call from Rufus, he is right behind us. In his unmarked FBI Chevy State of the art car. Looks fucking brilliant. He pulls over next to us.

He said, 'you trying to solve this case with Linda. I have spoken to my boss.'

I said, 'so what has she done?"

Rufus said, 'well, what hasn't she done?'

I said, 'come on, no more mind games. What has she done?"

Rufus said, 'pull up over in that parking lot.' I drove over to the parking lot. We got out. Lattes in hands, from The Mcdonalds.

268

Rufus said, 'she's committing Fraud.' I said, 'I suspected that. But isn't that a matter for the IRS?'

He said, 'no, you don't understand. It's not your standard forgetting to declare expenses fraud. Or the IRS, will fine your arse a $1000 dollars if a form is late fraud. We are not the nazi police.'

I said, 'well who is she defrauding?'

Rufus said. 'She has written bogus cheques. All over the county. All over the fucking county. She owes more than 100 grand. More like 300.'

I said, 'you serious?'

Rufus said, 'no I am fucking with you. It's not like that.'

I said. 'Enough of your lies. What has she done?'

Rufus said. 'She helped Giles kill the victim.' He said sordidly.

I said, 'but she's a criminal defence lawyer.'

Rufus laughed and said. 'So? That's just a ruse. That is just how they met in the first place.'

I said. 'So I get it. Rufus. Giles went to her for help. With one of his alleged misdemeanour charges at the time.'

Rufus said, 'bingo, you just won the lottery of answers. They met. At this bar. The old oak Tavern.'

I said. 'Oh shit. I go there.' James said,

269

'Me too.'

Rufus said. 'She told him to kill Louise Grey.'

I said, 'did she know Louise?'

Rufus said. 'Yeah, barely though.'

I said. 'So call in some units.'

Rufus said, 'we have her house bugged. Everything. The phone, the internet lines. Every time she types. It's recorded.'

I said, 'she's on a watch list.'

Rufus said, 'you know you spoke about MI5.'

I said. 'Yeah.'

Rufus said, 'they have her on a terrorist watch list.'

I said, 'why?'

Rufus said, 'oh come on man. I have been working hard. So fucking hard. I can't stand this.'

I said, 'I am not pulling your chain. I just want to know why she was put on a terrorist watch list?'

Rufus said, 'well, that is all the intelligence I was given.'

I said, 'bullshit, you know it. You are leading onto something bigger than this. What are you, the paranoid police?"'

Rufus said. 'Okay, okay. I will bite. She took a trip to the UK. Once. She flips. They get her to pay extra for her luggage. $100 dollars extra. She flipped out at security. She made a threat. To security. A threat that we took seriously, and help me. I cannot repeat.'

I said. 'Fuck.' Rufus said, 'we have had sniffer dogs over her house. She has been cautioned, but there is one problemo.'

I said, 'oh let me guess, the problemo lies with she's a fucking psycho.'

Rufus smiled and said. 'No, the problem lies with the fact that she's a criminal defence lawyer. She knows her law.'

I said, 'oh come on, you can find any excuse to lock her up. What is she? Some kind of Sociopath? What has she got in the kitchen?'

I said, 'it's scaring me.'

Rufus said, 'why do you think that we didn't involve you pencil dicks in the first place. Because we knew you couldn't handle the pressure of Federal Bereua Work.'

James said, 'look Rufus, cut the crap. I already knew.' He said calmly.

Rufus said. 'Did you?' James said, 'well yeah, it was obvious, the whole missing her taxi thing. Forgetting to pay. Getting the wrong day. It all added up, playing the stupid blonde lady. When we have someone smart on our hands.'

I said, 'so, you just carry on, questioning her. Will she face charges over her encouragement of Mr Giles Hemingway?'

Rufus said, 'look, no, because that guy

has to take accountability. But deep down. It's worser than that'

I said. 'You know what. I am sick of you. You keep talking in riddles.'

He said, 'you are out of your god damn depth, you know that?'

I said, 'no shit, so why involve us now? After all of this time. Why this here now?'

He said, 'because I wanted to scare you.'

I said. 'Bullshit man, you are not a friend of mine.'

We walked away, and so did James. James said, 'this is how you treat us?' Rufus said. 'Look guys, seriously. I am not trying to be a jerk here. Come on, and speak to me. In my house.'

So there we have it. We go into this guys house. He has a federal house in New York. Which is where all of us toe rags are staying until that Giles gets put away.

Rufus is divorced. Has children. They don't live with him. He makes us all sandwiches, and we talk in the living room.

He said, 'look, let me be honest with you here. There is going to be charges put on Linda Coleman.'

I said. 'Let me guess. Throwing a wobbly at that airport, and getting put on some list. That isn't going to cut it?'

Rufus said. 'Come on, you don't understand. She's a wanted criminal. We

272

read her, her rights. We have so many charges stacked up against her.'

I said, 'but throwing the wobbly at the flight. That has nothing to do with MI5. It has nothing to do with national security. She's a woman, she flipped.'

Rufus said. 'Maybe so, but we had to keep tabs. Besides. What harm is it going to do?'

I said. 'So after she threw that temper tantrum at the airport. And got fined for baggage overload. You followed her to her home address. Once there. You walked inside. You found evidence she was implicating. A vulnerable man. Giles Hemingway. Into something he couldn't handle. You arrest her. She threatens to sue. You release her. You find out she's in debt with the IRS. You make some enquiries. You talk to her lawyer. You find out that if you keep her under surviellance. Instead of charging her. You will get more evidence. More evidence, means more meat for the judge to chew on. Post prosecution. Is that right?'

Rufus said, 'exactly. We keep her under observation We keep her on all of these things. We wait, and we wait.'

James said, 'you get evidence, but you want to tell judge Alan Joseph Carter. You want to explain to him. What she has done.'

273

James said, 'please?'

Rufus said, 'he already knows. We are going to bring her in, last minute.'

I said. 'This is not how you run a trial.'

Rufus said, 'you got any alternatives.'

I said. 'Yes I do.'

Rufus shouted wait. I got into my Chevy I drove 12 blocks to Linda Colemans house. I said. 'Lina. I am arresting you for one count of perverting the course of justice. One count of fraud, and one count of conspiracy to commit murder. You have the right to remain silent. Anything you do say will be held against you. You have the right to an attorney. If you cannot afford one. One will be appointed to you.'

I get two female police officers to transport her back. To transport her back to the cells. I speak to Alan Joseph Carter, and I explain to him everything He laughed about the freak out at the airport. The DA are behind it. We got her.

We bring her into court.

Alan said, 'we can't exactly put her in the same courtroom as that psycho Giles?'

I said. 'As a witness. Then she can have her own escapade in a court after.'

Alan said, 'okay, we'll bring her in as a witness.'

I walk up the custody block. I said to Linda. I said, 'look, we need you to testify

274

against Giles. He will go away, and that will be the end of it.'

She said. 'What if I don't want to.'

I said, 'if you do, we will give you a reduction in sentence.'

She said, 'not convinced.'

I said, 'look, if you do it, we will pay your remaining bills. Overlook your charges of fraud. We will take you off that bullshit watch scheme. You shouldn't have even been on in the first place. We will sort everything out for you. Just promise me you will testify.'

She said. 'Exonerate me and I will.'

I said, 'okay. I will 'exonerate' you.'

So we get her in, and she testifies. She spills the beans and everything.

Chapter 36

The judge shouts. 'All rise.'

Alan, the judge said, 'we have a new witness. The witness is called. Linda Cole.'

She went to the stand. No questions were asked. She made a blanket statement.. She said, 'I took advantage, and I helped Giles Hemingway. Kill Louise. I helped him. It was all me. Who encouraged him.'

She stood down. Alan Joseph Carter said, 'does anyone want to cross examine?'

Kyle defending said, 'yeah, well I will.'

Kyle said, 'so Linda, what exactly are you. A gigolo A lawyer. A prior cop. What did you do?'

Linda said, 'I don't know if it's any of your concern.'

Kyle said, 'you, worked quite closely at law. You had a huge freak out at an airport. You had issues with the IRS. You have problems. Mental Health problems?'

She said, 'perhaps.'

Kyle said, 'so enlighten me. What are your issues?'

She said. 'Depression.'

Kyle said, 'is that all?'

She said, 'yes.'

He said. 'Are you sure?'

Linda said, 'yes.'

Kyle said, 'so in that case. I am not sure. What if it was you. Oh no wait. It couldn't be you. We have Giles on CCTV. Yet you put him up to it.'

Linda said. 'I encouraged him.'

Kyle said, 'did you threaten him, or blackmail him?'

Linda said, 'I told him, if he didn't commit the murder. Then I would kill him.'

Everyone was shocked. I said, 'this is outrageous.' Giles shouted, 'hey screw you.' At the court room.

I said, 'I have to ask you something. Just

276

for the record. Linda. What is actually happening here?'

Kyle said, 'look. I am asking the questions. You didn't go through with it. You weren't violent. You were vindictive. You played a prank on him?'

Linda said, 'I guess so.'

The judge shouted. 'Order, order, order.'

I said. 'Right, well I think the jury should make a decision now.'

Linda is re arrested I was lying about dropping the charges. It was just a ruse to get her in.

The jury is making the decision. So that is what happened. 11 hours of talking. 11 people.

Chapter 37

Judge Alan Joseph Carter, shouts, 'all rise.'

Everyone rises. Alan said. 'Please, jury, tell the verdict.' A big woman, not massive. With a high pitched voice. Ginger hair. She said. 'We the jury find Giles Hemingway. Guilty of first degree murder. Guilty of Grievous Bodily Harm. On 5 counts. Guilty of perverting the course of justice.'

So guilty on all counts.

Alan said, 'okay, Giles, you have manipulated this court. Left right and centre. I am sentencing you to 100 years in prison. Without the opportunity of parole. Trust me. This is generous under the circumstances.'

He then shouts aggressively. 'Bailiff, take this man away.' Giles is pushed into 6 security guards, prison guards. Who escort him to a prison van. He is driven off. In Police escort.

I am sitting there looking at Linda, and we charge her, and she is going to get many years behind bars also.

I return to the court block. I walk out. I drive back to my apartment. I am packing my things. Ready to head home to Detroit. My work is done. At least I thought my work had been done

Chapter 38

I am back in Detroit just finishing a few pieces. A few bits and pieces. I am stuck. I am feeling drained.

My position in this whole thing. Has left me feeling shocked. I feel aimless, and in a way. I feel like nothing good is going to happen.

I sit in my humble abode. With Alex in the military. My wife. I barely see her anymore. I am home. On my coach. Just

278

dotting some i's and crossing some T's. Thinking. Kind of like a debrief you would expect to have with someone. Yet with yourself.

I am thinking over everything, and I am thinking about things closely. I am wandering what kind of aims I have left. As I pop a pill, and attempt to go to bed. I have a few years left in the force. Until retirement. So that is good.

I think very clearly, I look at things clearly. It's different. It's different to what I expect. It's different to what I know.

I look at the world differently now. I always wanted to be the perfect person. With the best results. Yet that wasn't effecting me anymore. I always wanted to be someone who people could trust. Looking back over the boulevard, and looking over what I knew. I was just a civil servant. Just, just a civil servant.

With some kind of heart. Beating in my chest. I look at things differently. I look at the world differently. It just doesn't make sense. I resented Giles. I resented him for what he had done. I resented every bone in his body. That's what I resented.

Yet over the years. I would think more closely with how things were. Or how things change. Or maybe I was wrong. I don't know. Like people jump to conclusions and you go through all the

279

hard ache. The bitterness. Only to find out, you are on the wrong side of dreams.

It never really occurred to me that I had done anything that bad. I had done everything according to procedure. I had been ruthless in my aspirations but gentle in my intrigue. I had done things which had been a merit to the force. In some respects. I felt like I was leaving stuff behind.

My old wardrobe, full of things I no longer needed. The apple pie on the table. The Sprite drinks. My DKNY shirt. My leather belt. My sense of aspiration. My Chevy, outside, keeping my Honda company.

I sold the Cadillac I sold it. It all went away. Like clouds in the sky are leaving. It never really effected me anymore.

So cheers to what I knew and what people would really know. I was this civil servant that wanted justice. Of course. Yet looking back at this case. I would be inhuman not to feel some kind of pity and compassion. For Louise. I would be inhuman not to feel anger at Giles.

Yet all through my life, being passed through pillar to post. One thing after another. After another. You just got nowhere. You looked at life with some kind of dream. We all conceived the notion that some day life would end up

280

how it was.

In my own mind, my own aspiration. What I had done to expect nothing. Just a tap on the shoulder. Or something. It wasn't what I knew. Or it wasn't what I expected. I had known of who I was.

In some respects. I had known of this journey I was embarking on. It was something which I had seen from time to time.

Besides the entangled away, from my dry sense of wit. The dirty jokes, and sense of apathy. I really had to make progress. I really had to follow my dreams. I really had to follow my ambitions.

Having met so many good people out there, and it is wrong for me to feel regretful. It's wrong for me to resent people.

I look at things differently. It's always like that. My mind is made up. I am a detective. I am a warrior. I am falling asleep, as my radio is going off. I am partially drunk, partially drugged. I respond to an urgent 911 call.

I go to step inside my vehicle, and I shout, 'no, not this way.' I walk 3 blocks to the incident. Wearing my pyjamas, with my coat.

Senior commander. Ryan Jenkins, said, 'who brought this guy along?'

I said, 'I am a senior detective sir?'

Jenkins said, 'you are drunk, go home please.' Rufus tapped me on the shoulder. He said, 'it's okay, he's one of us.'

Jenkins said, 'anyway, we have a shooter.'

Rufus said, 'he's armed.' I said, 'what gun?' Rufus said, 'the fuck does it matter. The guy is armed. We are getting SWAT to take him out.'

I said, 'so why call me, what can I do?' Rufus said, 'my man, Lucas, now you are here. It's time for you to be the hostage negotiator.'

I said, 'what has happened to the real hostage negotiator.'

Rufus said. 'He's away, unwell.'

I said, 'what's wrong with him?'

Rufus said, 'I don't know. Some kind of food poisoning'

I said, 'fuck this, you expect me to hold this guys hand?'

Rufus said, 'you don't want to hold this god damn guy's dick.'

I said, 'no I do not, tell me what I need to know. This is stupid. This is like a fucking marathon. I can't believe you put me in this position.'

Rufus said, 'what are the alternatives? You have had some liquor, you have had some brandy. Now all of a sudden, you think you are god's gift?' I said, 'no I don't.

I don't think like that at all.'

I radioed in and I said, 'okay, I will take command.' I got my megaphone, and I shouted. 'Hey, this is The Police. Drop your weapon.'

He was a religious nut job. A far right extremist. He had some kind of AK47. Firing at us.

I was disappointed I said, 'anything you want, just come down, this is the police.'

Fuck, I was not going to play hostage negotiator I was not going to do it. I was not going to do anything like this. I just feel kind of stuck. Kind of very worried about myself. This whole situation.

I grab my pistol, and I fire one shot. He's dead, right in the head.

One shot. I get in close range.

I put my gun back in my holster. I order for a taxi home. I appear to have stubbed my foot.

Rufus said, 'well done.' I said, 'he's small fry.'

Charles Jenkins, FBI said, 'yeah, but the orders were not to shoot.'

I said, 'Internal Affairs will sort it out.'

Charles Jenkins said, 'you gonna call them, or should I?'

I said. 'Oh come on. If it was a suspect who wasn't armed. Chased him through the road. And I mistook his mobile phone for a gun. Maybe then disciplinary proceedings. The religious nut jobs. Orders were to shoot on impact.'

Rufus said, 'those were not the orders.'

I said, 'yes they were. I heard it on the radio. I have the intelligence. I heard everything. I saved your skin.'

I got into the taxi, and I was driven home. It was the same guy who was driving aimlessly in traffic. Before that whole Linda trial went square pegged, round holed.

I went home, and I slept very well. I woke up to all of my clothes trashed.

Chapter 39

Louisiana, felt I was having an affair. She put two and two together and got five. She thought I was having an affair. Fuck. Not me. No not me. Wouldn't have worked like that.

I said, 'what on earth is this about?' She said, 'who is Linda?' I said, 'she is a suspect. Well she was. She's in custody.'

Louisiana said, 'I got a phone call from her, telling me you slept with her. Is this true?'

I said, 'no, she's lying.'

Louisiana said, 'you swear to me.'

I said, 'of course I do. I swear to you.'

Louisiana said, 'in that case, sorry about the clothes, and looks like you need to put that bitch in her place.'

I said, 'I will don't worry.' I gather my clothes. I put them in a nice polite pile. I ring up the prison in which she is staying. I speak to one of the guards there.

I said, 'look, can I be honest with you here. This whole thing is a nightmare. I want Linda to be put in isolation for 6 months. She keeps spreading rumours.'

The celly was a bit apprehensive about this, but agreed, and he said, 'hey, that's what it takes to shut her up. She has been yapping her mouth in here. Making up rumours about people in here also. Thank you.' I hung up. Not maliciously, but I had to make sure which clothes were torn and which weren't.

Turns out one of my favourite shirts was torn. I turn to Louisiana and I said. 'Can't you just learn to trust me. Or at least wait for me to wake up. Before you trash my stuff?'

Louisiana is tearful. She said, 'I am sorry. I really am. I panicked. It was so plausible.' I said, 'don't be so gullible.' She turned around and she said, 'excuse me, gullible? What exactly are you trying to say?'

I said, 'oh come on, if I heard that same story I would laugh it off the phone.'

Louisiana said. 'So, if someone phoned you up, and said that I was having an affair with a man. You would think it was

285

a wind up?'

I said, 'of course I would. Look. I am a seasoned detective. I go on facts. Not hearsay. Get some rest.'

I pointed to the bed. I walked in and got some orange juice. Feeling ever more fed up.

Chapter 40

This Hemingway case had gotten to everyone. All of us. I hated it. It wasn't *funny. It wasn't clever. It wasn't what I wanted.'* I said sharply to Louisiana

It wasn't what I wanted. Yet, I know, deep down. Where my memory lies. I know deep down that all of the past had been bullshit. Now I was *here, now. With this*. With the same thing I had always wanted to do.

If things had not made sense. In the latter parts of the day. You would always worry about the small things. Yet, when life gets to you so much. You make perfect sense. Life isn't fair. We sometimes learn the hard way. Yet the same apprehensions are leading us astray. We have become the very epitome of what we had known.

When I look at the world, through the same lens I had always seen. Times were challenging. I get that. My suede jacket, my apprehensive look. My ability to decide where life is going. My ability to make snap decisions. I didn't know where life was taking me. Regressing back to the days of office duty. Or even being the cop I was. I was never punished, but we had paper work to do.

Now all of a sudden. Things change. The rules change. I was not laughing anymore. Not that I was in the first place. My whole world was spinning around. Some people seemed so grateful to see me. Someone they could trust. I was never selling anyone fancy gimmicks I was never doing that.

Deep down. In my own latter years of life. I had known the difference between sanity, and insanity. The difference between discretion, and choice. The difference between patience, and resolve. It was something I already knew. I had nothing else to compare that to. I had no kind of dream or no kind of outlet. I was not going to grind other people down. Just for my own appeasement. If something was giving me the wrong idea. Then that's something I could have known. Deep down. Beyond the challenges, the despair. The struggle. The same kind of things as you can hear people shouting a couple of blocks away.

People crying, and people making all kinds of noises. I was a known detective. Yet I knew if anyone came to my crimson house. My place of luxury. I would be okay.

Fred was on his way to come to speak to me. He was from the IRS. We had some tax returns to do. I gave him my tax returns, and showed him the tax I had been paying. I showed him receipts, and I showed him what I had done. I explained to him that all of my expenses came from the government. I told him I was an experienced detective. I told him my salary. I told him of my average weekly expenditure. He was happy, and he didn't need to do extra digging. As it's not self employment. He was just checking for anything that shouldn't be there.

Like anything. Like something I couldn't afford. I told him my Rolex was second hand, and came from my grandmother. Which is true. Which she paid. Cost me $2,000 dollars. He said, 'look, seriously, don't worry about it. I send over shmucks. Like secret IRS detectives all of the time to spy on people who break the law.'

I said, 'yeah we do the same.'

He said, 'yet the bottom line is, you are an honest cop.'

I said, 'I try to be.'

He was a slim man, with an amiable appearance. Maybe too slim, but I didn't want to say anything. He had some loose skin here and there.

288

I said, 'listen, since we are on the same team and all. I really want to have a discussion over. Linda.'

He sighed and he said, 'oh I know Linda. She is one of my clients.'

I said, 'I know, FBI gave me, the information. She's a very manipulative person. I am just wandering what kind of things are we looking at here.'

Fred said, 'well to be honest, if we can talk about this lady. Honestly. She was defrauding the government. Yet that's all I can say.'

I said, 'look, I know everything she did. I am just levelling with you and saying. If this is the case. If this is what you want to do fine. All politics aside. If you want to kind of speak, or research. About any of this. Then be my guest. Yet she is spreading rumours in jail. They locked her up in solitary. I did them a favour. Now you and go pay me a visit. Do you see where I am getting at?'

He said, 'I heard your theory about government ops, and this whole thing you got going on. Blaming people. All of the time. Blaming people. One thing after another. Like it's some orchestra.'

I said. 'It was never like that.'

He said, 'did you enjoy the military?'

I said, 'the military, ages, ago, for 4 years. Now this. You couldn't exactly be

289

reasonable with me? You couldn't dig up any files in relation to the credentials of Linda. If we are talking about corruption. Then we need to know. Every detail you have. Because this is federal. This shit isn't just some tea party we have on a Friday night. We have the FBI on this thing. Even MI5 are working on Linda. She's a nasty piece of work.'

Fred said, 'she worked with The Blakely's?' I said, 'did she?' He said, 'yes she did. That is why she's so high profile. Then you look into the drug trade. Which isn't my area of specialty. Yet there was drug smuggling.'

I said 'I have heard all about the drug smuggling. I have heard all about the airport freak out. I have heard all about FBI hunting her down. I was the one who made the arrest you know. Nothing else you can tell me. It just goes around in fucking circles.'

He said, 'isn't that part of the job we do.'

I said. 'oh no, we are not part of the same fucking department. Maybe the same team. Yet you had to know what was happening here. All of the time we made remarks. All of the time we kept silent on the things that mattered. We detectives, we are not giving up. We were not just assuming things were going to be okay. We look on the dull side of life, because

290

that's the training we get. Then I get you coming in. Telling me no tax returns were late.'

I felt angry. I felt like ripping his face off. I fell like throwing him down the toilet. I felt like throwing his leg down the toilet. I felt like setting him on fire. I felt like shoving him. I didn't know what else to do. I didn't know what else to say. I couldn't win with some people. The tides of my mind were just clearly effecting my judgement. I was going insane with worry. Insane with worry over the whole Blakely cases. Verses Hemingway. Even though it's different cases. Them verses the state Then me talking about government ops, like it's some big deal over here. It's nothing. It's not the life I wanted to know, and it sure as hell didn't fit in with what I was trying to say.

Chapter 41

The light in my eyes was blinding me. I fell asleep and for the first time. I couldn't wake up. I entered this world of sleep paralysis Which I am sure lots of people hear about.

I wake up and I look around. I look everywhere. I look at the duvet. The coverings. The mattress The bed. The overriding structure we have here. I look at the calm before the storm. I look at my croissants. I look at everything.

I am not just one person, and I am a detective, but at home I am a family man. What we tried pinning on Hemingway. Before he went stir crazy Some times we are our own worst enemies. You see the smiles, you see the good hearted gestures. You see the wrong, you see the corruption. But not me. I wasn't going to be prepared to have a migraine the size of a hockey puck. Just hanging over me. Like a constant feeling of guilt. I wasn't going to have it. I did nothing wrong and nothing else can surpass my mind.

I was going around the twist, and I couldn't cope. Back to the drawing board, and one last flight. To speak to Linda in solitary. I wanted to know more about The Blakely's.

Even though I couldn't decide to give up. I had to speak to her.

Chapter 42

So the days turned into nights, and turned into days. I spoke to Linda. Through a little screen. I said, 'look, in all fairness. I don't know what is happening right now. Spreading rumours. Not fair.'

She said, 'well I apologise.'

I said, 'how's solitary confinement?' She

said, 'it's okay, don't get picked on here.'

I said, 'oh playing the victim are we, because this is not going to wash. This isn't.'

I said, 'look, I am not here to grill you or anything like that. I want to know something. I want to know how much you knew about The Blakely's'

She said, 'a lot, why?'

I said, 'I don't know. I keep getting weird people showing up unannounced First the IRS man, there's been postal workers. Asking about them.'

She said, 'they are in jail aren't they? So am I.'

I said. 'Well, yeah, but what we have witnessed is copy cat versions. There is a huge drug smuggling ring.'

She said, 'well if people are copying, it's nothing to do with The Blakely's'

I said. 'I don't know. There are more out there. Fuck if I know. People copy people all of the time. You want to talk facts. I know there's more men out there.'

She said, 'bullshit, everything was washed up. Everything you knew was gone. You can't hide behind this Lucas. You can't just pretend that there are people conspiring against you. At every turn.'

I said. 'So what about the truth. Am I not allowed to search for that now?'

293

She said, 'of course you are, but it doesn't lie with The Blakely's'

I said. 'Then who does it lie with?'

She said, 'I don't know, you kept going on about government ops, and set ups, and MI5. Tell me more about that.'

I said, 'I am not entirely sure, but I know there has been strange people about.'

She said, 'you are going to have to be more informative than that.'

I said. 'Some things don't add up. I get the Blakely's I get what they did. I get what the other dude did. Hemingway. Yet I can't picture anyone else in frame. We talk about repercussions for crime. You lock someone up. You proverbially throw away the key. At least until parole. Yet The Blakely's had some government officials playing their fucking whistle. Their own tune.'

Linda said, 'everyone you have ever spoken to, in relation to The Blakely's. They themselves, 7 dead, 7 captured. One in witness protection. Don't know why you bothered. Figured he was an informant. That was the price you got. It's not the government. Besides. What are the FBI keeping from you?'

I said, 'they didn't tell me anything about you, until I pressed them. Then they keep saying there are some cruise liners. In Michigan. Full of drugs. Full of people.

Full of workers. We knew this. So we did some digging. We found nothing but these drugs. All lined up. Cocaine, heroine, and you name it. The victims and slaves. Were being drugged up. Being made to work without consent. They were working there. Slaving away. They were slaves. It's modern day slavery.'

I continued, I said, 'yet, something wasn't adding up. I didn't even bother speaking to the FBI sometimes I have my own affairs to sort out. I am intelligent enough on my own. I am sure I help from time to time. I looked around the cruise liner. The one we searched the night of the arrest I found two dead bodies in that ship. Maybe even three. Just everywhere. They were everywhere, and it was like ants crawling under my skin. I couldn't take it. They had been drugged to death. Which leads me onto my next point. The drug smuggling. They hire a slave. Give the slave some cocaine. Then we catch the slaves. Yet I was adamant, at every time. To claim duress. Lack of a sentence. Then we have the big fish. We have the people at the top of their food chain. Yet the slavery exists. And I can't shake it anymore. You see them. Working on that cruise liner.'

Linda started smoking a cigarette, she said, 'not anymore, not in here. Not with all of this going on. The only thing I see is mail, three square meals a day. Then nothing else.'

I said, 'yet when you worked with The Blakely's You saw it. You saw the level of destruction they were creating. All of this ties in. when the FBI say it's an isolated incident. You do know they just say that. To stop people from worrying. Yet deep down. We know everything is connected. Everything. The cruise liner. The Blakely's Hemingway, and you. And you are probably wandering, 'he got so smart', well I did.'

Linda said, 'I realise this, but you can't take the lid off the whole thing. If you don't realise where the facts are lying. You need evidence. Did you take swabs of the bodies. Call in forensics.'

I panicked and I said, 'no,'

She said, 'why not?' I said, 'oh come on, don't paint yourself as this remarkable citizen all of a sudden. Just because I didn't tell the FBI. They already knew.'

She said, 'they are not God, how could they know?'

I said, 'they had the whole place tapped, wired. Everything was under surviellance.'

She said, 'oh I see, just like with you. Those people end up in a body bag.' I said, 'well they would have done. I do things by the book. I am not buying this routine you have here. We have so many sick people in jail. You want to try and lecture me. About what is right?'

She said, 'never again, big mistake.'

Chapter 43

I continued to talk to Linda. Her blonde hair. Prison wasn't ageing her. Not yet.

I look inside the walls. I see how prison is treating her. Even though she is in a female's prison. It still pays credence to that fact. She is scared. Lonely. I get it.

I don't know what to think anymore. The room is spinning around my head. I feel confused. I don't know why. I have this idea of what I want to think. Linda, she had conversations with Blakely. He's now in jail. So is she. Yet that doesn't explain everything.

Linda started smoking, you could see the smoking blonde lady. Almost turn to proverbial ashes. Whilst smoking. Almost like the wind had been turned off her sails. If she was a boat. She would be up New Jersey. Up on the rocks. Floating away into the distance. Yet this wasn't New Jersey. Hell, I didn't even know why I was still in NYC. I didn't know what I could do to help. If anything.

There were female prisoners walking around. Libraries Book shelfs, and the place seemed well kept. Well, more than I would have expected. I look around and I see glimmers of hope. In the pale faces of the women in prisoned there.

I look to myself for the answers. Yet I look to Linda for the answers really. As her cold gaze was looking at mine. I didn't know what else to think.

I just wandered, you know. I just wandered about everything. The long nights I would stay awake. The sirens in New York blazing away in the background.

The jail cell screw guy, guard. Looking like he was angry. A female social worker was with us. Called Angelina. I was at a loss for even emotions at this point. As Angelina was securing the wounds. Of what appeared to be a severe self harm attempt. Linda had cut her wrists. When I say self harmed. I mean she went along the street. Not across it. Missed her main artery by mm's. It was a suicide attempt. Not self harm.

I said to Angelina, I said, 'she botched it.' Angelina said, 'yeah I know.'

I said. 'It doesn't make sense. When I look at it. Linda, are you still there?'

Linda was foaming at the mouth, and before I could even speak. Two female paramedics rush in. On call. As she is already on suicide watch. She is rushed into the infirmary, and treated there. As she has taken a drug overdose. I could see her getting CPR. Luckily it wasn't fatal, and I visited her the next day in the infirmary. She was a broken woman. Once was a flower, is now scattered petals on the ground.

I said, 'look, I don't think now is the time for any more questions. I just want you to get better.'

Linda Cole said, 'I know you do, and it's my own fault.'

I said, 'no, it's not. Blakely was using you. He's a son of a bitch. I will do some work.'

I handed her a card. On that card was a number of a suicide prevention helpline. Taped to the card, were several quarters. I said, 'look, if you are feeling desperate. Just ring up from the payphone in the hallway.' She smiled, almost like a gleaming smile. As I walked towards the infirmary door. I walked away. Into my Cadilac I had rented. Yet it was puffing away steam and smoke. I had no idea why. I get it checked out, as this two star MOT body shop factory. I go in and I said, 'this car I rented. What's with the smoke?'

This fat guy appears, I think he might have been half greek, and half Mexican. He shouts, 'ah good to see you.'

I said, 'excuse me do I know you?'

299

He said, 'you do now my friend. I come and fix your car yes?' I said, 'I want to know what's with the smoke?' He took a look inside. He said, 'your exhaust pipe.'

I said, 'what about the exhaust pipe.' He said, 'it's damaged.' I said, 'no shit, there is nothing wrong with it.'

He said, 'there is, look inside.'

I could see now. It was bent, in 4 places. He said, 'this is a petrol car. I don't know what has happened here.' I said, 'I don't care either. Can you fix it or not?'

He said, 'of course I can, give me a minute.' He climbs over. He grabs this big sized metal cutter. Sparks are flying. He replaces the exhaust, with a new one. He said, 'next time, don't drive so fast in New York. Especially with this heat. Keep it to 30.' He laughs.

I said, 'you are out of your mind, how much do I owe you?' He said, 'you are federal police are you not?' He points at my badge. I said, 'yeah, but I want to pay, how much?' He said, 'okay, well it's going to be around $500 dollars right now.' I coughed up 5 x 100's. It was easy for me. My wallet didn't even feel lighter. I said, 'thanks.' He said, 'you are investigating the Blakely's are you not?'

I said, 'how the hell did you know that?' He opens the even standard and he said, 'sons of bitches. They are still out there you know. You do realise his brothers are still out there.'

I said, 'well I thought we caught them all.'

He said, 'never, you can't, they are like ants. They just reproduce. They are still out there.' I said, 'thanks for the tip off.' I drove 80 miles per hour, to the cruise liner. All the way from New York. On the inner estate. Going all the way back to Michigan. I wanted to find out how many slaves were on that boat. I stopped outside.

It was empty. There was nobody there. Nobody. I walk in. No slaves. Nothing. They must have moved their operations.

Brian, one of the contractors, working on the site said, 'can I help?' I said, 'I am LAPD.' He said, 'the Blakely's' I said. 'Yeah, that is how it is. I want to know where their brothers are. There are more of them.' Brian said, 'well you won't be finding them here.' I said, 'mind if I take a look around on the ship?'

Brian said, 'by all means, but nobody or nothing is there.' I look around, and I can hear something. A gun shot. Then a voice shouting, 'help'. I walked over. To this man. One of the slaves. Trapped under some rubble. I pull him out, and I said, 'look, I am getting you to safety.' I radioed into control. I said. 'Yeah we have one

301

here. He needs hospital treatment, over.' I said, 'what is your name?'

He said, 'my name is Chris.' I said, 'I wanted to know your name. So how long have you been working on this boat. Chris?'

Chris said, 'for a year now.' I said, 'let me guess. You don't get paid.' Chris said, 'how did you know.' I show him a photo of Blakely, and I said, 'I know everything. I am the investigating officers. Well one of them. FBI are on this also. We are going to get you some medical help.'

Chris shouts, 'do you need any information?' I sit on this little bench, until paramedics arrive. I can hear the sirens crying in the distance.

I said, 'every day I am getting information. It's only a matter of time before I catch those sons of bitches.'

Chris said, 'well hurry up.' I said, 'why?' He said, 'they are driving over to the harbour. Right now.'

I said, 'I have every time in the world. Don't worry. Just look after yourself.' He said, 'this whole thing. The way they treated us here.' I said. 'I know, it's sick. But it's an ongoing investigation.' Chris said, 'Blakely was too deranged. Nothing more he could do. Nothing more anyone could. Let me tell you something. They are out there.' The paramedics arrive. I jump into my Caddalic, and I drive to the other bit of the harbour. To catch Justin Blakely. One of the brothers. Trying to get away on a jet. I punch him in the face. I punch him in the stomach. I trip him over. I punch him in the stomach again.

I said, 'not very easy after all is it?' He said, 'okay, you caught me.' He reaches for the pistol. The whole harbour is almost reverberating with fear. The lights are just shining in our eyes. As the sun sets.

I said, 'the game's up Chris. You have been caught.' I try to handcuff him, as he resists. I radio in, 'all units, all units.' He looks at me and he said, 'you stupid son of a bitch.' I said, 'you really want to know what I have been up to. Trying to find the rest of you lot. Whilst the main guy, is in jail. Russel. Russel Blakely. Now you. Chris Blakely. Just go figure.'

I handcuff him properly. Punch him in the face. As he punches me in the face back.

I said, 'you son of a bitch. Why couldn't you just tell the truth for once in your life?'

Chris looks at me and said, 'this is the truth.'

I said, 'cut it out. I caught you red handed. You want to know why I always carry my gun on me?'

He said, 'because you have to catch

303

people.' I said, 'that's right, but it's not empty. I can use it. I know what you are thinking.' He said, 'my mind is going a buck fifty. I can't think straight. I need an ambulance. I can't even breathe.' I said, 'look sir, we research what kind of ailment you have. Concussion or something.'

We bundle him into a police van. I drive, behind in this. Second hand rental Cadillac.

We arrive to the hospital. He is treated for minor wounds before we escort him back to a cell.

Me and Rufus stood, interviewing him. Rufus said, 'you don't get it.' We have been trying to find you Chris. For how long now. Year after year. Kept shifting your operations. Kept thinking you were smart. Kept trying to find out what you knew.'

Chris said, 'what if I have information, about Hemingway?'

I said, 'then you would be in a luck of surprises. Because the guy is behind bars.' He shouted, 'Giles Hemingway, this was his whole idea. This whole thing.'

I said, 'bullshit, and you know it. Be a man, stop getting people to cover for you.'

He said, 'oh really, you want to know what a real man looks like?' He starts struggling in the chair. I sit down on one of the chairs. The wrong way around. I said. 'Look, I want to know, why you even thought in the first place about cruise liners. Ships. Exploiting those workers. Chris, your story doesn't add up. Everytime we have spoken to you. Now we have you here. Your story always changes. All of the time. We can't take anything you say seriously anymore.'

Chris said, 'this whole thing was a shake down.' I said, 'it's not, that is not what we are trying to do.'

Chapter 44

I wrestled Chris Blakely to the floor. He tried punching me, and I said. 'Look, there's certain things I want to figure out. Certain things I don't know about yet. You can talk all day about right and wrong. Or what you did. It just doesn't make sense.'

Blakely said, 'we have a lot of guys working that cruise ship.' I said, 'how many guys?' Chris said, 'lots of us.' I said, 'so why don't you do the decent thing and hand yourself in? Why all of this?'

Chris said, 'because we are making money.' Rufus said, 'we make money, the lawful way. Your activity isn't going to last. We will make sure of it.'

Chris said, 'put me in jail. I don't care. Yet there is more of us.' I said, 'don't you think I know that. Don't you think I

305

realise there is more of you guys. You pop up, we detain you. Yet there was something about that cruise liner I hadn't seen before. I am not sure what.'

Chris said, 'it's a fucking cruise liner. What do you expect was going to happen? It wasn't for holidays. It was for importing drugs.' He said loudly, assertively.

I said, 'that cruise liner had been used to smuggle drugs. Yet I knew about the imports to England.' He said, 'oh come on, you know about imports to England. Customs were all over us. Why do you think Linda Cole freaked out at the airport. Because she was smuggling cocaine in her hand bag. They didn't find it. She gets put on a watch list for christ sakes.'

Chris was scratching his chin. He had bruises all over his face. He looked angry. Hostile even. He was looking around. Looking very sinister. Rufus, had his black braces on. He was his usual self. Then there was me. In my usual lightist-medium grey suit. Trying not to lose my temper. My pistol in my holster. Pens in my pockets.

Chris continued and said, 'look, lock me up. Be my guest.'

I said, 'that is what we are planning on doing. You are not helping our investigations.' He was escorted back to the cells. Rufus said, 'nice job, but he isn't talking.'

I said, 'you know. I don't think we want him to talk. We have the information.' Rufus said, 'oh really? Do you? You have all of the information on The Blakely's The drug smuggling. You have all of the information?'

I said, 'yeah sure. I mean it's what I do.' Rufus said, 'me, the FBI, my crew. We have been on this case for years. It's not a cut and dry case.'

The sun was shining through the station window. Birds were flying outside. The sun was shining in our faces. As we walked into the third floor. Detective suite. Rufus put on his blue FBI jacket. We walked upstairs where more sun was shining at us. Paperwork galore. People on the phones. People talking.

I said to Rufus, 'we have work to do.' Rufus said, 'nothing is springing to mind. The only other thing we can do is get forensics on the case. Do you know how much resource that's going to take?'

I said, 'we get forensics into that cruise liner. We get them in there. We get them to do swabs, and we might be closer to the other brothers.'

Rufus said, 'how many man hours are we talking about here?' I said, '2 days, 3, it could even be a week. But we would find vital information.'

Rufus said, 'all of the slaves on that ship have been moved. To witness protection, to immigration, they have left. Nothing, nada, some have run away.'

I said, 'so we will do a positive ID on the whole ship then.' Rufus said, 'okay. I will call in the FBI forensic unit. But your hunch better be right.' I said. 'Always is.' Rufus pointed and he said, 'your arrogance doesn't even offend me anymore.'

Rufus said. 'All units, can we get forensics over to Michigan harbour, Detroit please?'

You could hear the operator shouting, 'all units, please respond, we need forensics on board.'

We drove over there. Was your usual crime scene. We had the yellow tape on the perimeter We had LAPD officers outside guarding it. We had men and women in those white suits. Tracing the place.

We had forensic doctors involved, and we had a team of 12 FBI agents. Picking up evidence bags, that forensics had marked out. We had two sniffer dogs. Small little jack Russell sniffer dogs.

FBI Agent Kylie Clark, said, 'we have something.' As the sniffer dog tried eating the evidence bag. I said. 'What is this?'

308

Kylie said, 'cocaine.' I said ironically, 'well that surprises me.'

Kylie said, 'keep searching boys.' I said, 'sorry, Kylie, nice to meet you.' I shook her hand. I said, 'is that all we are finding is cocaine, drugs. Nothing else?'

Kylie said, 'no we have found lots of things. Shoes, pieces of clothing.'

I said, 'what types of shoes.' She said, 'military brown boots.' I said, 'probably belonging to The Blakeleys.' She said, 'yes maybe.'

I said, 'anything else?' She said, 'we have found lipstick, heroine, more cocaine. On the deck of the ship. That was where it was. We also found this.'

She held out a printed document. Almost like some kind of map or blueprint.

She said, 'this was inside the floorboards. It details their whole operation. To imports, to everything.' She placed it in the evidence bag. She had white sterile gloves on.

I said, 'so that is how it works then.' Kylie said, 'just doing my job.'

James Watkins comes along, wearing just trousers and a shirt. He said, 'nice to meet you.' I said, 'like wise. Sir, we have already met.' He said, 'we are getting evidence. That is good.'

I said, 'sure.' He said, 'fancy a ride in my

Cadillac?'

I said. 'Go on then.' We left the crime scene, and we went for a drive. James said, 'look, I am not sure about this anymore.'

I said, 'what, you are thinking of quitting your job?'

James said, 'no, I am not sure if that cruise liner holds all of the answers. What if it was a decoy?'

I said, 'it wouldn't be. The Blakely's aren't that smart. This is a bread and butter case.'

He said, 'ah you think so?'

I said, 'I know it is.'

He said, 'well think again, because they are smarter than you think.' We drove to the suburbs. I had never seen this side of Detroit. Not for a long while. There were lots of working class people roaming the streets. Muggers, car jackers. Prostitutes. All kinds of people.

People scoring drugs. Homeless people in alley ways getting mugged. Hookers in alleyways, getting raped. It was chaos.

I said, 'look, James. Why the fuck have you taken me down the suburbs. Are you trying to get me killed?'

He said, 'oh come on. It's not that bad.' I said. 'Come again, but what attracts you to this place?'

He said, 'we are just going for a drive.'

310

I said, 'maybe we are. But I don't understand why this place.'

He said. 'Just trust me on this.' We park up, next to this dialect building. We walk inside, and we find this man. Right upstairs. He looks homeless.

Chapter 45

The homeless guy is called Craig. I am getting agitated at this time. I said, 'look, I just want to know why we are here?' James said, 'well Craig knows The Blakely's.'

I said, 'is that right Craig? Do you know them?'

Craig said, 'I have been told not to say anything.' We lifted him up, whilst James punched him once square in the stomach. I looked at him, as he had some tape over his ear.

I said, 'you like sleeping in this shitty part of the estate?' He said, 'not really, no.' I said, 'then we can help you. Talk.'

Craig said, 'well I know where the rest of the brothers are.'

I said, 'go on, spill.' He said, 'right next door.' I said, 'you are shitting me. In that hotel?' He nodded. I pushed him. We both left. He was then begging for a meal, and some bagels. But we both said in unison. 'Later.'

We walked to the hotel. We went inside. Flashed our badges. I said, 'I have information some criminals are upstairs.'

The hotel desk clerk said, 'sorry, can't give any information on any of my clients. Data protection.' I slammed his head on the desk. I said, 'listen jackass, you don't know the day I have had. So you will tell me those names. Those rooms.'

He whispered aggressively. 'You mean The Blakely's?' He looked scared. I shivered sarcastically, and said, 'yes I am so scared of them. Give me the room key now.' He handed me over. Room 146. Second floor. Pistols ready. I had quietly called in for back up.

We walked in, there they were, all 5 of them. Playing poker. Rufus on his high horse said. 'Well hello there ladies. I am disrupting anything?'

I said, 'right that's it motherfuckers. You are all under arrest'

Damien, one of the brothers, said, 'hey fuck you man.' We fired some bullets into the windows. We could hear residents screaming. I said, 'don't fuck with us. We are the law. '

Armed police followed, SWAT, FBI, we had lots of men.

Rufus was reading them their rights. Into high secure prison vans. Back to the station.

312

Rufus high fived me, and so did James. James Coleman arrived, and he said, 'it's a fucking reunion. This is great. Great to finally get all of those bastards.'

I said, 'but it never would be over.'

Rufus said, 'oh come on, we talk all day about this.' James said, 'cut it out, it's over.' I said, 'no more shred of evidence. Nothing.'

I looked around. The floor boards had been cranked up. I could see cannabis underneath the floorboards. I could see crack cocaine on the tables. I could see porno flicks on the tables. The kitchen was in a mess. What little kind of diner kitchen, on suite little kettle they had. With the bathroom, and the mirrors smashed.

I said. 'Wow, this is some fucking party.' James said, 'pencil dicks. We will interview them in the morning. Are you okay Lucas?' I said, 'me, I could be better.' James said, 'I thought so, what is it now? Positive thinking you got going on or something?'

I said, 'positive thinking doesn't cut it.'

The more I looked at this motel. The more I looked at this hotel/motel. What ever you want to call it. With the lights shining. With people running around. Escaping. It just made perfect sense to me. Maybe at first nothing registered with

313

me. Now I am sure I know what is happening. It wasn't something you would dream up.

The sun, still kind of radiating on our skin. It was almost like we didn't know what else to think anymore.

Chapter 46

It was a new day, and it was morning in my house again. The Blakely's were all in custody. All behind bars. All going to jail. I was relieved. Of course I was. I just, didn't know what to think anymore. I spent my whole life just wandering what would happen once this case was all over.

I am reading the morning news that says Giles has had boiling hot water thrown over him. I turn over the page. There is the usual crime in there. Robberies, thefts, and other things.

Louisiana is looking over me worried. I am not worried. I am feeling complete because I know my job has now been done. Or has it? You know. You look all of the time for the answers. You look all of the time for things to happen. You don't just switch off. You become kind of immune to suffering around you. I wouldn't call it great by any expectations.

I knew work had to be done to convict The Blakely's With everyone running around loose. Just trying to get on with their lives.

The job of a detective, and in my case. The work I was doing. Full square face of it. I was not thinking straight. Not that I needed to at this time. It felt like a fucking vacation or something. Yet I wanted to know if anyone else was pulling our chain.

The cruise liner had been sent to a special compound to be demolished. It was now empty. Everything was taken off the streets. Everything.

We had seized kilos of cocaine, heroine, and we had done this by following our gut. Following through on what we believed. Yet it didn't make sense to me anymore. Not that it needed to.

I looked around, at all of the wide eyes, and glares of faces. All of the people I had known. Who had nothing better to do, than stare through my window. Then there was the press. 2 of them, wanting as god damn story. As if my work in convicting these sons of bitches wasn't enough. Two press people, looked like two jehovas witnesses. All grinning like Cheshire cats, just wanting to know how easy it was to convict. I sat them down, and I said. 'Nice to meet you. David, Brian.'

They both shook my hand. I said, 'look, what I need to know, is that are you pulling my chain or not? What kind of story can you make in 24 hours?' Brian said. 'Well we can put you in the front cover, and explain your whole operation. From Hemingway to Russel Blakely. To the cruise liner. We can have a 6 page special.'

I said, 'how much do I get paid for that?' Brian laughed and he said, 'well come on, it's public knowledge anyway.' I said, 'so why are you at my door.'

Brian said, 'okay, we will bite. How does ten thousand dollars sound?' I said, 'that sounds like daylight robbery. I want 100 thousand dollars.'

Brian said, 'okay, it's a lot of money.'

I said, 'I am bullshitting you. 10,000 dollars is enough. It's not like you guys have a lot of money. Do you?' They were a small newspaper crew. I said, 'so, like I have been saying all along.' I was telling the story. As I could notice something in Brian's hand. A pistol. Loaded. My pistol was on the table. He took off his hat, and his fake moustache He said, 'we are not news crew asshole. We work with The Blakely's We want them released from prison.'

I said, 'it's not going to happen.' Brian said, 'then I shoot you dead.' I said, 'then do it already.'

Brian looked confused and said, 'what? Are you serious?' I said, 'listen here. For one moment and I will tell you everything. If you think you can get away with this. You have another thing coming. You hear me?' He screeched

I said, 'it is not going to work like this. No?' I said, 'you have the guts to shoot me. Do it.' He cocks and loads the pistol. I walked towards him. I kick the pistol out of his hand. I wrestle Brian to the floor. Whilst the other one tries to escape. Turns out he is just a decoy. And I don't really need him anyway. Brian paid him $100 dollars to sit with him. The loner. I slapped Brian so hard, that blood came out of his ears. I said, 'no more games. My friend.'

Brian said, 'I am not your friend.'

I said, 'well you will be someone's bitch in prison.' He said, 'so be it, lock me away.' I put him in handcuffs, as I escorted him to my car. My white Chevy Fuck. I must have forgotten the keys. Until I realised they were on in my pocket. I preferred my silver Chevy. It was due an MOT. So I had this car, and I didn't mind if I broke it in places either. Because it wasn't the type of car I wanted as a replacement car. The dick jobs down the MOT office should be warned of who I am.

Brian said, 'where are you taking me?' I said, 'taking you to god damn jail.' Brian said, 'you have to interview me under caution first. I have rights.'

I said, 'yeah, the right to shut the fuck up. I know your games. Everyone here does. You are nothing but a stupid son of a bitch.'

He said, 'fuck you, coming in here.' I said. 'You came inside my house. My fucking house. I have a say in all of this.' He said, 'maybe so, and maybe I can tell the DA of how much of an asshole you have been.'

I said, 'maybe, yet they are not going to believe you. We are going to sit tight. Because for once in my life. I feel dangerous.' He said, 'you are scaring me.' I said. 'that is the point.'

LAPD arrive, you can hear the commander Nicholas shouting, 'is everyone safe in here?' I shouted, 'yeah I got the son of a bitch.' Rufus and Charles Jenkins, with Ryan Coleman and James Watkins. We were all debriefing, as FBI took him away. With SWAT.

I said, 'so boys, what is it now?' James said, 'hang on a minute. We need to talk about this.' I said, 'what else is there left to say.' I said, 'I don't know. Okay. I don't fucking know but something. Something is going wrong. These people are playing *mind games with us.'*

James said, 'yeah they are, but it's all

sorted now.' I said, 'Giles Hemingway. Giles Hemingway, yesterday, last night, whenever it was. He had boiling water poured over him. Right on top of him.'

James said, 'well the guy is in prison.' I said, 'I know that. I know he's in prison. Yet, we can't get certain people back from the dead to forgive his sorry ass. I don't want to be speaking to Charlotte anymore.'

James said, 'well don't speak to her. Don't speak to her because that is all that's going to happen. You will get the same story. This is done. It's an open and shut case. Back to the drawing board.'

Rufus said, 'look, I know it's hard for us to handle all of this. I know it's difficult for us to understand this. Yet you take a closer look. Not everything meets the eye.'

I said, 'what do you mean?' Rufus said, 'the whole thing, stinks of organised crime. But it's not just here. MI5 are on this.'

I said. 'Government Ops.' He said, 'damn right, government ops. That is what is happening. You think we are the only people on this?'

I said, 'I spoke to MI5. They knew nothing about this case. Nothing about Blakely, nothing about Hemingway. They knew nothing. The only thing they said is if they find drugs with customs. They get

319

seized'

Rufus said, 'oh come on, that's a load of baloney. You know it. MI5 had this thing down to a fucking T. They had everything. The murder weapons, the guns. Everytime those assholes met customs. They had them on watch lists.'

I said, 'the prime asshole award watch list or something?'

James said, 'watch list, like Terrorist watch lists. You don't understand the lengths these men went to.'

I said, 'oh come on, you two are not making sense. They weren't terrorists were they?'

Rufus said, 'they were put down as a terrorist organisation.' I said, 'what? The Blakely's?'

Rufus said, 'we found something in that ship, explosives. Lots of them. At first we thought nothing of it. Then we took a closer look. We even found some quotes in their books. Linking them to AL Qaeda'

I said. 'You have to be shitting me?' Rufus said, 'would I make this shit up?' I said, 'oh come on, they had not had that planned. That wasn't part of their agenda.' Rufus was angry and he said, 'look, we do our damn jobs here. They had links to AL Qaeda, that is what I am saying.'

James said, 'if that was the case, why was it all below board. Why didn't we hear about it until now? They could have been more flamboyant about it. Made some kind of remark, and expressed it. At first. We didn't know. Thought they were common law activists. They were twisted fucks. I wouldn't put anything passed them. Yet I did some digging also. They have been using the dark web. Not once, not twice. Every day, and you know what I have plucked out.'

Rufus said, 'you tell me.' James showed screenshots of their dark web activity. The kind of stuff they bought on there. There was an itemised list. A bill.'

'100 rats, $199
An old plane black box $1,000
Viagra $400 x 5 boxes, jumbo
Ribbed condoms, x 5 $5
Machine guns x 3 $1200
Eavesdropping device, $400
GPS Tracker $400
Wire cutters $100
Live Mice $100
Crystal Meth $400
Rogaine $400
Gucci jackets $200
Bongs $300
Whips $200'

I was shocked, I said, 'seriously? This is what they were buying?' Rufus said,

'James, you are amazing. Where did you get that?' James said, 'I did some digging on the national police systems. We were able to track there whereabouts. I logged into the data tracker. Found a legal warrant to view emails. Went inside. Printed it out.'

Rufus said, 'FBI knew they were buying off the dark web, but we weren't able to find lists. Well done.'

I said, 'well that solves that mystery.' I rolled my eyes, in sarcastic humour. James said, 'no it does not. Come on. Live rats. What the fuck were they doing with those? Lacing them with cocaine?'

I said, 'I don't know, I am not sure what the mice are about either. It's either to intimidate the witnesses. Do something to the victims. Or to lace the drugs in.'

James said, 'unless they are just fucking weird. You ever brought that to your attention?' I said, 'it's possible I guess.' James said, 'oh come on, it's possible. Do you know what kind of people they are? You think you are interested in the low down. If you want to play devils advocate be my guest. It ain't gonna work.'

He snatched the paper. It was a print out. Double sided. Still warm from where he had printed it out. No smudge whatsoever. He put it back in his brief case. I said, 'so they are twisted, that is all we have accomplished from those details.'

Rufus said, 'no, I mean, we look at things logically now. It's organised crime. It's the underworld. It's not opportunistic crime. Like someone leaves their car unlocked, and Mr Thief comes and robs it. It's not like that.'

I said, 'it's organised. I know, but all of this stuff.'

I said, 'was this why MI5 were on this? Going on the dark web?' James got angry and he said, 'listen. MI5 have denied everything. This is federal. This isn't anything to do with them.'

I said, 'maybe not, but I still wanted to know.'

James said, 'well shut your mouth. I am tired of your god damn lies.'

Rufus said, 'listen boys, it has been a long day. Time to meet Sarah down the Old Oak Tavern.

Chapter 47

We walked into the bar. It was cold, and there was a mysterious look about the place. There was a look I had never seen before. We walked in and I was surprised. Not at first. Didn't know why. Like I wanted to be inspired. That is when I see Sarah again. For some reason it wasn't shaking well with me. Just seeing her. In

323

some yellow attire.

Things seemed different now. Things changed. The whole routine was different. I went into get a drink. Wasn't the first time this was going to happen. I just wanted to know where I stood with this whole thing. Rufus and James looking kind of discontent.

I said, 'Sarah, I hear there is someone else. Someone else involved.' She said, 'like who?' She said, 'I don't know. Someone. Someone who I know.'

I said, 'well you know well and clear what I am talking about. Heard The Blakely's were not the only ones on this organised crime charge.' Sarah said, 'well who else was involved?' She said in a disconcerting way.

I said, 'I don't know. I have scoured everywhere. I have checked everything. I have no idea what is happening. I did hear this is a man called Kyle. Not the defence attorney. Kyle had access to weapons, he had everything.'

James said, 'Kyle, the guy behind this whole cruise liner.'

Sarah said, 'what was his second name?' I said, 'Kyle Jones.' I continued, 'everyone was scared of Kyle. I never minded him. I thought he was okay. Yet everyone else was apprehensive No idea. Kyle apparently was the guy who bought this ship. He is living in Detroit, but we don't know exactly where he is.'

Sarah said, 'so you are wandering if he ever comes in here?'

I said, 'I kind of want to know that, yeah.'

Sarah said, 'I get so many customers. So many of them. It would be impossible to tell straight away.'

I said, 'maybe, and maybe you are right. The whole thing just seems negative. But Kyle was someone nobody messed with. Helped them buy explosives. The night we seized that cruise liner. It was up on high, mighty express load of fire, surrounding the entrance. It wasn't vandals. I checked inside. Where all of the slaves were. Figured someone had any reason to know. Now these guys were smokers, there you go, force of habit. The whole cruise liner, was stinking of cannabis. When I got inside, nothing.

We searched the premises, if you wanna call it that. We found the usual Class A, mostly. Some Class B. Yet no cannabis. No lighter fluid, even though there had been a fire. Then Kyle is nowhere needed to be seen. Even though he is the kingpin. He was using the Blakely's.'

James said, 'yeah, he was using them. Kyle, leather jacket. Big shit tonne of a guy. Looked like the guy you would run

325

away from in an alley way. Up in Detroit, Michigan. You name it. Never would have made sense.'

Sarah said, 'yeah well, I think I remember him coming in here once or twice.'

I said, 'well there you go.' Sarah said, 'don't take this as information. Because the guy you are on about. Never spoke. Even when people spoke to him. Nothing. No information. He was alone. That was where he was staying. Deep in his leather jacket. His smokes, smoke everywhere. He carried a pistol. He had no rolex. He wasn't poor. He had a white vest. Black boots. Polished of course. He was a tough guy. Kyle. So tough he didn't even have a fuckin' second name.'

I said, 'I don't care how resilient this guy was.'

James said, 'yeah I mean, if we wanna know what his nickname was?'

Sarah used to say, 'they used to call him O'Ryan?'

I said, 'was his second name O'Ryan?' She said, 'no.'

I said, 'So, O'Ryan, Kyle. Whatever the fuck his name was. The king pin in all of this.'

Sarah said, 'you know, maybe they called him KingPin.' I laughed and I said, 'I highly doubt they called him kingpin.'

Sarah said, 'anyway, Kyle O'Ryan, was in here. Sprouting some story. At first it was believable. He was into some kind of garden centre trade. He was just trafficking garden centre material.'

I said, 'what, is this guy serious? So all of this time he was feeding people a load of bullshit. What has this guy got on anyone we have nicked anyway?'

James said, 'we want to know where O'Ryan is? Transport. Anything. Anywhere?'

Sarah said, 'he's not hiding behind a tunnel. For all I know. He's in New York.'

I said, 'no, Detroit is the information we have.'

Sarah said, 'could be both, gonna have to call it in boys.'

I said, 'if you see him again, are you going to call us.'

James said to me, before Sarah nodded. He said, 'look, this is insane right now. You expect me to believe there is a guy, we haven't got. We got everything on that ship, and now someone else is there. In the picture. No, no way, not like this.'

I said, 'because it makes sense. If the Blakely's were just there in the background. They had to have someone to answer to. The place was like a surrogate family. It sucked, but there you go. That's organised crime for you.'

327

Me and James drove off, looking for this mysterious O'Ryan.

Chapter 48

Me and James were driving into this warehouse. Ironically between the warehouses of New York and Detroit. Feds were all over the place looking for this guy. Nothing was showing up. I said to James. 'This guy is a myth. I see nothing on him. No clue on the name. Everyone is wandering around like they don't know. If we all just want to remain some calm here. I will be shitting coffee tomorrow. Or puking it up. Because it's the anxiety of this whole thing. We get on a boat. We seize drugs. Everything. So why this now? This guy? No way.'

James said, 'we are going to have to check out this warehouse.'

We walk inside, and we see this Kyle dude. We want to know what is alias is. I am not buying the name Sarah gave us. Thought it was too fucking ordinary. I go out there and I said, 'look Kyle, if that is your real name.' I take a balaclava off his head. That looks like a pear of woman's tights

I said, 'who are you?' I shouted. Kyle said, 'I am the man in charge of this whole operation.' He did a little moving gesture with his hands. He was smoking and puffed some in my face.

I said, 'cut it out, you are nothing special. So what are you doing here? Out in this warehouse? Wanted some fresh air. I kick him in the leg, as he points his pistol towards me.'

Me, and James, point our pistols towards him also. With Rufus in the background just smiling. Holding his magnum. FBI in the background, just laughing, not even drawing weapons.

I said, 'oh dear, oh dear, oh dear. Kyle. Kyle. Kyle. You truly have messed this one up. The imports. Everything.'

Kyle said, 'I had you fooled didn't I.'

James said, 'we knew all about your operation. We knew what you were doing.'

I said, 'we knew everything. This whole thing. This shake down.'

The warehouse looked half empty. Boxes everywhere. Empty fork lifts. People walking around paranoid. Running away. The smoke detector was shot out by a pistol. We had some crystal meth seized. We looked everywhere. All around the place. In every corner you wanted to look at. It was all the same. This 'tough guy' had it all. All of the cocaine. All of the heroine. It was exporting all of these ships. The Blakely's were just following his command. I would know Kyle would have something to say. I walked up to him and I said, 'look, I wanna know who else you are working with. We have every ship in the city marked with your name on it. What kind of plan have you got?'

I continued and said, 'kyle, my man, it's not Kyle. It's Diego Vega.' Kyle said, 'bullshit, that name doesn't exist.' I said, 'oh right? Then fine. That is it. That is the kind of thing we are looking at here. You go away for a bit. You spook out. You make some decisions I haven't even heard of. Yet it all comes back to us. Like some kind of miracle.'

Diego said, 'what? So you think I am involved in this now? You got me cruising all over this. I am not this guy you are looking for? Found me crossing the border.'

I said, 'are you okay?' He said, 'yeah, I am.' I said, 'what's with the tough guy image then Diego Vata.

He said, 'what you talking about?' I said, 'you come across as a local states man. New York, maybe New Jersey. Maybe you were, but why this whole organised crime thing you got going. It doesn't fit in with what we have here.'

Diego said, 'I don't know. It's kind of how it is right. The same conversations, playing around in our head.'

I said, 'we will take you to custody.' We

slam him in the cell..

Chapter 49

The next day. Diego was interviewed. In an interview room. Wired. Phones, contact. Video. Audiographs. Everything.

It was me, and him. Nobody else. Well, okay. It was me and James also. Yet James wasn't doing any of the talking.

I said to Diego, 'look, I wanna know some facts here. You get these ships. These cruise liners in. You import them. Then what?'

Diego said, 'we import the cruise liners over, then nothing. We sell heroine, wrap sheets. Mixes, spice, anything you can name. In some of our business.'

Diego stank of cannabis, and we found some on in. He had this look about him. This look like life had put him in a bad situation. I was not feeling sorry for him. I wanted to get to the bottom of what he was doing.

I said, 'Diego, I talk to you endlessly, about what is right, what you had to do. What I am supposing you are talking about. We knew everything now. Yet something isn't gelling. Hence why we have brought you into questioning.'

Diego said, 'I am clean, I just did some time out of the state. Came back. Was the usual shake up. At first, when you look at it. It wouldn't compel you to second guess. It wouldn't compel you to be anything other than normal. I mean everyone does things differently. At least I think. Nobody was standing up for what we were selling. The industry was going bust. Nobody was talking. So we started asking questions. At first, little things. Little questions. Then all of a sudden, when life got too hard. We started trying to find out meaning. The meaning behind things. Even though at times there was nothing.'

I said, 'you used to score dope?' He said, 'I used to, still do, but it's the kind of reflection we have made here. All of the time you try and make sense of the world. Thrice, three times, nothing.'

I said, 'so the harbour and all of these mind games you had been playing. Giving us the slip. Making us jump through hoops. For what reason?'

Diego said, 'I don't know. I just like to believe in something. Deep down. Even though this industry was killing me. Me and Russel go back a long way. Russel Blakely.'

I said, 'yeah I know Russel, but I don't know anything about you two. Combined, your relationship.'

He said, 'he's a solid man. I got him to do my dirty work. I took vacations.

Everywhere. France. Germany. Nobody touched me. I keep my phone on silent. I come back. I meet you two guys.'

James huffed and looked annoyed, for a moment. I said, 'we are just talking to you because we don't believe everything you are telling us. It's okay to speak to us in this way. It's okay to believe in what we are talking about. Yet nothing else is happening.'

James said, 'yeah.'

Diego said, 'we are just trying to find out some interests here. The dope game was hard to score. We were doing it. Doing everything we could to make it work. We knew where life was coming to us.'

I said, 'so you won't speak to the DA, you won't let them blow smoke at you. You are looking at many years. Without parole.'

Diego said, 'I don't care.' I said, 'so you never had dealing with any people.' He said, 'what is this? You serious?'

I said, 'I just want to know what you are on about. Because most of your dealings are in the US. You never even went to Mexico. Sure, you were brought up there. Never had anything to do with their drug trade?'

Diego said, 'no, never really dealt with them. This was all in the US.'

I said, 'but those cruise liners. Do you expect me to believe they were always just kept in the harbour. Never moved. Feds checked it out all of the time. Not always there.'

Diego said, 'we did some visits.'

I said, 'where?'

He said, 'New Jersey, mostly, went out of state. Went over to other places. California. East side places.'

I said, 'that's a stretch, on a cruise liner.'

He said, 'not really, doesn't take that long. We had to import the drugs somehow. We had dealers on the east. That is a different ball game. Good luck in catching them.'

I slammed my hand on the table and I said, 'we don't need your shitty luck. Do you know how much trouble we have been in? Looking for you. Just to find out. You were dealing to the east. For what reason? You think we don't talk to Cali police? You don't think that?'

He said, 'I am sure you do, but you know about this.'

I said, 'I have every drug dealers name in this book.' I handed this book out. It was a small black book.'

He said, 'you ain't scaring me man. I know nothing about those people.'

I said, 'so you just trade with them. No social time.'

He said, 'exactly, it's a business, not a fucking social club. You got me down to a

T.'

I said, 'what I have got down to a T is all of this is just how you responded. You push the drugs. You knew everyone. Socially, business. Don't want to mix those two together You had dealings with Giles Hemingway, once didn't you. Across the block from when he was rough sleeping, you sold him cocaine. On one occasion. We have it on CCTV.'

He said, 'sure I did, the guy was quiet as a mouse.'

I said, 'on the subject of that, we found your little list you have been buying on the dark web. Some of the items are bit weird. If you don't mind me saying so. Like, the viagra pills. The Rogaine. Then you bought, 100 live rats, 100 live mice. What was your purpose in that?'

He said, 'we put drugs in the mice and the rats?' I said, 'you fed the animals cocaine, and then what?'

He said, 'taunted the victims.'

I said, 'bullshit, this is crazy I don't believe this. You just wanted to buy them so you could dunk them in the water. Throw them into the sea. It was just cheap entertainment for you.'

He said, 'maybe.'

I said, 'did you slice a mouse's head off, and put it online. I heard you were engaging in animal cruelty. Like I don't

335

give a fuck about mice. But I heard there were other animals involved. Cats, and dogs also. What interested you so much in animals?'

He said, 'they were our middle men.'

I said, 'so you used them for what purpose. To traffic drugs? To abuse them.'

He said, 'look, we buy on the dark web. What you buy is what you get. What was on that list didn't tally up. Because if you buy something on the dark web. Say you buy smokes. Sometimes other things happen. We had large shipments coming in. We had to store the cocaine somewhere.'

I said, 'you are so full of shit.'

James chimed in and said, 'what if that bill we found, was just a fake. You wrote it to try and take us off the hook. I don't believe this for a second. I think you dabbled in stuff you are not telling us. What, you faked an invoice. Had us running around in circles. Fuck with that. Tell me what you really were doing. What were you buying. I want to hear facts. Not stupid fairy tale stories. I could tell my grandchildren in 20 years from now.'

Diego said, 'okay, the bill was made up. There were no animals.' I said, 'thank fuck for that. Now tell me what you were really doing?'

He said, 'honestly, you don't think we

have everything covered. There was no way we were even using the dark web. We had all of the supplies. Went from different warehouse, to warehouse. Supply chains. Faked businesses. Committed fraud. Did some things. Nasty stuff. Pretended to be this banking company. Or a contracting company. Went to one supply chain. Bought a shed load of material. Went to another supply chain. Kept buying things. That appear random, or usual, or normal to the supplier. Then it kept going on like that. Until we finally went on the dark web. But it wasn't anything you had spoken about. It was more than that. Cocaine, heroine, mainly. We were buying all of that stuff online. We were also buying fake number plates online. Fake ID's, fake passports. That bill was a red herring.'

I said, 'so that is why you have an alias. Your street name is Kyle Oriely, But your real name is Diego.'

Chapter 50

Still in the interview room. Grilling this guy. I said, 'look Diego, what I want to know, is were the fake passports all set. Did you have to sew. Stitch them on?'

He said, 'all set, no sewing involved. Obviously, we had to get the fake number plates in. We tear off the plastic. Take off the old plates.'

I said, 'so you were linking up with garages, warehouses to do your operations. The ship was the only place you could store your dope. What about Hemingway? Do you expect me to believe you only met him once? That butchers knife, 10 inches long. Do you seriously expect me to believe Louise Grey gave that to him. With no help whatsoever. She was a college grad, wet behind the ears. 21 years old. I think you orchestrated that. Let them all along, sold them all the cocaine. It was you. Your the main guy.'

He said, 'yes, I gave Louise the blade, I told her to give it to Hemingway. If she didn't do that, there would be aggressive consequences. Like killing her. You know.'

I said, 'yet that was a bluff, because there is no way you would kill of a college student. It would lead us to you fast. So you just used empty threats?'

Diego said, 'if I want someone dead. I can kill them. I don't care who they are.' I said, 'so, Louise Grey. You goaded, with the help of Linda, and the Barkley's You goaded him to use that blade?'

Diego said, 'we are making progress. Guess where that knife came from?' I said, 'was it a butcher's shop by any chance? There was one down the road.'

He said, 'close, but don't you think it would be suspicious if I just took a blade off a butcher. He would be asking questions. Phoning you guys. I got the blade off the dark web. We sprayed it down to avoid finger print detection. We then put on some gloves. We gave it to Louise, told her to pass it onto Hemingway. We said if she didn't. She would cut sliced the fuck open.'

I said, 'and you think that is an appropriate way to talk to someone?'

He said, 'it's the business I am in?'

He said sarcastically, hence the question mark. I said, 'what, killing people? You are into that shit? How many people have you killed? Are you going to lie about that also.'

He said, 'I haven't killed anyone.'

I said, 'but you just threatened to kill someone, then handed them a murder weapon. Who have you killed?'

Diego said, 'you don't wanna know who I have killed.' I said, 'tell me.'

Diego said, 'there was a corrupt cop on the harbour.' I said, 'all of my police officers are straight. It wasn't a cop.' He said, 'no, not in Detroit. It was an NYC cop. Nothing to do with your men. You do a clean job. But this cop was dirty.'

I said, 'the killing and murder of Paul Thomas Anderson.'

339

He said, 'made the news. He was harassing me for ages. Always wanted to know what I was up to.' I said, 'we do that with convicted felons.' He said, 'you are missing the point. This guy was dirty. He was into the dope game. Selling drugs. Sometimes, we even exported to him.'

I said, 'bullshit, no NYC cops would be in the dope game.' He said, 'do you want a bet? Because I can link this guy to it.' I said, 'the guy you are talking about was a family man. Well respected. He wasn't dirty. He looked into your cargo cruise liner ship. You got paranoid. You drugged him and shot him dead. It's all forensics have said,'

Diego laughed. James said, 'next time you call one of our police officers dirty. You better stop with your lies.' I said, 'he wasn't dirty, you killed him. Once. A bullet in the head. Coming from a semi automatic shot gun. 12 gauge. One bullet, you threw him in the ocean. He was found the next day by sniffer dogs and helicopters. He was hoisted to the nearest hospital. He was dead when he arrived. We have done a full autopsy, and we know the guy you killed. There was nothing to link him to the drug game.'

Chapter 51

James said to Diego. He said, 'look, you are leading us down paths we don't want to go down. First of all you say dark web, and you mention fake items. Then you tell us the truth, something different. You try to call one of our officers dirty. Turns out that wasn't the case. You come in here smelling of arrogance, sweat BO, and that cannabis you have been smoking. We check you out, and we have enough to put you away. Yet you are talking, and we appreciate that. Yet you are going to have to start talking some more. Because maybe we can get you immunity. In prison. We can't exonerate you for this shit. But we can make things a little more comfortable for you.'

Diego said, 'then what's going to happen. I did a 10 year bit before I did this game. In and out of jail. Like you wouldn't believe. I know the prisons you are talking about. If you can get me a deal that would be great.'

James clapped, and said, 'listen, this isn't like tennis, you can't just throw us a god damn line. Expect us to throw it back. We have to make solid rules here.'

Diego said, 'you want more information. And then what? I become one of your informants. You lesson my charge, and you put me in a minimum security prison Opportunity of parole. You give me 10 years.'

I said, 'maybe, maybe we can do that. But we want a list of names to bring this whole circus to an end, if you don't do this. We will throw the book at you.'

Diego said, 'so you want me to write down every drug dealer I know in the USA. Man, this is what you want?'

I said, 'it's a start, you got into this mess. You want to clear your name. Now would be the perfect opportunity to do this.'

Diego said, 'I will write the list down. Yet we keep talking.'

James said, 'okay.' He paused the CD.

I couldn't believe my ears. I couldn't believe what I was hearing. I couldn't believe anything. Nothing was working anymore. We look at Diego. We look at him. We see him for who he is, and that is the best interest I can have. He was using us. He hated us cops, and it did leave a sting. There was nothing to even think of anymore. The whole thing had been a set up from start to finish. The whole thing. Now was the time to wander, to gain knowledge. Like I was doing that in the first place.

I was changing all of the time and getting emotional. Yet that wasn't the end. I was going to put this in a minimum security. Level 3 facility. If I did that, then he might escape. I wasn't going to turn him into a rat. An informant. Not like I had planned. It was no use for him there.

That Diego had killed one of ours. A cop, for what purpose. The whole thing stank of a set up. I was pacing all of the time. Trying to make sense of this. Then I couldn't. His smug and arrogant face and the look of disbelief on the face of James. I couldn't even recall what it was we were charging him for. The charges were all over the place. The laughter wasn't there anymore. What was a good line of business. Was a fact remaining that we had work to do. We had things to prove.

We had to show who we were. We were cops. Even though that cop he claimed to kill was dirty. That all of the stuff he had bought on the dark web. It pointed fingers to the fact, that if we did use him as an informant. He would do less time. Yet he had accountability to that fact.

I remember the interview room well. I remained there, and stood there in disbelief

Chapter 52

Whenever I used to go into a gun shooting range, I used to shoot. One at a time. One straight in the bulls eye. One straight over. With the glasses on and the phones around my ears.

343

Yet in this range, we met some incredible people. Lee Graham Clive Johnson. Lee Johnson was a man who could shoot a clay pigeon out of the ground.

We went to his farm, in Detroit. We would be there all day. With beers. Just shooting clay pigeons. We moved onto real pigeons, and the fact still remained why Lee Graham. Went dirty. What was a loveable guy. Was now a crooked cop.

Still in the interview room. I spoke to Diego. I said, 'you have met Lee, haven't you? He turned dirty. I used to go shooting with him.' Diego said, 'yeah that guy, a corrupt cop.' I said, 'the irony is, you killed the wrong guy. The cop you killed wasn't dirty. But Lee, he was. He slipped through the net. He was working in Michigan for a bit. I would never let him in my force. He applied and I rejected his application. Because I knew what kind of scumbag he was. Yet when I went shooting with him. Absolutely nothing. No word of a lie. Nothing we could pin him to. Yet, he gave us pathetic tip offs. Just trying to cover his own back. He moved to Detroit, and I even contacted the IRS. Convicted him of fraud. He spend 2 years in a level B facility. He was beaten so heavily. Being a cop in prison and all. He then served an extra year in prison for beating up a cell guard called Rushman. Nevill Rushman. An Irish man. We spent ages just trying to figure out why. It would never wash.

He was released, and he walked down the corridor. An old junky, and he used to think he would see that lorry. The Baskin and Robbins lorry. The ships, the warehouses, the trucks. It all made sense to me. Yet we kept this guy under lock and key. We always would get a bad rap for this guy's attitude. His work performance. He failed the academy three times, before getting into the police. He forged his Resume, and said he had qualifications he didn't. He was the only dirty cop amongst these ranks. Even if I could say that. The city of Detroit. The state of New York. Could never have him. He was stuck in lots of police forces. Always getting transfers. He did a bit in Ohio for a year. Chasing after bandits and crooks. He then went to jail a second time for armed robbery. He bit into the leg of a truck driver. He was sentenced to 5 years. Got out in half that time for good behaviour.'

Diego looked at me. Looked at me. I wanted to drown that rat. I wanted to make his life a living hell. I looked at Diego and I said the following. 'There is no way, you are getting immunity from us, you asshole. I am going to recommend to the DA that you serve maximum security. Your tip offs are just like blowing smoke into a chimney.'

Diego looked shocked, and he said, 'I can't roll with you boys. I tell you everything. So I killed the wrong cop. Big deal.'

I said, 'the wrong cop, the wrong story. It keeps adding up. We knew what you were doing. Right away it wasn't making sense. Yet we kept evaluating what you were saying. You always led us off onto these tangents. Never really knowing where it was going. You always wanted us to believe you were going straight. Went into the high road. Didn't know where the gas in your car was, when you switched off the ignition. This was your hobby and your job. You are a methodical criminal.'

Diego said, 'what's your point?'

I said, 'well in my opinion, if we are going to use you as a rat, or a human intelligence source. Which is pathetic, because you are better than that. Then you ought to start talking. I want to hear proper sentences Not some bullshit phrases. I also want you to work with us, and go clean. You killed the wrong fucking cop. Lee was the one who was dirty. Yet you never would go near him.'

Diego said, 'there is more than one cop who is dirty.'

I said, 'prove it, see, you can't, you can't prove anything. We have undercover officers. We have people patrolling the streets all of the time. Every butcher, everyone who knows me. Who keeps a close eye on this. Every vigilante roaming the street. Reading the news. Giving us tip offs. Is reading about you. Your case. Your interests. Your pathetic obsession with breaking the law. You are not worth a match sticks, and a bottle of piss.'

James said, 'in all respect, if we let you go, and send you on level C minimum security. You could escape. On the other hand. We want you to work with us. Help us find the other dealers. So I am going to speak the DA about getting a deal. You will still go to trial. We will have a word with the jury, and the judge. We will make sure you are dealt with accordingly. Providing you, tell us, what the fuck is happening. Stop pissing us around with the same stories. We want facts. Not gospel tales.'

Diego said, 'okay. I will start talking, and for real this time. I knew every drug dealer in the USA. Who was dealing with me. They all owned boats. Cargo ships. Taxi drivers. Everyone you could think of. It was a massive ring, corruption at it's finest. I used Russel Blakely, and played him like a fiddle. I painted him as the bad

347

guy. Whilst I was in the background getting dope. Yet it wasn't low level, and it wasn't low crime. We had every cargo ship loaded with elite products. Big massive warehouses stacked to the brim. With fake numbers plates. Heroine. Cocaine. And anything else you can think of. We transported cargo ships with heroine. Under the guise of genuine businesses. Even cloning some businesses along the way. We checked out of customs, that is how we managed to travel from state to state. There were trips to the UK. Where we successfully smuggled cocaine and heroine in food boxes. Lunch boxes, and other stuff. It went unnoticed for a bit. Until Linda Cole started stressing out at the airport. She was put in a terrorist watch list. And she was investigated night and day. The feds wouldn't leave her alone. It was me who set her up to have that fit. I wanted the distraction away from me. She was small fry in those days. She wasn't anything I had heard of. Until we met time and time again. She helped me unload some elites, and some cargo ships. She helped me secure things, like drugs, and other products. She was able to do this. Yet we remained on board, and we helped. We were all knowingly involved in this. The only time I could ever speak to someone was under morse corse, and I don't mean that literally. We spoke in ways, in which people couldn't understand. You want to see how my record plays out. It doesn't blow enough smoke under those dashboards. The chrome plates. The fake tyres, with no tread. The pictures of fake celebrities up on the walls. The porno flicks painted on the walls with graffiti. The way we structured everything. This wasn't just crime. This was an elaborate fucking adventure I was loving every minute of it.'

I said, 'you were playing an elaborate adventure, out. Like some road trip. So you went to Ohio. Then what? You just vanish off the map? For how long?'

Diego said, 'for a bit. Nothing real concrete. Made some kind of way about it. So I wouldn't get caught. Changed my mobile phone every 4 months. Different number and provider. I knew I was going to get caught, but I was enjoying the reality. Of not knowing when.'

I said, 'so you liked living on the edge.'

Diego said, 'basically, but come in here, and you want names. I can give you names.'

James looked confuses and he said, 'so those cargo ships. They were just a front. A disguise. You weren't using them, or were you?'

Diego said, 'we were using the ships to

349

transport cocaine and heroine. We were doing this night and day. It wasn't a fucking disguise.'

I said, 'so what about all of the taxi drivers you pimped out to transport all of the drugs?'

Diego said, 'they were in on it. It was how it was going. This whole thing, and you think this is simple.'

I said, 'look, I have been a detective for the best part of around 30 years. I have never met anyone like you. Your story changes all of the time. You blow smoke on the truth and you create lies. I just don't know if I am the right person, to be talking to you. What are you? Some kind of psychopath or something? You knew you were going to get caught. You just didn't know when. Prison for you is just like a hotel. Is that how you want your life played out? Just be some massive cog, in a machine that tries to bring down the whole city of New York. How about the respect we have. This isn't personal, and I never meant to be. If we are to take you on board.'

James said, 'my colleague is right, you are going to have to work with us, and take the deal. Yet in my terms. This is all we say. The DA will do the rest. We sit here holding our dicks. Just like you can set yourself on fire if you want to.'

Diego said, 'oh I see, it's like that. Different sides of the fence. Like a game, almost.'

I said, 'I never mentioned games, I just mentioned how it was for you.'

Diego said, 'look, in all honesty. I know what's going to happen now.'

I knew what was going to happen. I knew what this guy was up to. I knew we couldn't give him immunity. I knew that. Wrapped around in my mind, was the same level of confusion I already had. The same level of quiet and what I thought of. The predicted life I had and the way I was investigating things now. Through the twists and turns of my world. It would be a time when I had to be serious. I had to know what kind of life was.

The crime, in other words. If I am talking correctly. If I wanted to wander of in the wilderness, and think poetically about life. I could do. Yet my badge, and what the department represented. Was how I was feeling. In other words. My own thoughts and feelings. Were how I was feeling.

Diego was a nasty piece of work. We had guys on him trying to figure out what his game was. He was treating us like were pieces on a chess piece. I was not going to have it. I left the interview room. And James was babysitting To find out if I could speak to the DA. District Attorney lawyer, and heavy weight attorney. Hugh Jones. Nicknamed the sharp shooter, because he never missed. We went shooting together a few times. On the farm near the petrol station. The same one Lee went to.

I spoke to Hugh, and we get a plea bargain arranged for Diego. I walk right in again. I said to Diego. 'You meet us, night and day. You give us intelligence. Even if it's a small thing. You let us know.'

I gave him a login code, and a password. I said, 'you use this database. Now don't go thinking this is the Police's database. This is just for you to write. We will have a link to it. To read. When we want. I want logs of all kinds of things. We can use. That is what we are doing.'

I hand him a security clearance. I said, 'you will serve 10 years in a minimum security prison. I have everything set up, the judge and the jury all agree. I have made sure when you have access to the internet in there all of the time. Visitations. Going out as long as you want. Yet we want at least 5 pieces of information a week. We will give you access to the internet. I would like 5 pieces of information a day. But 5 a week will do. You will go online. You will trace things. We will watch you. You will be our

352

informant. If this fails, and if you pull a stunt. Kick off, act like you aren't interested. We kick you with 150 years in a maximum security prison. No visitations. No chance of parole. Do I make myself clear Diego?'

Diego said, 'yeah I understand, so I will agree to this.' He signs some paper. Diego said, 'out of interest. What made Lee turn dirty? When he went shooting with you. In the yard, the farms. Baskin and Robbins. The cornflower shops, the cornflower ties. Wasn't that a sign, that he was alright. Way before he went dirty.'

I said, 'I knew him for ages. I didn't know what kind of man he was before I met him. After he had changed. I had become what I knew. To him. He had gone off the rails and had led to believe. That he could do whatever he could. Then the whole force got a bad rap for what he did. I was not letting him anywhere near our operations. We wouldn't go near him. He was bad news, and was working security. Yet it was how it panned out. Give it some interest or not. Paint it with a vibrant picture or with not. It makes no difference to me because he hasn't been in the force for some time. Only security would even dream of taking him now. Yet if you look towards the sky. If you look towards what we know. We knew who he was. Our entire investigation was like a pack of cards. Or some kind of lighter or match sticks. You could just burn up a cigarette with him. Back in the days when I smoked but packed it in. Even though he was bad news. I felt sorry for him. I don't know why. I just did. So I knew that, it became part of who I was. The time to even think for a minute. About all of the dirty stuff he did. In my mind. Was not going to cut it. I went home to the wife. I made sure I was okay. I made sure I had enough time to reflect. Not all of the time either.

Yet sometimes it was not the same. You look out of the window for hope, and instead of that. You get these trials. Some of them are bad news. Then we find people who commit organised crime. Then we expect them to be okay. Even though they compromise our security. I do everything I can to ensure you are on the right tracks. Yet you have to face up to what you did. I am sure you will be aware of this. Yet the road to recovery for a criminal. Is like the road to recovery from any ill or wrong doing. You had to make steps. In the right direction. Yet the wrong moves you made. You had accountability.

I woke up in the summer if 93, and I would almost smell some kind of reason. Why I never caught Lee. Now, I am sitting

354

with you. In this desk. In this office. In this time. Just hoping that something will work out. That we are able to make informants out of crooks. And lesson their sentences Then we talk about the press. They are a piece of cake. *For me anyway.*

I would never even know what kind of action you would take Diego. In terms of your rights. They become different when you prostitute the laws that are ready and available to you. I guess I never even wanted to know why some people sold off their freedom. For a pack of cards. A lighter. Some kind of match sticks. The eagerness wasn't there anymore. So I would know. No more hard ball or no more going off the topic. I had to do my work, just as you knew.

Yet don't go thinking this is a vacation, because it's not.'

James looked sternly at Diego, and said, 'you give us all of the names of all of those pieces of shit who deal. From the east coast, all the way to New Jersey. Mexico. New York. San Fran Cisco, all the way to Detroit. Boston. We want every bit of information. If you hear about anything.'

Diego said, 'I understand, but you are not going to be able to catch all of these drug dealers. Just by utilising my help alone.'

I said, *'Why not? What is this? You*

know what a reputation is for you?' I said aggressively.

He said, 'no, and as far as I know. I can either be the felon, or the rat who helps The Police. On any adventure you have. It pays no fact to me. Yet I will do it. And I will kick the balance. Between what you wanted to know.'

I said, 'rat, informant, human intelligence source, nobody. I wouldn't even care. You want to be part of a society. We are giving you that choice.' He said, 'you know what happens to snitches in jail or even out of jail. In this climate?'

I said, 'it makes you a prime target. I get that. Yet we will give the the skills to defend yourself. Maybe when this is over. You can do security. Join the military. You will never be able to join us. With your record. Yet the military might take you. You will be all over the world. Yet all you think about is now.'

Diego said, 'Who the fuck would take me into the military?' I said, 'what are you on about sir? The military accepts anyone. No matter of race or religion.'

James said, 'yeah most of the military guys we meet, are from good families, anyway. Doesn't make you a democrat, if you are an armed soldier.'

Diego said, 'is this funny to you? Do you really think I give a shit about the military. You miserable little shit.'

I said, 'I don't know, you tell me. Because as far as I am aware. We had to talk to you. Do your time and come out better. You are not just distant. To anyone.'

Diego said, 'oh come on man. You talk to me all day about this. I want to know what you think. Deep down. I couldn't care. Because I know the down time you are giving me in jail. Yet it's the press that scare me.'

I said, 'they will to a jerk off like you. They will try and intimate you. Well don't let them. I will let you in on a secret. I know some republicans, some far right neo nazis. And I hate them. Yet, I read books, who are the same. Then the people in the books. Acting. Yeah. I get it. Yet listen to me. If anyone makes your life hell. You come to us. We ain't fucking around anymore. We are not taking sides. This is police business. This isn't political. You have done the crimes, and we are there. Working with the DA. To make sure you are safe. Any political matters aren't worth anything to us. Like match sticks it goes out in flames. Remember what I am saying.'

Diego said, 'so I know, that you are there to look out for me.'

James said, 'hey listen. I will be clear to

357

you, on a level. I have seen so many wrongs in this world. I have seen so many people wind up dead in jail. I have friends in England. They have different crimes to what we deal with here. If you want to think, long and hard, about the decisions you have made. Prison is for you. But if you want to be arrogant, and think you can fuck with us on this. We will discard you to the wolves. Like a piece of flesh. We mean business.'

I said, 'yeah, I mean what you did was fucked up. You even shot the wrong cop. That guy had family. Lee was the dirty one all along. You are going to do time for that also.'

James said, 'well, murder, third degree, we will make it look like it was an accidental fire round. You mistook him for a robber. It will go down as a piss weak manslaughter/self defence charge. Yet, we are doing this, because we want all of the other people who are dealing. Brought to justice.'

I said, 'yeah I mean I want the USA to be safe. I go in my home a lot in Detroit. I remember the times it was different. Then I could sleep. When the psych just gave me loads of pills. I could sleep easy. Yet never forget your past. The younger, and more foolish you. The young and dumb you. The one who went out, half naked at night. Just to buy a pack of smokes. You learn the hard way.'

Diego said, 'look, you two pieces of shit. Is this whole thing over now. I am not standing here, trying to have a social with you.'

I said, 'yeah it's over, but I wouldn't put anything passed you. You have a new life now. Remember that, you post bail when we say so. Every parole board that I knew. Will hear from you. Just like I knew. I took one look at you. You treat this like a vacation, and I will hang you by the balls. This is not.'

James said, 'well it isn't, and what I know is. When you are going in the convenience store. In this low level, theatrical fucking prison we have. Where they are going to sell you coca cola products. For the price of a lollipop. You walk home, along the reservoir You think to yourself where you life was. That was what I did, when I was younger. A trip to the shop. Some coca cola. A walk along some abandoned lake. Straight in the car when the sun was scorching.'

Diego said, 'I understand what you are saying. Don't fuck with me on this. I know 2020 has been tough, but this is the last thing I need. Bringing me back to 94. Who do you think you are?'

I said. 'We are The Police, we own this

land. Which means we own your ass plus every one else's. One wrong move, and you become someone's bitch up in California Maximum security prison.'

Diego said, 'you want to know the real truth?'

I said, 'go on then.' He said, 'Giles Hemingway, doesn't even exist.' I said, 'he does, we have him in custody.' He said, 'no you don't understand. I know he exists. I mean his legacy. Is not worth a box of piss.'

I said, 'well his life was a bit strangled at the end. He is not leaving a legacy. Like all of those people who worship pieces of shit like him. We will make sure he is reputed. As a man who is psychopathic. Of course then you have to deal with the left wing media.'

James said, 'well it's not the left wing media I hate. It's the god damn democrats. Who like to say these criminals are just helping our economy. Because the more people in prison. The more profit.'

I said, 'no I thought that was the republicans.'

James said, 'you know what I mean. The whole thing is watered down with piss. You all know it. So what do I have to do to make it happen. Do you want another song and dance. Or back to the fucking custody suite.'

We slam that guy away. Into the custody block. I am left just with nothing. Except for the main suspect of course.

Chapter 53

I return home to my wife. I return home, and I leave. Everything is in place. I don't leave her. I distance myself from everything. My own kind of place.

I file some notes, and I try and put Diego out of my head. Just for the time being. The postman arrives, with a package. I open the package. It's from Giles, he has said, he 'feels very guilty for what he has done.' Which is understandable. Then he then writes the letter. Like this.

'Dear Lucas. I feel like I made a friend. I lied to you, which I cannot forgive myself for. I can't say too much right now. Yet I am glad I can still send mail. I was scolded with hot water. I spent 4 weeks in the infirmary I feel ever so guilty for the crime that I had done.

There is nothing I can do to repay you for this. Or the victim.

See you soon. Signed. Giles Hemingway.'

I sighed. I didn't know what to think. That guy was genuinely sorry. I radioed into control. I said, 'look, I feel for that guy.' It was on channel 2.

I look at life differently now. My colleagues, that managed to keep me afloat. It was how it was. I see above the smoke. I see above the criminals. I see the light. I am not just a cop. I am not just a detective. I am not just a sworn officer of the law. I am a law abiding family man with a heart. A sensible person. Someone who understands what life had done. I realise this. My overriding thoughts, and feelings. In this case.

My contempt for the criminals who have committed the crimes. My overriding confusion as to why some people do this. Even after 31 years. The TV, the remote, those channels. It was home for me. So was what I had already thought of. In my mind, at the time. I kind of think about things logically.

I look over, and I look at myself, in a way nobody else was. I didn't want to think about Diego anymore. I didn't want to think about Hemingway. I didn't want to think about Russel Blakely. The court cases. The DA. Or anything I had done. It had been done for a reason. Which, was how I was.

My whole life. I learnt from the ability to help the victims I met. The people nobody took a shine to. I could resonate with.

I could connect with the people who were victims. People with mental health. People being neglected by the system. Even though I knew deep down it was bullshit.

I wanted to find closure in the fact that sometimes words would be meaningless. The heart is what is important. Yet I had to know where my life was.

It was not in the pale expressions. The versatile notions. The long drives into the boulevard, and the sun just radiating in my face. It wasn't the obstacles we had, in the face and adversity of crime. It was the realisation that despite the wrong doings of others. I could remain just tolerant.

I knew I had to be tolerant of people's views. That interview with Diego got heated. I had to show cultural sensitivity with him. Deep down. I just wanted to help. He needed a second chance at life. I wanted to change his world. Yet the cop he killed, was the wrong one. Then I look at all of the allegations he made against the force. I wasn't lying when I said I was going to cut him a deal. It was happening. Yet the force was changing. My radio was going off. I was not willing to answer it.

363

Not yet anyway.

Everything I had fought for. I didn't want to be absolute bullshit. I wanted a happy existence. Yet that meant tolerating the pieces of shit that stood in my way. Listening to all of the negative people. It wasn't going to cut it. I had to live life by my own design. I had to lead by example. I was a leader. That was who I was. People looked to me for answers.

The radio is going, and I am leaving the house again. Driving down in my Cadillac, and I am driving up to a mental health related shooting. The man is armed, and is threatening to kill a passenger; In his car.

I smash the window. With the edge of my gun. I load my pistol. I point my gun at his head. At the suspects head. As the civilian runs out of the car screaming. And running. I said to the suspect. 'I am giving you one minute to put your gun down. Or you will turn to juice.'

He is sweating and nervous. I don't know how else to help him. I am sweating, and nervous. He reaches for his gun, and I slowly push on the trigger. Second by second, by second. Until one final rush of wind, or one final press. Would send a bullet into his head and destroy him. He reaches for his gun and points it towards me. I press on the trigger of my gun. I hear this 'clicking' sound. I shout, 'fuck'. The suspect laughs, and he said, 'you forgot to load it didn't you?'

I said, 'one of my cardinal sins, yeah.' The suspect said, 'luckily this gun is loaded. He points it towards my head.

I shake my head. He relinquishes it to his head, in an effort to shoot himself. Every second now counts. I am reaching over him wrestling him to the ground. The gun fires off into the edge of the car. The car is going to blow up in 10 seconds The petrol fuse has been hit.

I put him on a fireman's lift. I carry him 100 yards away from the car. LAPD, divert traffic very quickly. I look back and the car explodes. Like a mushroom of smoke just vaporising in the air. Rushing towards the oxygen around the son. The car smashes into a thousand pieces.

Not one person was hurt.

I look at the suspect. As I cuff him. My last words to him before he's taken away by uniform. To be interviewed. I wasn't going to interview him. He was being transferred to a different detective unit. My case load was full.

My finals words to him on that day, before he left were this.

'I can't imagine what you have been going through. I know I saved your life. However, you are going to have to turn yours around.'

I will never forget the hard work I put into securing all of these convictions. I will never forget all of the hard work I put into making sure. Detroit. And New York. And the USA. Were free of drug dealers. Right now I had Diego in jail. Informing on the giant drug dealers. It was a blessing. Detroit was my home. I was happy to be back. This was my ground.

This was my city. This was my whole life. Detective, family man, law abiding and armed. Pistol. Cadillac And prisoners galore. My life had just started. My life had just had 'hope' written all over it. I was the best. Yet not without my team.

THE END

Printed in Great Britain
by Amazon